SPECIAL MESSAGE TO READERS

THE ULVERSCROFT FOUNDATION
(registered UK charity number 264873)
was established in 1972 to provide funds for
research, diagnosis and treatment of eye diseases.
Examples of major projects funded by
the Ulverscroft Foundation are:-

- The Children's Eye Unit at Moorfields Eye Hospital, London
- The Ulverscroft Children's Eye Unit at Great Ormond Street Hospital for Sick Children
- Funding research into eye diseases and treatment at the Department of Ophthalmology, University of Leicester
- The Ulverscroft Vision Research Group, Institute of Child Health
- Twin operating theatres at the Western Ophthalmic Hospital, London
- The Chair of Ophthalmology at the Royal Australian College of Ophthalmologists

You can help further the work of the Foundation
by making a donation or leaving a legacy.
Every contribution is gratefully received. If you
would like to help support the Foundation or
require further information, please contact:

THE ULVERSCROFT FOUNDATION
The Green, Bradgate Road, Anstey
Leicester LE7 7FU, England
Tel: (0116) 236 43?⸍

website: www.foundation.ul

D1521869

Wendy Soliman was brought up on the Isle of Wight in southern England but now divides her time between Andorra and western Florida. She lives with her husband Andre and a rescued dog of indeterminate pedigree named Jake Bentley after the hunky hero in one of her books. When not writing she enjoys reading other people's books, walking miles with her dog whilst plotting her next scene, dining out and generally making the most out of life.

Visit her website at:
http://www.wendysoliman.com/

KITTY BENNET'S DESPAIR

Lizzy Darcy's spring house party is becoming a Pemberley tradition. This year her family and friends will meet four-month-old Marcus Darcy, as well as celebrating Georgiana's engagement to Dominic Sanford. Lizzy will have the pleasure of all her sisters' company — but is apprehensive at the thought of her mother and Lady Catherine being at Pemberley at the same time . . . Recently-promoted Major Richard Turner plans to propose to Kitty Bennet during the course of the party. But when his father accompanies him to Pemberley, Richard knows that he won't approve of Kitty. Must he choose between familial duty and his heart's desire?

Books by Wendy Soliman
Published by Ulverscroft:

LADY HARTLEY'S INHERITANCE
DUTY'S DESTINY
THE SOCIAL OUTCAST
THE CARSTAIRS CONSPIRACY
A BITTERSWEET PROPOSAL
TO DEFY A DUKE
AT THE DUKE'S DISCRETION
WITH THE DUKE'S APPROVAL
PORTRAIT OF A DUKE

MRS. DARCY ENTERTAINS:
MISS BINGLEY'S REVENGE
COLONEL FITZWILLIAM'S DILEMMA
MISS DARCY'S PASSION

WENDY SOLIMAN

KITTY BENNET'S DESPAIR

Complete and Unabridged

ULVERSCROFT
Leicester

First published in Great Britain in 2014

First Large Print Edition
published 2016

A catalogue record for this book is available
from the British Library.

ISBN 978–1–4448–3086–6

Published by
F. A. Thorpe (Publishing)
Anstey, Leicestershire

Set by Words & Graphics Ltd.
Anstey, Leicestershire
Printed and bound in Great Britain by
T. J. International Ltd., Padstow, Cornwall

This book is printed on acid-free paper

1

'It seems remarkable.'

Will gazed at his sleeping son with so much pride in his expression that Lizzy had to smother a spontaneous laugh, for fear of disturbing the child.

'That you have a son? Naturally, I think Marcus is remarkable too, but then, I'm as biased as you are.'

'As parents, we're permitted to be biased. I believe it's expected of us.'

'And I'm perfectly willing to play my part, but still, facts must be faced. Women have been producing babies for millennia and there really is nothing particularly remarkable about our son.'

'Ah, but I can't claim credit for any of those other babies, whereas — '

'Now I understand you.' Lizzy had understood him perfectly well the entire time, but was unable to resist teasing her husband. 'Despite having secured the continuance of the Darcy name, Marcus's birth has also compelled you to contemplate your own mortality.'

'Nothing nearly so introspective, my love.'

Will's smile, this time directed at her, was a tender caress. 'My mind was full of admiration for our son's fighting spirit. It seems remarkable Marcus is now so healthy, so . . . er, robust — '

'He's certainly that,' Lizzy agreed with feeling, thinking of his readiness to demonstrate his lung capacity whenever he felt hungry, uncomfortable, or simply because he felt like it.

'When I think . . . that terrible night when I thought . . . I thought I would lose you both.'

'Hush.' Lizzy reached for her husband's hand and gave it a gentle squeeze. 'I'm not so very easy to do away with.'

Will shook his head. 'Had it not been for Sanford — '

'Who happened to be here and was pleased to make himself useful.'

Will ran a hand abstractedly through his hair. 'Lizzy, how can you make a joke out of almost dying *and* frightening me half out of my wits?'

'I'm usually able to find something diverting in the direst of situations. Besides, it all ended well and you can now take pleasure in Marcus, who makes it all so very worthwhile.'

'Which brings me back to my original

point. When I consider how tiny Marcus was, how weak and sickly. Sanford warned me he might not survive, and yet look at him now. He's as plump as a pudding.'

'My son, after all the trouble he put me to, wouldn't dare to do anything other than thrive.' Lizzy smiled. 'Besides, he cannot help himself. He's a Darcy through and through. He shares his father's steely determination, to say nothing of his eyes, his hair . . . ' Lizzy grinned. 'Well, what he has of it,' she added, thinking of the tufts of soft dark down concealed beneath the bonnet that covered her infant's head. It insisted upon standing up at different angles and gave him the appearance of being permanently astonished.

'But he has your smile.'

'That is most likely wind.'

'Be that as it may, I still have grave doubts about this party and your ability to withstand the strain of having the house invaded. You've been through a terrible ordeal and have not yet fully recovered your strength.'

'Oh, I'm as strong as that new horse of yours you set so much store by.' Lizzy and Will had been through this argument countless times before Will gave his grudging permission for the house party to go ahead. 'Would you have me make myself a perpetual invalid?'

Will barked out a laugh. 'Not you. That is

precisely my difficulty.'

'Then you must be disinclined to entertain because you would prefer not to go to the trouble of making yourself agreeable.' Lizzy smiled to take the sting out of her words. 'Even you cannot entirely escape your social responsibilities, especially since we owe it to Georgie to celebrate her engagement to Dominic Sanford in a manner befitting a daughter of Pemberley.' Lizzy knew that reminding her husband of Pemberley traditions and the expectations of the local populace in that regard was the only reason why Will had capitulated. But he was clearly still unhappy about his decision. 'Would you have it any other way?'

'No, of course not, but it could have waited a little longer. Georgiana would not have minded.'

'*I* would mind. We have already left it for four months. The spring is here, your aunt and cousin are both keen to meet Mr. Sanford and give their approval, or otherwise, to the match. Besides, my family have waited quite long enough to meet Marcus.'

Will grimaced. 'Lady Catherine's approbation is not necessary. As to Fitzwilliam, he and I are Georgiana's guardians and I already know my cousin approves of Sanford.'

'You can remind Lady Catherine that she

has no say in the matter, if you like.' Lizzy shuddered. 'I do not dare.'

'Ah, so I have found a way to keep you in line at last.' Will's triumphant expression made Lizzy smile, causing her heart to burst with a mixture of exasperation and pleasure at his overprotectiveness. 'I need only to threaten you with lady Catherine and you will do precisely as you should.'

Lizzy sent her husband a playful look of reproach. 'You are certainly welcome to try, but as it happens, Lady Catherine and I understand one another perfectly. She knows I don't respond to bullying and no longer tries to bend me to her will. And as to her approving of Georgie's choice, I am sure your sister will be very upset if Mr. Sanford doesn't pass muster, but can't imagine that will be the case. He possesses great charm, and will doubtless show Lady Catherine sufficient deference to satisfy even her exacting ideas of protocol. And if he is able to suggest a remedy for her stiff joints — '

'My aunt does not have stiff joints. She has never, to my precise recollection, admitted to weaknesses of any kind.'

'She may not admit to them, but that doesn't mean they don't exist.'

Will conceded the point with a sigh. 'I dare say you're right.'

'Certainly I am, just as I was right about Georgie losing her heart to Mr. Sanford upon first making his acquaintance.'

'At Colonel Fitzwilliam's wedding to Celia Sheffield?'

'Exactly so.'

'I must defer to your expertise in such matters. It is a subject upon which all females appear endlessly knowledgeable.'

'I am delighted that Mr. Sanford is not a fortune hunter and genuinely returns Georgie's affections. She was worried she would never find a gentleman who would like her for herself rather than her money, you see.'

'Really?' Will seemed genuinely surprised. 'She never mentioned anything to me.'

'Of course she didn't. You already kept her on a tight enough leash. If you had even suspected she had concerns of that nature, you never would have let her set foot outside of Pemberley.'

'Am I really so draconian?'

'When it comes to your sister's wellbeing, to say nothing of mine — '

Will spread his hands. 'If loving you both, wanting to protect you and keep you safe, is a crime, then I plead guilty.'

'Yes, but in your desire to keep us out of harm's way, you don't always credit us with the sense we actually possess. However, I cannot fault you for that. And as to Georgie, I assured her she would know it when she met a gentleman who genuinely admired her, but I don't think she actually believed me, until she saw Mr. Sanford.' Lizzy closed her eyes and sighed. 'I am very glad to see her so deeply in love since I am quite determined everyone who is dear to me will be as happy in marriage as you and I are.'

'That is a very ambitious desire.' Will gently rubbed his knuckles down Lizzy's cheek. 'Few men could possibly love their wives as passionately as I love you. However, Sanford and Georgiana seem genuinely suited, which is enough to satisfy me.'

'And Mr. Sanford's estate abutting Pemberley makes it easier for you to part with your sister.'

'That, too. I think very highly of Sanford, as an old acquaintance, as a doctor and as a man. She has thought herself in love with lesser men.'

Will scowled and Lizzy knew he must be thinking about his sister's unfortunate attachment to Wickham.

'Perhaps so, but if the circumstances had been different, would you have agreed to the match so readily?' Lizzy sent her husband a sideways look of censure, teasing him into forgetting about Wickham. 'Yes, I can tell from your expression that he would have had his work cut out because no one, in your estimation, is good enough for Georgiana. But Mr. Sanford had the good sense to not only save Marcus and me but also rescued Georgie when the odious Major Halstead tried to kill her.' Lizzy shuddered. 'It still makes me go cold all over when I think how close he came to succeeding.'

Will flexed his jaw. 'But we must try not to think about it. Halstead cannot harm us now.'

'Will he hang, do you suppose?'

'Either that or he will be transported.' Will squeezed her fingers. 'The judicial system will decide his fate.'

'Yes.' Lizzy shook herself. 'On a happier note, we are both agreed that Georgie and Mr. Sanford are ideal for one another.'

'And to celebrate their betrothal, we shall have a houseful of friends and relations for a sennight, just as we did this time last year.' Will shook his head. 'Our spring house party is in danger of becoming a tradition, but with less drama than at the previous gathering, I sincerely hope.'

Lizzy shuddered. 'As do I.'

Lizzy reflected upon that first, disastrous, occasion upon which she had greeted friends and relations as Pemberley's new mistress. Some amongst their number considered Will had married beneath himself and were watching her, hoping to see her behave inappropriately so they could tell one another they had always known she would give Mr. Darcy reason to regret their hasty union. Lizzy was equally determined not to give her critics reason to find fault. She could not have anticipated that trouble would be visited upon her by Wickham, her own sister's husband, and Miss Bingley, who was intent upon breaking up her marriage and taking Lizzy's place.

'Your parents ought to arrive this afternoon.'

'Poor Will.' Lizzy leaned her head on her husband's shoulder. 'Your aunt and my mother here at the same time. They will drive you demented, unless they kill one another first.'

'Your mother has not seen Pemberley, nor has she seen her grandson. I shall not mind her, especially since she will only be here for a week before going on to stay with Jane.' Will kissed the top of Lizzy's head. 'And as long as I have you to myself every night I dare say I shall survive the experience.'

'The Gardiners will be with Mama and Papa, and at least I don't have to apologise for them.'

'You don't need to apologise for any of

your relations, Lizzy. How can I make you understand that?'

'With Mary and Lydia coming, too, it will be pleasant for us five sisters to be all together again, as we will be when Jane and Mr. Bingley arrive tomorrow. That I cannot deny.'

'Don't lose sight of the fact that Caroline Bingley will be with them. I know we have seen her several times since she came north to stay with Bingley, but she hasn't been to Pemberley since trying to make trouble between us. I most emphatically do not wish to see you overset. If she sets one foot out of line, or makes even one disparaging comment, I shall ask Bingley to remove his sister. I would rather be at odds with Bingley than have you discomposed.'

'I'm sure it won't come to that. Miss Bingley has lost her spirit and seems subdued to the point of being impolite. I don't envy Jane and Mr. Bingley having to keep control of her.' Lizzy frowned. 'It is very hard to know what's going on her mind. However, she won't attempt to make any mischief, especially now she understands that you really do care for me.'

Will shook his head. 'How she could have thought otherwise is beyond me.'

Lizzy bit her lip to prevent a smile from escaping. The subject was too raw, and her precious Will still too unaccustomed to being teased, for her to explain what ought to have been obvious.

'Just make sure you smile at me when we are in company.'

'You may depend upon it.'

Lizzy lifted her head from Will's shoulder and checked the baby when she heard him gurgle, thinking he was about to awaken.

'He can't be hungry again already, can he?' Will asked dubiously.

Lizzy smiled as she adjusted the baby's covers. 'He shares his father's voracious appetites.'

'I shall take that as a compliment.'

'It was intended as one.'

Lizzy glanced through the window and noticed her sister Kitty wandering aimlessly across the lawn, her ever-present sketchpad beneath her arm.

'I am glad Lydia and Mary will be here. Kitty must feel lonely since Georgie's attention has been taken up by Mr. Sanford and mine by Marcus. It was kind of you to let Lydia come, Will.'

'Your uncle wrote recently and told me Wickham is doing well, managing his warehouse. To the best of his knowledge he has not fallen back into his dissolute ways.'

To the best of his knowledge. 'I credit

Lydia for the improvement in his behaviour. She has grown up, understands this is her husband's last opportunity because everyone is losing patience with him, and is making sure he behaves himself. I'm glad she won't be excluded from this family gathering. She is still so very young but already understands the extent of her folly and how it's likely to be for her, married to an unsteady man like Wickham.'

'She is no longer in love with him?'

'That I couldn't say, but from the odd remarks she has made in her letters, I do believe she no longer harbours illusions about his character.' Lizzy sighed. 'While he was in the army, she wasn't constantly in his company, and he could hide his excesses from her. Now her eyes have been opened. You don't need me to tell you how dangerous and manipulative he can be, but I do worry he might try to deceive my uncle.'

'Your uncle is awake on every suit and well aware of Wickham's black heart. He will not be taken in by his charm and flattery.'

'I hope you're right about that.' But Lizzy still felt uncomfortable whenever her thoughts dwelt upon Wickham. She knew how ambitious he was and how unjustly he felt he had been treated. She couldn't imagine him remaining satisfied with a career that he looked upon as being beneath him. However, now was not the time for such introspective thoughts and she shook them off. 'I feel excessively for Lydia and blame my mother for the way she turned out. If she had not been so spoiled, allowed to run wild and her every whim indulged, then things might have been very different.' Lizzy sighed. 'However, what's done is done and I am glad she is to have a short respite from her travails.'

'Lydia is always welcome at Pemberley.'

'Kitty will enjoy her society. She seldom talks of her Captain Turner, but I know she's upset to see so little of him. I really thought he would declare himself after the débâcle with Major Halstead, but she tells me he is much taken up with his duties, to say nothing of his father, who will interfere in the captain's life every step of the way.'

'I haven't noticed any particular changes in Kitty. She seems as obliging as always.'

Lizzy shook her head. 'Oh, she seems like her normal self on the surface, but I know she's unhappy. Anyway, Captain Turner wrote me a charming note, accepting our invitation to the engagement dinner, and apologising for not having called for some time. His duties have kept him fully occupied. There must be a great deal to do, I suppose, after Major Halstead's arrest. It can't have been easy for the captain to do his duty when the major was his particular friend. No wonder he's been so preoccupied. However, he did mention that his father is in the district and plans to remain here for several weeks. Ought we to invite Mr. Turner to join the party as well?'

'It sounds as though Turner was angling for just such an invitation when mentioning his father's presence. Why not ask Kitty what she thinks?' Will stood up, his precious time alone with Lizzy and the baby over for now since his steward awaited him. 'Whatever you decide,' he added, leaning over Lizzy to bestow a slow, lingering kiss on her lips, 'will meet with my approval.'

★ ★ ★

The regimental dinner droned endlessly on. Richard Turner's shoulders throbbed from the number of congratulatory slaps they had received from his fellow officers. Richard was being hailed as a hero for arresting Halstead and saving the regiment's honour. He didn't feel very heroic, disliked all the fuss and hated being the centre of attention. It was not a situation he was accustomed to and always made his stammer more pronounced.

His father, on the other hand, seated beside

Colonel Brigstock, basked in reflected glory. For the first time in his recollection, Richard had made a favourable impression upon his irascible parent. Not once during the course of his childhood had he ever managed to achieve that ambition. Any parental praise — and there was precious little of it — was always directed towards one or other of his older brothers. It had seemed grossly unfair to Richard since *he* was the only one out of the three of them who behaved as he ought *and* yearned for acclamation.

Noticed by his father he most certainly was — but only to be ridiculed for his stammer, or other aspects of his character over which he had little or no control. A diligent student, blessed with an enquiring mind and a love of learning, he strove for perfection but was held back by shyness and his wretched stammer. His brothers were both idle brutes, intellectually challenged but able to get away with their inadequacies because they were strapping fellows in possession of guile and charm which they were proficient at dispensing to cover their deficiencies.

Richard, with modest independent means thanks to a bequest from his grandfather whose speech was also blighted by a stammer and who presumably understood the agonies of such an affliction, need not have taken up a career if he had preferred not to. Both of his brothers preferred not to, but Richard had a point to prove — to himself, but more especially to his father. He purchased a commission as lieutenant and had been promoted to captain on merit. And now, he was to be promoted again.

The regiment lacked a major, thanks to Halstead's arrest, and the colonel wished to prefer that rank upon Richard. It felt unchivalrous to benefit from his friend's fall from grace and his first notion had been to refuse the promotion. But common sense prevailed. Such opportunities did not come along every day. It was not his fault that Halstead's greed and love for an unsuitable woman had caused him to act so abominably. Richard berated himself for his inability to see Halstead's true character. In retrospect, he had shown glimpses of it during the course of their friendship, but Richard had not made the connection. Besides, he was not alone in that regard. Everyone in the regiment had thought Halstead to be a first-rate chap.

Be that as it may, the regiment needed a major and if Richard didn't accept the promotion it would go to someone else.

And by accepting the commission, finally . . . finally, Richard had earned parental approval.

Perversely, now that he had it, he wondered why it had been so important to him. He didn't like his father very much, and he had done nothing to earn Richard's respect. He had always been a tyrant, ruling his family by intimidation, making his displeasure apparent at the mildest transgression of his draconian rules. His mother's death ten years previously saw the end to any restraint he might have exercised out of deference to her finer feelings. Richard's buttocks still stung from the regular thrashings he had received, designed to literally beat the stammer out of him because no son of The Honourable Angus Turner, the Earl of Cheshire's younger brother, could possibly go through life with such an impediment.

Military life, the camaraderie he enjoyed with his fellow officers, had seen his stammer almost disappear. But the moment he was anywhere near his father, he became a babbling idiot again. It was infuriating. Almost as infuriating as it was now, listening to his father's booming voice as he all but told Richard's new colonel how to run his regiment. Richard looked away, disgusted. His father had not spent a single day in a red coat and knew nothing whatsoever about military tactics, but that did not stop him from being an expert on the subject.

'Damned good show that your pater joined the celebration,' the officer seated beside Richard observed.

'Quite so.'

But the question was, why *had* he chosen to come, and for so long? He had made a journey of almost two hundred miles from the family home in Cheshire and Richard wasn't foolish enough to imagine he had done so simply to celebrate his son's promotion. Come to that, he had no idea how his father had heard of it. Richard certainly hadn't enlightened him.

But his father, ear to the ground as always, *had* heard about it and inflicted himself upon Richard, seemingly in no particular hurry to return home again. He wanted something of Richard: that much was plainly apparent. But what? Richard shrugged, accepting that he would not remain in ignorance for long. His father had never been one to dissemble when it came to getting his own way.

The pater had recently tried to force Richard into marriage with a woman of his own choosing: a member of the aristocracy who, from his father's perspective, would raise the family's profile. Richard's two brothers had dutifully married the women chosen for them. His father must have assumed that Richard would also toe the parental line.

He now knew better.

A serious argument had ensued when, for the first time ever, Richard stood up to his autocratic father. Whatever he wanted of Richard this time, he couldn't possibly harbour hopes of his marrying another suitable female of his choosing.

Besides, Richard had already settled upon the lady he wished to spend the rest of his life with. Kitty Bennet was the sweetest girl imaginable. They had interests in common, never ran out of things to talk and laugh about, both suffered from shyness and, significantly, Richard's stammer didn't return while in her company as it normally did with members of the fairer sex.

Frustratingly he had been too busy to get over to Pemberley very much in the months following Halstead's arrest. He had been detained at the garrison in Newcastle, which was too far from Pemberley to make calling convenient. The regiment had been on manoeuvres and his time had not been his own. But there was to be a house party to celebrate Miss Darcy's engagement and Richard was invited for the entire week. He planned to use the opportunity to declare himself to Miss Bennet and was nervous about his reception. Richard thought she could do a great deal better than him, but if she had decided against him he would prefer to know it, even though it would break his heart.

He had mentioned his father's presence in his reply to Mrs. Darcy. To his surprise, she had replied, inviting his father to attend the party as well. Richard sighed, wondering if she knew quite what she would be letting herself in for. The pater wouldn't be intimidated by Pemberley's splendours, nor would he be content to keep his opinions to himself. Still, if that was what it would take for Richard to be able to spend more time in Kitty's company, he would just have to make the best of things. He managed a brief smile when he considered the possibility of Lady Catherine, Darcy's formidable aunt, being present. Even an estate as extensive as Pemberley, Richard suspected, would not be big enough to accommodate two such forthright characters.

To his detriment, he had considered withholding the invitation and merely sending his father's regrets, but if the pater's path should cross that of the Darcys in future, as it would if Richard persuaded Kitty to marry him, he couldn't risk it being mentioned. Therefore, he had told his father about it and, naturally, he had accepted, knowing of Darcy by reputation. A letter to Mrs. Darcy, accepting for both of them, had been duly sent to Pemberley.

'Well, my boy, that went well, I think.'

Richard, lost in thought, had not heard his father approach. He stood up, along with everyone else, since the dinner had finally come to an end.

'I shall return to my lodgings now,' his father continued. 'Call upon me there in the morning. I need to speak with you about a matter of importance.'

2

Kitty Bennet stood beneath Pemberley's entrance portico with her sister Lizzy, Mr. Darcy and Georgiana, watching her mother and father's carriage, and that of her aunt and uncle, wend their way up the long Pemberley driveway. She had accompanied her father on a visit to Pemberley about a month after Lizzy's marriage and was invited to remain indefinitely when her father left again after just a week. At first feeling homesick, out of place and anxious, slowly Kitty had become less awed by Pemberley and now actually felt as though it was where she belonged.

'Well, Kitty,' Lizzy remarked. 'We are about to be a family again.'

'What if Mama expects me to return to Hertfordshire?' Kitty asked, linking arms with her sister, alarmed when the thought popped into her head. 'I am quite settled here at Pemberley and have no desire to leave.'

'And nor shall you.' Lizzy patted Kitty's hand. 'Your home is at Pemberley now and anyway I couldn't possibly spare you.'

'But I don't do anything.'

'On the contrary, you are moral support

and make me feel less of an imposter.'

'Lizzy!' Kitty lowered her voice so that Mr. Darcy, in muted conversation with Georgie, would not hear her. 'Your husband adores you, and so do all the servants.'

'Who probably compare me to Will's mama and find me wanting.'

Kitty flapped a hand, unable to believe that Lizzy, who was always seemed so sure of herself and her opinions, could possibly have insecurities. 'Really, you talk such nonsense sometimes.'

Kitty was glad her place at Pemberley was secure, even if Lizzy was only being kind and had no real need of her. At first petrified of Mr. Darcy, whom she had considered haughty and aloof, Kitty had slowly become accustomed to his ways. Since the terrible night when Lizzy had struggled to give birth to Marcus, she had seen Mr. Darcy in an entirely different light, and had come to like and respect him very much indeed. He had given vent to his emotions and actually cried in front of her and Georgie when he thought Lizzy might die. Only imagine that.

Oh, what Kitty would give to inspire such total adoration in a gentleman!

She had thought that Miss Darcy, whom she had heard described as being as aloof as her brother, would resent Kitty's presence.

Much to Kitty's astonishment, the reverse had proven to be the case. Georgie was not aloof but lonely and shy, and she and Kitty had formed the most unlikely friendship. Their lives up until then had been diametrically opposed and Kitty felt like a poor relation with little to offer that would interest the refined daughter of Pemberley.

She and Georgie, frequently thrown into one another's company, fed from one another's experiences. They gasped with astonishment at the activities the other described. Georgie could hardly believe the amount of latitude Kitty and Lydia had enjoyed. Kitty thought the rigid restrictions surrounding Georgie's every movement were unnecessary. She sympathised with her new friend and asked why she had not rebelled. Georgie claimed rebellion would not have occurred to her. Her cousin Anne's movements were similarly restricted, and she assumed that was how it was for all young ladies in her position.

Kitty imagined it probably was. Not being an heiress herself, she wouldn't actually know.

Mixing in such refined society had had a beneficial effect upon Kitty and she was now very glad indeed that her father had not been persuaded to let her go to Brighton, along with Lydia: a journey which had resulted in Lydia's hasty marriage to Mr. Wickham.

Lydia had lived with Wickham before they were married. It still shocked Kitty to think that her headstrong sister would go *that* far, wondering what had compelled Wickham to marry her when he need not have done. She got the impression that Mr. Darcy had somehow been involved, just as he must have persuaded her uncle to give Wickham a position when he left the army. It was an oddity and Kitty wished she was party to all the particulars.

Still, all in all, it was fortunate for Lydia that Mr. Darcy happened to be on hand when she made such an appalling mess of things. He was so much in love with Lizzy that he involved himself in the affairs of a man he obviously despised to save the reputation of the lady he adored. His selfless actions had benefited the Bennet family collectively. As Mr. Collins, the clergyman who would inherit Longbourn upon Mr. Bennet's death, had taken delight in reminding them, who would have wished to know them had Lydia's scandalous behaviour become common knowledge?

Such thoughts rattled through her brain as the carriages drew closer. So too did concern that her mother's ceaseless chatter and . . .

well, foolishness, would embarrass them all. How much she had changed in one short year. It would not previously have occurred to her to find her mother embarrassing, or wonder how Lydia's domestic felicity had come to be.

So much had changed in her life for the better. She had a closet full of fine clothes that her father would never have been able to afford to provide her with. Her manners had improved beyond recognition, she had been encouraged to indulge her love of sketching and was now moderately comfortable mixing in all levels of society. And yet . . .

It seemed churlish to have complaints when she was so very fortunate; the envy of her friend Maria Lucas, with whom she still corresponded. Not that she would ever voice her dissatisfaction. That would be a sorry way indeed to repay her sister's kindness. She was genuinely happy that Georgie had found her heart's desire, but the bald truth was that she missed her society now that so much of her time was taken up with Mr. Sanford's activities. It left Kitty with too much time to think what the future might hold for her. Unlike Georgie, she did not have a large dowry, or any fortune at all, to attract would-be suitors.

Kitty now understood how Georgie could

have been lonely at Pemberley and felt guilty for harbouring such feelings herself. She had ample reason to count her blessings and ought to shake off such unworthy thoughts. If only Captain Turner would . . . but she knew he would not. His absence from Pemberley spoke volumes and she would be best advised to forget her ambitions in that regard. She had got it wrong and there was an end to the matter.

'I heard from Captain . . . I mean Major Turner this morning,' Lizzy remarked, as though sensing the nature of Kitty's thoughts.

'I still think it odd to hear him referred to as *major*. I am sure he's been promoted on merit. Even so, I can't imagine he takes much pleasure from his elevated rank since it's only because of Major Halstead's transgressions that the opening arose.'

'Yes, I dare say you're right.' Kitty wondered why Lizzy was looking so . . . well, nervous. 'What is it? Is Major Turner not coming after all? Is that why he wrote to you? You don't need to worry about me. I am perfectly indifferent and I'm sure the major can do as he pleases.'

'Oh no, he's coming.' Lizzy paused. 'So is his father.'

'His father!' Kitty clapped a hand over her mouth, all pretence at indifference forgotten.

'But why . . . what?' She shook her head. 'I don't understand.'

'I told you he was in the district for a while.' Kitty nodded. 'I felt obliged to include him in the invitation when I became aware.'

Kitty trembled. 'I wish I had known.'

Lizzy smiled. 'Which is why I didn't tell you. I knew how you would be, and didn't feel the need to worry you if Mr. Turner declined the invitation.'

'Well, I suppose . . . but what if he takes me in dislike?' Kitty shrugged. 'Although that doesn't really signify, I suppose, since the major has no special interest in me.'

'Ok, Kitty!'

Lizzy had no time to expand since the carriages had just rattled to a halt in front of the entrance portico.

'Are you ready?' Lizzy asked.

'Of course,' Kitty replied in a falsely bright tone that caused Lizzy to send her a quizzical glance.

'Everything will work out for the best,' Lizzy said, patting Kitty's hand as she detached it from the crook of her arm.

Kitty wondered if Lizzy was referring to their mother's visit or to Major Turner's father. She had no opportunity to ask her as she and Mr. Darcy had stepped forward to greet the new arrivals. She could sense

Lizzy's mixed feelings at seeing their mother for the first time in over a year: feelings that closely mirrored Kitty's own. Unworthy feelings that persevered in spite of Kitty's best efforts to banish them.

A footman lowered the steps and assisted Mama to alight from the first carriage. She was red in the face, her bonnet askew and her travelling clothes hopelessly crumpled. She waved at them all, then stared up at Pemberley's magnificent façade and her jaw dropped open, rendering her temporarily speechless.

'Mama!' Lizzy gave their mother a hug and then transferred her attention to their father, whom she greeted with far greater warmth. Kitty suspected Lizzy had still not entirely forgiven Mama for trying to force her into matrimony with the odious Mr. Collins, her determination to secure her own future taking precedence over her second daughter's happiness. Lizzy and Mr. Collins would have made one another miserable, and Mama was the only person who couldn't see it. 'How was your journey?'

'It seemed interminable, Lizzy,' Mama replied, even though the question had been addressed to Papa. 'And I am absolutely sure the beds were not properly aired in that last inn we stopped at. The landlady assured me they were. She was most uncivil and all but accused me of making difficulties.' She flapped a hand. 'As though I would do such a thing. I told her Mr. Darcy of Pemberley was married to *my* daughter and she would hear from him if she did not show more respect. However, she didn't seem to believe me and I am absolutely sure the linens were damp. I dare say I shall catch a chill and my poor nerves will be affected as a consequence. You know how I suffer. Not that I ever complain. This house is absolutely enormous. I had no idea. You did not explain it to me properly, Mr. Bennet. How do you do, Mr. Darcy.' Mama paused only to dip a curtsey but gave no one else an opportunity to speak. 'Kitty, my dear. I almost didn't recognise you. I'm sure you have grown taller and I have not seen that gown before. Miss Darcy, I am very glad to see you again.'

Kitty inwardly quailed. Her optimistic expectation that Mama would be cowed by her surroundings were already proving to be without foundation. Lizzy left their mother to run on and quietly greeted everyone else as they spilled from the carriages.

Kitty followed her example. Her aunt and uncle looked upon her with kindness and said they were very pleased to see her again. Her sister Mary looked different: more elegant.

Her clothing had improved, as had her manner, and she had done her hair more elaborately. It was as though being the only Miss Bennet in residence at Longbourn had given her more self-confidence. Kitty was glad. Mary had always been a solitary person, but perhaps not through choice. Jane and Lizzy had been close, as had she and Lydia. Poor Mary had been left out. Kitty felt ashamed not to have realised it before now and vowed to spend time with her while Mary was at Pemberley.

Lydia came next and Kitty braced herself for a boisterous greeting. Much to her astonishment, Lydia appeared subdued and made no attempt to put herself forward. That was unusual enough to cause Kitty concern. She wondered if being cooped up in a carriage with their mother for several days had worn even the indefatigable Lydia down.

Mr. Darcy proffered his arm and escorted their mother into the house, leaving an army of footmen to fall upon the luggage. Following behind, Kitty winced at Mama's constant loud exclamations at everything she saw and her verbal estimations of their value. Poor Mr. Darcy! Kitty couldn't imagine anything other than the deep, abiding affection he felt for his wife compelling him to endure such uncouth behaviour with equanimity.

Mama made a terrible fuss about removing her outer garments before settling in a comfortable chair in the magnificent drawing room. She had a footman reposition the chair several times before she was satisfied that it was exactly the right distance from the fire. And all the while, Mama's gaze continued to rove around the room, taking in every small detail. Kitty suspected she was attempting to commit to memory as much of its contents as possible, the better to boast about them to Lady Lucas when she returned to Hertfordshire.

Refreshments were served, which gave everyone something to do with their hands, and conversation was temporarily suspended. But, since their mother was present, that situation did not endure.

'Kitty,' Mama said in a loud voice, as though Kitty was in another room, not seated a few feet away from her.

'Yes, Mama. What is it?'

'That is what I should be asking you. Why did you not tell me yourself about Captain Turner and his interest in you? Why did I have to hear it elsewhere?'

Kitty glanced at Lydia, who mouthed an apology. 'There is nothing for you to know,

Mama. He is merely an acquaintance. Oh, and he is a major now.'

'A major. Well, he sounds like a remarkably steady young man and I should like to meet him. His father is an earl's brother, no less.' Mama's bosom swelled in direct proportion to Kitty's desire to melt into the wainscoting. 'Just imagine, my little Kitty being related to an earl.'

'Mama!' Kitty felt her face flaming. 'You assume too much.'

'I do not make unrealistic assumptions, child, and shall know as soon as I meet the major if his intentions are serious. Still, it would do no harm to give him some encouragement.'

Kitty glanced helplessly at her father, who merely shrugged, the ghost of a smile flirting with his lips. As usual, he was diverted by Mama's silliness, didn't seem the least little bit embarrassed by her rambling tongue, and clearly had no intention of putting a stop to it.

'I was sorry to hear we were all deceived in Major Halstead's character,' Aunt Gardiner said, kindly diverting the attention away from Kitty. 'I was shocked when Lizzy wrote, explaining it all. I gather you and Mr. Sanford were instrumental in bringing him to justice, Miss Darcy.'

'Yes, ma'am,' Georgie replied. 'But not intentionally, and it was Mr. Sanford's dog who actually saved the day.'

'I am glad to hear you did not put yourself in danger deliberately,' Mama replied before Aunt Gardiner could respond to Georgie's comment. 'I don't approve of young ladies taking unnecessary risks.'

'Mary,' Lizzy said. 'You're very quiet. Have you fully recovered from the fever you caught last year? We were quite worried about you.'

'I have a strong constitution and don't give in to infirmities,' Mary replied.

Perhaps Mary had not changed so very much, Kitty thought, wondering if she realised how pompous she sounded.

'It is such a shame that dear Wickham could not be spared from his duties,' Mama said into the ensuing silence. 'Really, brother,' she added, glaring at Uncle Gardiner. 'I am perfectly sure he could have been. I am surprised you didn't think of me before insisting he remain in London. How delightful it would have been to have all my daughters' husbands in the same room.'

A penetrating silence greeted this oration, but if Mama felt the tension her words had created she gave no sign of it.

'Poor Lydia. No wonder you are so downcast,' she added.

'I am not downcast, Mama.'

'Only eighteen and such fortitude in the face of adversity.' Mama shook her head in admiration and beamed at Lydia, her favourite child. 'Really, Lizzy, I am surprised that Jane isn't here. Whatever were you thinking?'

'Mr. and Mrs. Bingley will be here tomorrow, Mama. Mr. Bingley has business to keep him at Campton Park until then.'

'Oh well, I suppose one more day won't signify.'

When everyone had refreshed themselves, Lizzy rang the bell and asked for Marcus to be brought down. Everyone admired the baby, who behaved impeccably. Everyone except Lydia who, Kitty noticed, barely looked at him.

'Only fancy my Lizzy giving you such a fine son, Mr. Darcy,' Mama exclaimed over and over again, as though she took personal credit for Marcus's existence. 'I am sure none of Lady Lucas's daughters will produce such a good-looking child.'

Oh dear, Kitty thought, momentarily catching Lizzy's eye. It was going to be a long week.

★   ★   ★

Richard presented himself at his father's rented rooms at the agreed hour and was admitted by Marsden, his father's long-standing valet and general factotum.

'Please come in, Major.' He opened the door to his father's sitting room and stood back to allow Richard to pass through it.

'Ah, there you are, my boy.'

His father was being jovial, immediately putting Richard on his guard.

'G-good morning, Father,' he said in a neutral tone.

'A glass of sherry?'

'N-no thank you.'

'I shall have one, Marsden, and then you may leave us.'

His father seated himself and accepted his drink from Marsden. Richard took the chair opposite his pater and waited, not troubling himself to make conversation.

'We have a family difficulty, my boy,' his father said, breaking the uneasy silence that ensued. 'And you are the only one who can uphold our honour.'

'Really?' Whatever his father had wanted to say to him, Richard hadn't expected him to admit to familial shortcomings of any sort, but especially not ones that only Richard could resolve. He was highly suspicious. 'I d-don't have the pleasure of understanding y-you, sir.'

'Then I shall speak plain. My brother

despairs of his worthless son ever producing an heir to eventually assume the title.'

Worthless? Richard's cousin, Reginald, had always been held up as the example that Richard ought to aspire to, even though it was made equally apparent that he would never achieve that ambition. Whatever could Reginald have done to fall so spectacularly out of favour?

'Reginald has three daughters. S-surely a son will follow?'

His father shook his head. 'Their youngest is almost ten. Reginald's wife is almost certainly beyond child-bearing age.'

'Yes, I s-suppose she must be.' Richard's mind had not previously been troubled by such trivialities. Reginald was close to forty and Richard seemed to recall that his oh-so-suitable wife was several years older than he was. 'Presumably either Edmund or Percy w-will produce a son,' he added, referring to the brothers whom he had never been able to emulate. 'A-and the title will pass to him.'

'I would much prefer it if you sired the heir.'

'Me!' Richard was astounded. 'E-excuse me, s-sir, but I am surprised to hear you make the suggestion. I have never done a-anything to win your approval. Or my u-uncle's, either.'

'I was too harsh.'

Yes, you were. But still, Richard had never imagined his father would make such an admission. 'I s-still don't see why Edmund or Percy can't oblige.'

'Do you not?' His father expelled an elaborate sigh. 'I had hoped not to have to spell it out.'

Richard was genuinely in the dark. 'I r-regret, you must e-explain.' Damnation, his stutter was getting worse.

'We have to assume Edmund's wife is barren.'

Richard bit his lip to prevent himself from reminding his father how suitable she, too, had been deemed, and how he had bragged at having arranged the match.

'They have been married for five years and have no children.'

E-even so — '

'And as for Percy . . . well, he is a complete disappointment. The damned boy prefers young men. Surely you realised,' his father said, presumably in response to Richard's astounded expression. 'He assures me he has done his duty and continues to do so, but it wouldn't surprise me if the marriage hasn't even been consummated.'

'What happens if none of us has a s-son?'

'The title dies out, since there is no one

else for it to pass to.' Richard's father ground his jaw. 'That cannot be allowed to happen. It has been in our family for three hundred years and ensures we are looked up to and respected wherever we go.'

Richard refrained from reminding his father that none of that respect had ever been accorded to him. He had been an embarrassment to his father, and his brothers, too; a stuttering fool to be ignored or made fun of. But now, if his father had his way, he would be the saviour of the earldom.

'So, my boy, it's up to you.'

'I am n-not married.'

'No, but that situation can soon be remedied. I have discussed the subject with your uncle at length. He, in turn, has been in talks with Lord Rainham. His daughter is — '

'No!'

Richard belatedly realised that his father had invented a new, more compelling, reason to choose his bride for him. Blinding fury gripped him and he was temporarily unable to say more than the one word of denial, but at least he said it with enough emphasis and cold determination to make his father flinch.

'Excuse me?'

'I said *no*, Father. We have discussed your interference in my affairs before now and you are acquainted with my feelings.' In his anger,

Richard overcame his stutter.

'That was before you understood the seriousness of our situation as a family. You have always had a strong sense of duty and I call upon you now to remember your obligations in that respect. Lucinda Rainham is a kind, biddable young woman who won't give you a moment's regret.'

'If I choose to marry it will be to a lady of my own choosing and I will then do my very best to sire a son. T-that is *all* I can promise you.'

'We cannot have just any lady producing the next heir.'

'It will not be just *any* l-lady.'

'You have someone in mind?' His father sat forward and fixed Richard with a probing gaze. 'Do I know her? Who are her people? Why have you not mentioned the matter to me before now?'

Richard stood up. If he did not leave now, immediately, he would say something he might later regret.

Or worse, not regret.

'You must excuse me, Father. I have duties to attend to before leaving for Pemberley tomorrow. In view of our difference of opinion, if y-you no longer wish to c-come with me, I am sure Mrs. Darcy will a-accept your apologies.'

'I underestimated you, boy,' his father said pensively. 'I can quite see that now.'

'I am dining with the colonel tonight but will c-collect you in the morning, unless you have a change of h-heart in the meantime.'

'You seem inordinately keen to go to Pemberley.' His father's expression became pensive, calculating. 'And I myself should not dream of reneging. I shall be ready for you in the morning.'

Yes, Richard thought, as he strode away from his father's lodgings. That was what concerned him.

3

Kitty tripped along the corridor and knocked on Lydia's door, thinking it would be like old times: the two of them huddled together in a bedchamber, exchanging confidences, giggling about something silly, sighing over a gentleman who had attracted their interest; finding fault with their neighbours and friends.

Except it could never be like that again. Lydia was now a married woman with responsibilities and Kitty wasn't the same person she had been as recently as a year ago.

It was half-an-hour since the party in the drawing room had broken up and her relations had retired to their rooms to rest before dinner. She fully expected to find Lydia's room strewn with clothing from an open valise while the room's occupant gave Nora specific orders about precisely how her gowns ought to be handled. Nora was Kitty's personal maid and would be looking after Lydia as well during her stay at Pemberley.

Her very own maid! Kitty still sometimes felt convinced she must have imagined such a luxury. Growing up at Longbourn, the five sisters had routinely squabbled over the services of one harried maid. Now Kitty had Nora all to herself but had readily agreed to Lizzy's suggestion that she share her with Lydia, who had always been fastidious about her wardrobe and clever in reinventing old gowns as fashions changed.

But when Kitty entered Lydia's chamber, Nora was nowhere in sight. Lydia herself was huddled on the window seat, still wearing her travelling clothes, arms wrapped around knees pulled up to her chin.

And she was crying.

'Lydia,' Kitty said in alarm. 'Whatever's wrong?'

Lydia blinked back fresh tears as Kitty sat beside her. 'I have made such a mess of everything, Kitty.'

'I'm sure that isn't the case. You succeeded in marrying the man of your dreams, just as you assured me you would the first time you saw him.'

'You should have stopped me. I didn't know my own mind and now it's too late.'

'I'm sure it's not as bad as all that. Have you had a disagreement with Wickham? Tell me what's wrong and I will help you if I possibly can.'

Lydia looked at Kitty for a long time. 'You're different. More refined.' Lydia made it sound like an accusation. 'I don't know . . . something.'

'I have lived here for a year. It's very different to Longbourn and I must have adapted.'

'This could have been me.' She plucked at the fine muslin of Kitty's afternoon gown. 'If I had been more sensible, or listened to Jane and Lizzy when they tried to warn me.'

'You're jealous?'

Kitty tried to hide her annoyance. How typical of Lydia not to be able to suppress her envy. Lydia sighed, seeming as though she was older than Kitty, which she was not. Only this time her eyes didn't sparkle with mischief but with weary resignation, as though at eighteen, she had already seen more of the world than ought to have been the case and didn't much enjoy the view.

'Our aunt and uncle have been generous in giving Mr. Wickham employment.'

Lydia shrugged. 'He hates it. He says being the equivalent of a shopkeeper is beneath him and talks of giving it up.'

Kitty frowned. 'At least you're in London, which is what you always wanted.'

'We never go out and enjoy ourselves. Our uncle watches us like a hawk.'

'Why should you not go to the theatre and assemblies? You're not making sense, Lydia.'

Kitty grasped Lydia's hand. It was ice cold, even though the room was pleasantly warm. 'I can't help you unless I know why you're so overset.'

Lydia sighed. 'It's complicated and talking about it will achieve nothing.'

'Lydia! Talk to me.'

'You know Wickham was old Mr. Darcy's favourite?'

'I also know there's bad blood between him and Lizzy's husband. What I don't know is why.'

'The dispute between them dates back to before we were married.' Lydia gazed out of the window while she spoke but Kitty suspected she didn't even see the magnificent view. 'He told me old Mr. Darcy made him certain promises of monetary reward which his son didn't honour. Wickham insisted his life had been ruined by my sister's husband, as though he expected me to intercede with Lizzy on his behalf. I did try. I wrote to Lizzy, dropping very obvious hints. She ignored them but sent me money when she could, so there didn't seem much else I could do.'

'Of course you could not.' Kitty patted Lydia's hand. 'I don't think Wickham told you the entire truth, but he's your husband and so of course you had to take his part.'

'I believed him, but convinced myself I could be such a good wife to him that he would forget about his disappointment. And it worked, to start with. He was in the regulars, safely garrisoned in this country, and there were lots of parties and smart assemblies for us to attend.' She shrugged. 'You know me. I never could resist a party, but Wickham likes them too and I thought he enjoyed showing me off.'

'Why should you not have fun? Young people like to dance and enjoy themselves.'

'Perhaps, but I should have stopped to think about what we had to live on; even though it's not a subject I'd ever had to concern myself with before then. Looking back, it's obvious we were living beyond our means. We both have extravagant natures and he did nothing to try and curb mine. This time last year, at Lizzy's first house party, we were in dire straits. The debts were mounting and could no longer be ignored. Wickham decided to leave the army and seek employment as a barrister in London, which he assured me he was adequately qualified to do.'

'I am sure he is. He had a fine education, thanks to old Mr. Darcy.'

'In spite of that he couldn't find work and with each door that was slammed in his face, so his resentment towards the current Mr. Darcy grew.'

Kitty's mouth fell open when Lydia went on to describe, in a dull monotone, the actions Wickham had taken to gain revenge upon Mr. Darcy.

'Let me get this straight,' Kitty said when Lydia ran out of words. 'Wickham and Miss Bingley joined forces to entrap Lizzy in a compromising position with your husband. Wickham expected Mr. Darcy to pay him to keep the matter quiet and, if he did not, Miss Bingley would pay him instead.' Kitty remembered Lizzy fainting at the party a year ago and being carried back to the house by Mr. Darcy. There was a lot of tension and raised voices, but everyone had assured Kitty there was nothing for her to worry about. She had been enjoying Captain Turner's attentions too much at the time to give Lizzy's difficulties further thought. 'I can understand Wickham's warped thinking, but why would Miss Bingley do such a thing?'

Lydia wrinkled her nose. 'She wanted Mr. Darcy for herself. She thought the marriage would not survive such a scandal and she could take Lizzy's place.'

'Well, she didn't try to hide the fact that she thought Lizzy was beneath Mr. Darcy when she was in Hertfordshire *and* clearly always wanted him for herself. But even so . . . '

'I fell for her ruse. I honestly had no idea what she and Wickham had planned.' Fresh tears coursed down Lydia's face. 'I grew up that day and finally saw Wickham for what he really is.'

'Oh, Lydia!' Kitty hugged her sister. 'And yet you are bound to him in matrimony.'

'Oh, why did Papa allow me to go to Brighton? I knew I was behaving badly, but rather enjoyed the notoriety and didn't think any real harm would come of it. Nor would it have done, had not Wickham been obliged to run away from his debts and offered to take me with him. He promised me marriage and I thought it would be the greatest fun imaginable to be the first of us married when I was still only sixteen.' She shook her head. 'How naïve I was.'

'So, explain to me how Wickham came to be employed by our uncle?'

'Our uncle offered him the position after Wickham's plot to compromise Lizzy was exposed. There is history between our uncle and Mr. Darcy that concerns Wickham.'

'What history?' Kitty was fascinated. This was all news to her.

'Between them, they forced Wickham to marry me. I still have nightmares when I

48

think of the consequences for the rest of you if they had not done so. I was so very thoughtless and selfish.' She expelled a long breath. 'Anyway, I think Mr. Darcy must have paid Wickham to marry me. It is very demeaning to think he had to be bribed into taking me, but that's no one's fault but my own. Our uncle probably wanted to foot the bill but Mr. Darcy wouldn't let him. I wondered why he of all people would do such a thing, but as soon as I heard he was to marry Lizzy it all made sense. Anyway, our uncle must have felt it was his turn to do something for Wickham and offered him the opportunity to manage one of his warehouses.'

'Given what he tried to do to Lizzy, you must agree that was very generous of him.'

'Oh, I do agree. But there are strict terms attaching to the offer. Wickham is not allowed to gamble, enter any of his old London haunts or mix with his less salubrious acquaintances until he has worked off his debts. And so we live a very quiet life. We dine with our aunt and uncle once a week, and they often have other guests present, which provides Wickham with an opportunity to be his old, charming self, but I can see that charm now for the sham that it is.'

'Poor Lydia.'

'I'm not supposed to know how extensive our debts are, but I'm no longer a blind fool and made it my business to find out.' She sighed. 'I shall be in my dotage before Wickham works them off.'

'You are only eighteen, Lydia,' Kitty said, squeezing her hand, hating to see her vibrant sister so downcast. 'It seems unfair that you're saddled with such a life, but at least you love Wickham, even if you no longer respect him.'

'Do I?'

Kitty widened her eyes. 'You are no longer in love?'

Lydia lifted one shoulder. 'After what he tried to do to Lizzy, is it any wonder? Besides, he never loved me and now . . . and now I am increasing.'

'Oh, Lydia, that's wonderful news! I am to be an aunty for a third time.'

'Wickham is furious about it. He won't speak to me.'

'Why? You've been married for two years. What else can he have expected?'

'I told him last week, thinking I couldn't leave it for much longer. But I should have waited. He was already in a terrible mood because I was coming to Pemberley while he would be obliged to stay in London and, as he puts it, continue with the drudgery. Any mention of Pemberley sends him into the most terrible rages, especially as he knows I will no longer allow him to talk to me about how badly he's been treated.'

'He has lost his most devoted sympathiser.'

'Yes, along with my respect, and he knows it.'

'Does he . . . excuse me, but does he entertain other women?'

'Probably. I really don't care. My more immediate concern is the baby. I haven't told anyone else, other than you, and don't plan to until Wickham calms down a little. *If* he calms down.'

'He will. Of course he will. All men wish to be fathers, deep down.'

Kitty wondered if she was giving her sister false hope. She had absolutely no idea if Wickham would actually calm down, but didn't see that he had much option.

'Your Captain Turner has proven to be quite a hero,' Lydia remarked, abruptly changing the subject.

'Major Turner, and he is hardly mine. I've barely seen him these past four months.'

'Is he coming to this party?'

'Apparently so. With his father.'

Lydia brightened. 'Do you imagine his father plans to look you over and give his seal of approval before Major Turner proposes?'

'Lud, I hope not.' She smiled at Lydia. 'Besides, what you have just told me has put me off the thought of matrimony.'

'Don't dwell upon my example.' Lydia smiled through her melancholy. 'Think of how happy Lizzy and Jane are in their marriages.'

'Well, there is that.' Kitty frowned. 'It starts to make sense now. Jane was wondering for a long time why Mr. Bingley's sisters didn't join him here in the north. Presumably they stayed away because of what Caroline Bingley tried to do to Lizzy.'

'Yes. Mrs. Hurst helped her sister to recover. Supposedly she had a breakdown, although I have my doubts about that. I think she pretended to be demented in order to excuse her despicable behaviour.'

'And yet she will be here tomorrow. Poor Lizzy. And poor you, Lydia.'

'I doubt she will try to seek me out and that situation suits me perfectly.'

'Do Jane and Mr. Bingley know the particulars?'

'Yes, I believe they've recently been told.'

'Goodness, Jane and her easy-going husband having to think badly of someone.' Lydia managed a wan smile at Kitty's words. 'How terrible for them.'

'Do you remember our friend Denny?' Lydia asked.

'Very well, but why mention him?'

'He too has left the army and is actually one of the few people who owes Wickham money, rather than the other way around. He still keeps in touch with Wickham and will be in Lambton later this week. I've promised Wickham I will call upon him to collect the money he owes. Will you come with me, Kitty? Wickham said I was to go alone but I'd prefer you to bear me company.'

'By all means.'

'I don't want to tell Lizzy where I'm going, or why. In fact I would prefer to avoid all mention of Wickham's name while here as much as I possibly can.'

'Not so easy when our mother constantly sings his praises.'

Lydia rolled her eyes. 'Mama is too self-obsessed to realise just how thoughtless some of her remarks can be.'

Kitty smiled. 'Diplomacy is not one of Mama's qualities, it's true.'

'You mustn't despair over the major, Kitty,' Lydia said, grasping her hand. 'I've seen him with you. I know how much he admires you and feel persuaded there must be a very good reason for his absence these past months. Once he arrives, I dare say everything will be explained.'

'I'm not in the least despondent, Lydia.'

Which wasn't precisely true. Kitty had set her heart on the major and was so sure he felt the same way about her that it was difficult to disguise her despair. But pride prevented her from making that admission, even to Lydia. It was astonishing that Lydia, the most self-centred of them all, should be so perceptive.

'These things have a way of working themselves out,' Lydia said, in a worldly-wise tone that belied her tender years. Given all the things that had happened to her since her marriage, Kitty supposed that shouldn't have surprised her. 'But returning to the question of Denny, Kitty. If we go together, you can ask for a carriage without arousing suspicion.'

'Of course I'll go with you. We could go tomorrow, if you like. What with everyone else arriving during the course of the day, we won't be missed.'

'Thank you, but Denny won't be here until later in the week.'

'Very well. That will give you time to regain your strength. You look very pale.'

'Oh, I shall be fine. I'm never ill.'

Kitty shook her head. 'You have never been in a delicate condition before.'

'Oh, don't remind me.'

'Come down to my room and take a look at my gowns,' Kitty said, seeking a diversion that would take her sister's mind off her unhappy domestic situation. 'I can still scarce believe how many I have acquired since coming to Pemberley and you are more than welcome to borrow one to wear to dinner.'

A subject which would once have captured Lydia's complete attention had little effect on her despondent mood. Even so, she moved from the window seat and linked her arm through Kitty's.

'Lead the way,' she said with a heavy sigh.

★   ★   ★

George Wickham scowled at the column of figures he was totting up. This was his third attempt to balance a simple ledger but he was so angry, his brain fogged with such a debilitating mist of rage, that he was unable to complete the task. Gardiner's clerk, whose job this ought to have been, sat on a high stool immediately outside of the cramped cubbyhole Wickham called an office, ostensibly hard at work but in reality spying on Wickham. Things had come to a sorry pass when his wife's pedantic uncle considered he needed a nursemaid to oversee his duties.

Ha! If Gardiner thought old Simcock would prevent him from doing precisely as he pleased, then he had grossly underestimated

Wickham's determination to be his own man. Wickham would take orders from Gardiner, if he must, and somehow raise an obliging smile, but he was damned if his actions would be impeded by a busybody old clerk who seemed to think that years of drudgery in Gardiner's service afforded him respectability on a par with Wickham's own.

Wickham was a gentleman, had enjoyed a gentleman's education and developed a taste for the finer things in life. Simcock was nothing by comparison.

Thoughts of the finer things in life reminded Wickham, if any reminder were necessary, that all of Lydia's family were now at Pemberley, enjoying the very best of everything. Wickham was left behind like a worthless poor relation; his humiliation complete. It made his blood boil. He thumped his desk with his clenched fist, causing the ink well to wobble and ink to spill on his ledger. Wickham didn't even bother to blot it up.

Since being cast into the role of a glorified warehouseman, Wickham had been at leisure to think more deeply about his circumstances, and old Darcy's special interest in him. Had that been because Darcy was his actual father, he'd taken to wondering. Wickham had quickly come to the conclusion that he must have been; which made sense of everything and reinforced Wickham's determination to have what was his due — the inheritance that Fitzwilliam Darcy must have spitefully withheld from him.

A lot of men in old Darcy's position had illegitimate offspring whom they didn't acknowledge and took no interest in. Darcy would have been too aware of his position to openly acknowledge Wickham, but had implied it in so many other ways that their relationship now seemed obvious and undeniable. Except that the current occupant of Pemberley was doing everything he possibly could to deny it. He had always been jealous of Wickham's popularity and closeness to old Darcy.

At last Wickham understood why.

Wickham's mother had been a comely lass. He recalled old Darcy spending more time in her company than was necessary and held her in obvious affection. Very obvious, now Wickham thought about it. He rubbed his chin, wondering why the idea had not previously occurred to him. There was a marked resemblance to the old man in Wickham's own countenance, and in some of his mannerisms, too, whereas he looked nothing at all like the man who was supposed to be his father.

It would explain Darcy's special regard for a boy who was supposed to be his steward's son since, even Wickham had to admit, old Darcy had been very aware of his position; aloof and a stickler for protocol. The rest of the estate's children had been below his notice, and rightly so. It did no good for the upper classes to mess with the hoi-polloi, giving them ideas above their station. Wickham wished now that he had thought to ask his mentor probing questions about his parentage when he had still been alive. He probably would not have answered him truthfully, but if he had prevaricated instead of issuing a straightforward denial, that would have been evidence enough.

Well, if Wickham's conclusion was correct, at least old Darcy had enjoyed the satisfaction of producing one son of whom he could be justifiably proud. And Wickham was not thinking of the strutting peacock who was now master of Pemberley.

Damnation, why wouldn't the figures add up! Wickham threw his quill aside and devoted his entire mind to contemplating his next move. Not that it actually required much thought since the die was already cast. Lydia's condition had seen to that. The devil of it was that she seemed to think he would be delighted at the prospect of fatherhood, but nothing could be further from the truth. It was bad enough living in a cramped apartment above a warehouse. To have that space invaded by a squalling infant who claimed Lydia's attention away from him would be insupportable.

Wickham had been prepared to tolerate his straitened circumstances for a year or two more while he laid his plans. But the fates had decreed otherwise. It was time to act and the house party at Pemberley would be perfect cover for what he had in mind. He would leave this mind-numbing toil behind him and live the life he had been born to lead, free from the constrictions of a loveless marriage and a wife who no longer seemed to appreciate his true worth. Damn it all, if a man could not look to his own wife for unconditional support, it was a sorry state of affairs indeed!

Wickham leaned back in his chair, thinking there was a perverse sort of symmetry in acting almost a year to the day since his last blighted attempt to secure justice for himself. A man had his pride and Wickham would not be able to lift his head up again if he didn't follow his conscience. Every misfortune that had befallen him was the fault of Fitzwilliam Darcy. Without the restrictions placed upon his movements by that jealous, petty-minded individual, he could have achieved anything he set his mind to.

Miss Bingley was to blame for his previous failure. She had had a very small part to play, and the incentive of being in a position to console Darcy when he caught his wife in an indiscretion to spur her on. And yet she had bungled it. She had obviously said or done something to alert Darcy. How else could he possibly have seen through Wickham's artful stratagem? Damn it, Darcy had walked into the summerhouse exactly when he was supposed to: at the precise moment when Wickham held Lizzy in his arms. He could not possibly have doubted what he saw.

And yet, somehow, he did. Instead of taking his wife to task, he swung a lucky punch at Wickham. Wickham had not been prepared for such a reaction and so hadn't been ready to defend himself, or fight back, and Darcy had managed to break his nose. It hadn't set straight and every time Wickham looked in the mirror he received a visual reminder of his grievances to join forces with his catalogue of injustices. A man of honour, dealt such a loaded hand, could not be expected to let matters rest.

Life was so unjust, Wickham mused. Miss Bingley had given them away, and her own part in the scheme to discredit Lizzy was known to Darcy. And yet . . . and yet, she was being welcomed back to Pemberley for the duration of this party while Wickham languished in a warehouse in Cheapside, discredited, *persona non-grata*.

The injustice ate at Wickham's insides like corrosive acid.

It really was a shame that Darcy had married Lizzy Bennet. She was the only woman Wickham had ever entertained serious feelings for. Her lively wit and sparkling eyes never failed to enchant him. Had she possessed a fortune, Wickham would have wooed her. She would have taken him, too, since she liked him very much when they first met; before Darcy poisoned her mind against him.

And now she had given Darcy a son, which further weakened Wickham's position. Lydia had been beside herself when she heard how narrowly Lizzy and the child had escaped death. Much as he admired Lizzy, Wickham was less pleased at the outcome. Against all the odds, Darcy had come to adore the woman he had probably only married to spite Wickham, having been made aware of Wickham's interest in her. It would have broken his heart to lose her, and given Wickham considerable satisfaction to contemplate his suffering.

He threw his reclaimed quill aside in frustration for a second time, tired of the numbers dancing in front of his eyes, changing columns whenever they felt like it and playing havoc with Wickham's calculations.

'Let Simcock deal with them,' he muttered. 'It will give him satisfaction to feel superior.'

Wickham opened the drawer which contained the cashbox, provided by Gardiner to cover day-to-day incidentals. He was expected to account for every penny he spent in the execution of his duties, and those accounts were meticulously checked by the pernickety clerk seated outside his door. God's beard, Gardiner had only left him with a little over twenty pounds. Wickham managed a wry smile. Anyone would think he was untrustworthy. He pocketed all the cash and left a promissory note in its place. Never let it be said that he was dishonest. Twenty pounds wasn't much, but enough for a good night's gambling, a tumble with a willing female, with enough left over for his fare to Derbyshire.

He reached for his hat and gloves and left his office.

'Where are you going?' Simcock asked. 'Sir,' he added, very much as an afterthought.

'I have business to attend to.'

'What business would that be?'

'I do not have to account for my movements to you.' Wickham looked down his nose at the foolish man, who stared insolently back at him. 'Finish these,' he added, throwing the accounts he had been struggling with onto Simcock's desk.

With a spring in his step, Wickham left the despised warehouse and ventured into a street clogged with fine carriages as ladies of quality flocked to the warehouses, looking for the latest silks and muslins imported from overseas. He hailed a cab — a rare luxury nowadays — and told the jarvey to take him to Covent Garden. He anticipated that an express would be sent to Gardiner when he didn't return and the cash was missed, but what could his employer do about it from Derbyshire?

4

Lizzy rested her head on Will's shoulder and expelled an elongated sigh.

'Tired, my love?' Will asked. 'It has been a long day for you.'

'And an even longer evening, what with my mother's determination to dominate proceedings at table.' Lizzy shook her head. 'Some of the outlandish things she said to you ... I didn't know where to look.'

'I didn't mind her.'

'I know you did not.' Lizzy wiggled into a more comfortable position, using Will's broad chest as a pillow. This conversation was taking place in Lizzy's bed, which was where most of their conversations took place at the end of the day. 'You tolerated her for my sake, which only makes me feel ten times worse. Still, at least she didn't go so far as to mention Wickham's name again.'

'Oh, she will return to the subject before the week's out. She senses the rift between myself and her favourite son-in-law and lives in expectation of bringing us together again. You know how she likes to make herself useful.'

'Heaven forbid.'

'I shall not fly into a rage at the mention of the man's name; that much I can promise you. If she raises it, I shall look down my nose at her in the haughty fashion you used to accuse me of having perfected and make no response.' His lips quirked. 'There, will that do?'

'Admirably.'

'Don't try to warn her off the subject. If you do, she will ask you all the questions she wouldn't dare put to me.'

'I won't say a word.' Lizzy pulled a face. 'We have survived one evening of my mother's mindless prattling, but I can't decide if it will be better or worse when the rest of our guests arrive tomorrow. At least tonight it was only her own family who were embarrassed by her.'

'Your mother becomes less trying upon better acquaintance.'

'Oh, Will, how can you say such a thing? I wanted the floor to open up and swallow me whole on several occasions. And yet you sat at the head of the table, Mama on your right-hand side talking your ear off and you remained perfectly composed the entire time.'

'I have decided to take a leaf out of your father's book and be diverted by it.'

'Much as I admire and respect my father, I

cannot help thinking he is as much to blame as Mama. If he had taken more trouble to check her wild talk in the early years of their marriage his daughters would have had a much easier time of it.'

Will kissed the top of her head. 'We only have her here for a week.'

'A week can seem like a very long time.' Lizzy shook her head, breathing in her husband's musky, addictive aroma as she resettled her face against his shoulder. 'Poor Kitty. Mama would keep talking of Major Turner as though their union had already been agreed upon. I do hope we can persuade her to hold her tongue when the major and his father arrive, but that's probably a futile ambition. Such restraint is not within Mama's capabilities.'

'There will be a lot of other guests and your mother will be less obvious.'

'It's very kind of you to pretend you don't mind, but I know better.'

Will sent her a wicked smile. 'Thanks to your guidance, I now have a more sociable disposition and far greater tolerance for stupidity.'

'Which will be severely tested this sennight.' Lizzy lifted a hand and touched his face. He caught her fingers and kissed each one in turn. 'And now, not only do I tremble at the prospect of what Mama might say tomorrow, but that she will say it in front of Lady Catherine.' Lizzy grinned. 'Even Pemberley is not big enough for two such opinionated ladies to cohabit in harmony, especially now that Mama has decided Kitty is to marry into a titled family. She probably thinks that eradicates the differences in rank and consequence between herself and Lady Catherine, allowing her to speak her mind in front of your aunt.'

Will flinched. 'I doubt whether Lady Catherine would agree.'

'Precisely.'

Lizzy felt Will's shoulder move beneath her cheek as he shrugged. 'My aunt is a very different person since Sir Marius came back into her life. Far more agreeably disposed and less inclined to interfere in the affairs of others. Sir Marius will be a member of the party joining us from Rosings and will doubtless keep control of her in his usual unassuming manner.'

'But he can't control her private thoughts. Lady Catherine can justify looking down upon Mama because of the way she expresses herself; indeed I feel the same way. But Mama is still . . . well, my Mama. It's one thing if her daughters criticise her, and I admit to being her fiercest critic, but I still want to spring to her defence when I hear her denigrated by others.'

'I have told you many times, my love. The fact that you and Jane rose above your mother's example does you great credit. And now Kitty is learning to do the same.'

'We have you to thank for that.'

'Me?' Will elevated both brows. 'What have I done?'

'You agreed to have her live here at Pemberley, where she has benefited from superior society and your sister's example. Kitty has always been impressionable, and for once the right impressions have made their mark on her character and behaviour.'

'She is your sister and therefore my responsibility.' Will idly twisted a strand of hair, escaped from Lizzy's braid, around his forefinger.

'I wish Mama didn't know about the major's interest in Kitty. I haven't said anything about it in my letters, and I am sure Kitty hasn't either. Lydia or our aunt must have mentioned it.'

'Undoubtedly. Ladies like nothing better than to speculate about such matters.'

'Kitty pretends indifference about seeing the major again, but her reticence doesn't fool me. She likes him very much and I thought her feelings were reciprocated, which makes his absence that much harder to explain.'

'His regiment is headquartered in New-castle.'

'Yes, but they are not very often there. They have been quartered just outside of Derby for the entire winter and still are. That's not so far away.'

'The major has had a lot to deal with following Halstead's arrest and his own promotion.'

'Yes, but even so.' Lizzy sighed. 'I wish Mr. Turner had declined my invitation. Kitty knows the major and his father don't see eye to eye and that he's a hard man to please.'

'Then she would do better to simply be herself. It's the major she needs to impress; not his father.'

'If only it were that straightforward.'

'If Turner is swayed by his father's opinion, then he's not worthy of your sister's regard.'

'Which would be all well and good, if she hadn't lost her heart to him.'

Will elevated a brow. 'You think she is that far gone?'

'I'm perfectly sure of it.' Lizzy leaned up on one elbow and fixed her husband with a playful smile. 'It's far easier to notice the signs when one's own feelings are not engaged. I didn't have the first notion you looked upon me with anything other than a critical eye. I was tolerable, but not handsome enough to tempt you.'

'Oh, don't remind me of what I said then!'

'My concern is that my mother, in a misguided effort to promote the match, will corner Mr. Turner and sing Kitty's praises. Nothing is likely to earn parental disapproval faster than an ambitious mother's determination. And so instead of helping Kitty's cause, Mama will only give Mr. Turner legitimate reasons to object to the match.'

'If Turner's half the man I think he is, and if he's in love with your sister, then he will overcome all obstacles placed in his path.' Will pulled Lizzy into a tighter embrace. 'Take it from one who was once in that position.'

'Once?' Lizzy pouted. 'You no longer love me?'

'Witch!' Will kissed her. 'You know better than that.'

'Yes, you're right.' Lizzy felt the tension drain from her body in the face of Will's persuasive words and even more persuasive lips. 'Besides, despite Mama's worst efforts, Mr. Turner cannot fail to be impressed by Pemberley.'

'Are you becoming property-conscious, Mrs. Darcy?'

'Certainly I am, Mr. Darcy.' She grinned up at her husband. 'Why else would I have married you?'

Will punished Lizzy by pulling her into a tighter embrace and an even more passionate kiss.

'I am concerned about Lydia,' she mumbled breathlessly when he released her. 'Have you noticed how withdrawn she appears?'

'She's probably tired after the long journey.'

'No, it's more than that.'

'We know the events of last year opened her eyes to Wickham's character.'

'Do you think she's embarrassed because Wickham is not invited?'

Will shrugged. 'I doubt that. She knows how things stand between us.'

'It's funny, I never thought I would miss the lively, irreverent, selfish, opinionated Lydia. But I do. She's a shadow of her former self, at least outwardly.' Lizzy paused, frowning. 'Do you suppose she's increasing?'

'If that was the case, would she not have said something?'

'If she is, I can't help thinking it's too soon, even though they have been married longer than we have. Lydia, for all her new-found maturity, is still barely more than a child herself.'

'Lizzy,' Will said, with an exaggerated sigh. 'You can't take on all your family's problems, or invent problems where none exist.'

'No, you're right. I'm sure Lydia will rally. She and Kitty were closeted together for a long time this afternoon.'

'Just as you and Jane will be tomorrow.'

Lizzy grinned. 'Most likely. Only nowadays we will use our time alone to complain about our respective husbands' tyranny.'

'Tyrannical, am I?'

Lizzy squealed when Will threatened to pounce upon her; disappointed when he didn't make good on that threat.

'Anyway, I'm persuaded that if there's anything seriously amiss with Lydia, Kitty would have confided in me at once.'

'And the fact that she did not won't prevent you from worrying.'

'I feel responsible for Kitty. We *are* responsible for her, and I wouldn't have her throw her cap at a man who doesn't return her affections, if it can be helped. And Lydia . . . well, nothing you say will convince me she's not in some sort of trouble.'

'At least you don't have to worry about Mary.'

Lizzy shook her head. 'She's as serious as ever. She spent every spare second this afternoon closeted in your library. She was reading Homer's *Odyssey* when I found her there. When I remarked that it wasn't exactly light reading and that she might strain her eyes, she informed me that she fully intended to take advantage of your library while she's here and that the rest of us could take turns to entertain Mama.' Lizzy smiled. 'Poor Mary. I think, secretly, she has enjoyed being forced more into society now that she's the only daughter still at Longbourn, but she will never admit it.'

Will laughed. 'Now that she's not being compared to you and Jane and being found wanting, I dare say she enjoyed society a deal more.'

'Oh, Will, what a thing to say.'

He shrugged. 'I speak as I find.'

'Mary looks frail since her illness last year. Improving her mind is all very well but in her pursuit of knowledge she should not neglect her body.'

'I don't neglect yours.'

Lizzy gave her husband a playful punch. 'I could never level *that* accusation at you.'

'Then I have fulfilled my duty.'

'Is that what I am to you?' She drew a pattern on his naked torso with her forefinger. 'A duty?'

'Absolutely.' His eyes shimmered with hot intentions. 'And we Darcys are slaves to duty.'

'I wish I could disapprove,' Lizzy said dreamily as Will's hands roved over the body under discussion. 'But you are not the only person in this marriage to possess an acute sense of duty.'

Will sent her a smouldering smile that caused her heart to beat faster and her pulse to race in anticipation of what she knew would soon follow.

'At last you have hit upon my true purpose in marrying you,' he said.

* * *

Kitty's concern for Lydia's situation diverted her thoughts from Major Turner's impending arrival and how best to greet him. Aloofness, polite indifference, or should she allow her pleasure at seeing him again to show? She had never felt the need to put on airs, or be anything other than herself when in the major's presence, but if his feelings had once mirrored hers, they had clearly undergone a change. Kitty was hurt by his neglect and would find it difficult to disguise that fact from him. It wasn't as though she had pursued him, or encouraged his attentions. *He* had singled *her* out.

And then, having awoken her expectations, neglected her quite shamefully.

'Mama, is something wrong?' Kitty asked in alarm when her mother burst into her chamber without bothering to knock. 'You look quite flushed.'

'It has taken me an age to find your room and I'm now quite out of breath. I took a wrong turn on three separate occasions. This house is so vast that one could become lost for a month. Not that one could really become lost, of course, because there are servants at every turn ready to do one's bidding. Lizzy really has been remarkably devious, managing to snare Mr. Darcy without saying a word to anyone about her aspirations. I cannot understand why she didn't tell me about the scheme. I could have helped her. However, it seems she required no help.' Mama tutted. 'You are not dressed, child. Whatever could you be thinking? Major Turner could arrive at any time.'

'Lizzy and Mr. Darcy will receive him. They don't require my help.'

'Well, of course they must greet their guests first but you ought to be on hand, too. It wouldn't do for the major to forget what you look like.'

'Mama, please, I beg you not to say or do anything to embarrass the major, or me.'

'Embarrass you, child?' Mama looked bemused. 'When have I ever done anything that would embarrass any of you? It is the most natural thing in the world for a mother to look out for her children's interests and I'm sure I have done nothing to justify being branded an embarrassment.'

'There really is nothing more between the major and myself than mutual friendship,' Kitty said, striving for patience.

'Tsk, I shall know as soon as I meet the gentleman which way the wind blows. A mother has a sixth sense in such matters. Besides,' Mama added, a calculating look in her eye. 'Has it not occurred to you that the major's father must be accompanying him for a specific reason?'

'I can't say that it has.'

'Oh dear.' Mama shook her head, causing her multiple chins to wobble on either side of the ribbons tied beneath them to keep her cap secure. 'I can see I didn't arrive a day too soon. Lizzy ought to have prepared you, but perhaps she couldn't be bothered to take the trouble. That would be typical. However, Mr. Turner is obviously coming to give his seal of approval before the major declares himself and we must ensure that he likes what he sees. It's such a pity that you don't have a dowry, but still, you live in this great house, which must count for something. Now what shall you wear?' Mama pulled open the doors to Kitty's closet and examined its contents. 'My goodness, what a very large selection of gowns. How generous Mr. Darcy has been. How about this pink percale?' Mama pulled the gown in question from the closet and examined it more closely. 'The material is remarkably fine and pink has always suited you.'

'If you like.'

Kitty rang for Nora and agreed to wear the gown her mother had selected. It would be a lot easier than arguing the point.

'It is all very well Mr. Darcy being so generously disposed towards you, Kitty. I should expect nothing less, what with him being so very rich and you now being related by marriage. What I cannot comprehend is why he is so *ungenerous* towards Lydia and my dear Wickham. He ought to be especially liberal in their case since Wickham grew up here at Pemberley and quite looks upon it as his home. I don't suppose you know that, but he once confided in me.' Mama's bosom swelled, presumably because Wickham had used her as a confidant. It would do no good to tell her he confided anywhere he expected a sympathetic hearing. 'People do that, you know. They tell me all sorts of things because they know they can rely upon my discretion. However, as to Mr. Darcy's attitude towards my dear Wickham, I don't understand it at all; really I do not.'

'I expect he has his reasons. And Mr. Wickham now has a good position with our uncle.'

'Pray, don't speak of such matters!' Mama placed her hand over her heaving bosom. 'That position is beneath Wickham's dignity. I can't imagine what my brother must have been thinking, or why Wickham was persuaded to accept it. But then Wickham is cut from the same cloth as myself and never complains if his circumstances take a turn for the worse. However, Wickham ought to be here with the rest of his family. There was no need for him to remain in London.'

'Mama, we cannot — '

'But when I suggested, most politely, that Wickham accompany us, your uncle was adamant he couldn't be spared. Lydia, when applied to by me, took your uncle's part. Really, I don't understand what has got into that girl. She seemed unconcerned about leaving Wickham behind but now that she's here, she's mopes about and I can barely get two words out of her. Really, it's too much for my poor nerves.'

'We shouldn't interfere, Mama.'

'Interfere? What nonsense! I'm sure I've never interfered in anyone's affairs. However, as I was saying, Lydia ought to have insisted, explained to her uncle how much she relies on Wickham to keep her spirits up. I feel assured Wickham would have been permitted to come if she had taken the trouble to insist.' Mama shook her head. 'Wickham himself said he was perfectly content to remain behind and be of service to your uncle, it's true, but I could tell he was not being sincere. He's just too well mannered, too obliging, to put himself forward. Lydia is really very lucky to have such a conscientious husband. If your major is even half the man that Wickham is, then you are to be envied.'

'Mama!'

'Don't look at me like that, Kitty. I am merely offering you the benefit of my advice, as every mother ought.'

A little too volubly. Kitty could tell that Nora's ears were flapping as she dressed Kitty's hair but knew it would be a waste of breath to advise her mother to mind her tongue. Mama always said precisely what was on her mind and even the splendour of Pemberley had not stemmed her flow for long.

'There, you look very pretty, Kitty,' Mama said when Kitty was coiffured and dressed. 'Very pretty indeed. Now let's go down and sit casually in the morning room with Lizzy.

We will be able to see the arrivals from that window if we do.'

Lizzy, Georgiana and Aunt Gardiner were in the morning room when Kitty and her mother entered it. Of Mary and Lydia there was no sign. Mama dominated the conversation, expressing her certainty that Major Turner would declare himself, causing Kitty to wince and Georgie to send her a sympathetic smile.

'And when are we to make Mr. Sanford's acquaintance, Miss Darcy?' Mama asked when she had finally exhausted the subject of Major Turner.

'He dines with us this evening, ma'am.'

'And we ought to refer to him as Doctor Sanford now, Mama,' Lizzy said, 'since he is ready to practise medicine in the district.'

'Well, I am sure I shall call him whatever suits him best. But I can hardly contain myself — '

At the prospect of meeting Doctor Sanford?' Lizzy asked, raising a brow.

'No, of course not, although I am perfectly sure he is everything he ought to be. But, excuse me, Miss Darcy, I am more anxious to meet my first granddaughter. I am very glad you were able to give Mr. Darcy a son, Lizzy, but personally I must express a preference for baby girls. All five of you were so good, so sweet, and didn't give me a moment's trouble. I am sure boys are not nearly so biddable and feel obliged to make as much mischief as they possibly can. Lady Lucas's hair has been turned completely white by the antics of her sons.'

Lizzy was saved from giving an answer to this rather astonishing assertion — astonishing because Kitty couldn't remember a time when her Mama had not lamented her inability to produce a son and heir, thus cutting off the Longbourn entail — by the sound of carriages arriving.

'That is Jane and Mr. Bingley now,' Lizzy said, standing.

'Jane must be anxious to see me again,' Mama replied. 'We have never been separated for so long before. I cannot imagine what possessed Mr. Bingley to take a house so far away from Hertfordshire. To my precise knowledge, there was nothing wrong with Netherfield. But then, I suppose gentlemen of wealth and consequence are accustomed to doing precisely as they please without stopping to consider the feelings of anyone else.'

'I understand Netherfield was not for sale,' Aunt Gardiner remarked. 'And Mr. Bingley had his heart set upon purchasing an estate.'

'There are many perfectly acceptable estates for sale in Hertfordshire,' Mama replied, sniffing. 'I don't see what's so remarkable about Derbyshire.'

Lizzy shared a resigned glance with Kitty as she led the way from the morning room at the same time as Mr. Darcy emerged from his study and joined her in the vestibule. He took her hand, placed it on his sleeve and Kitty noticed him squeeze her fingers. Such devotion! Kitty was envious. Mr. Darcy knew Lizzy must be anxious about greeting Miss Bingley at Pemberley again and wanted to reassure her.

Kitty suspected that Lizzy was actually grateful to their mother when the reception party spilled onto the front step and Mama pushed herself forward. She dashed past Mr. Darcy and Lizzy before they could exchange more than a word or two with the new arrivals and threw herself at Jane the moment she stepped away from her carriage.

'Oh, my dear girl, let me look at you!'

'Hello, Mama,' Jane said in her usual placid manner. 'I trust I find you well.'

'Oh, you know how it is for me.' Mama waved the question aside, but also answered it. 'I am plagued by my nerves but never make a fuss. How do you do, Mr. Bingley. Miss Bingley, Mrs. Hurst. It is a pleasure to see you again. Now, where is the dear baby? I long to see her.'

As usual Mama gave no one the opportunity to utter more than a few words. Lizzy hugged Jane, shook Mr. Bingley's hand and led the party back inside. She acknowledged Miss Bingley with cool politeness. Miss Bingley, as far as Kitty could see, had not changed in any particular manner. If she had suffered a nervous episode, there was no sign of it in her manner. She cast covetous glances at Mr. Darcy, until Mrs. Hurst touched her hand, whereupon she simply followed everyone else inside.

Little Emma was produced and admired at length by Mama. Lydia and Mary had joined the party and for the first time in over a year all five sisters were in the same room together.

5

It felt as though a conspiracy had been hatched to prevent Richard from reaching Pemberley in a timely manner. A serious disagreement had sprung up between two junior officers regarding a debt of honour that required Richard's intervention. Then the new colonel detained him. He was a stickler for protocol and didn't seem to pick up on Richard's desire to be away; or that less than half his attention was taken up with business that could easily have been dealt with by his adjutant.

Eventually, three hours later than planned, he rode to his father's lodgings, from whence they would travel in the pater's carriage to Pemberley. Richard's frustration was in danger of bubbling over when his father decreed they would take luncheon together, refusing to depart until they had been served a full meal by Marsden with all the time consuming ceremony that ritual entailed. His father's petty revenge for having been kept waiting, no doubt. Hardly the best way to persuade Richard to toe the family line and rethink his position on matrimony.

'You seem awfully keen to arrive,' the pater remarked, when Richard, driving the conveyance himself, gave his team the office.

'I t-told Mrs. Darcy to expect us this afternoon. As matters stand, we shall be f-fortunate to arrive in time for dinner.'

'If she has a large party of guests, we shall not be missed. There's no need to risk turning the carriage over in your haste.'

Richard checked his horses, slowing infinitesimally, not sharing his father's view that he had been driving especially fast, or recklessly.

'Bad form to spoil her seating a-arrangements at table.'

Implying that their manners might be at fault had the desired effect and the pater made no further comment about Richard's driving.

'I know of Darcy by reputation,' his father said a short time later. 'But nothing about his wife. Who is she? Who are her people?'

'Her family come from Hertfordshire, I u-understand. Her father is a country squire. You would not know him.'

'Not of our circle, huh? Darcy married beneath himself?'

'H-hardly that,' Richard replied laconically, wondering if his father had somehow got wind of his interest in Miss Bennet and was attempting to undermine his decision. He

85

would not put it past him. 'Mrs. Darcy is a lady in h-her own right.'

'All manner of rumours circulated in London at the time of Darcy's marriage. There were two schools of opinion. He was either out of his senses, or had been compelled to marry.'

'Evidently not,' Richard replied, refusing to allow his father's words to irritate him. 'Mrs. Darcy's sister is m-married to Darcy's greatest friend, Bingley.'

'Bingley.' The pater shook his head. 'Never heard the name. Lady Catherine de Bough is Darcy's aunt, is she not? What does she make of Darcy's marriage?'

'You will be able to ask h-her yourself. I hear she is to be at Pemberley to celebrate her niece's betrothal.'

His father fell silent, leaving Richard free to concentrate on his driving. It wasn't until they entered Pemberley Park that the pater found his tongue again.

'Damned fine estate,' he said as they made their way at a more sedate pace up the long drive. 'Very fine indeed. Makes you wonder about that wife of Darcy's and the hold she must have over him. A pretty face, I have no doubt, but I'm surprised a man of sense allowed something like that to sway him. You would do well to remember that, my boy.

Beauty fades, pleasing figures spread, but breeding never ages.'

Richard made no reply to a comment that was clearly intended to either rouse him to indiscretion or make him rethink his decision about choosing his own bride. He had not realised his father's social pretentions were so deeply seated that even the grandeur of Pemberley could not, in his eyes, excuse Darcy for marrying beneath himself. This latest display of inflexibility set Richard on his guard as he realised the enormity of the task he had set himself, and the diplomacy he would have to employ to persuade his father to accept Kitty. The rest of her family would be here — her mother and father and all of her sisters — which could only help his cause. He understood they were close, presumably they were also genteel and their affectionate interaction would help to convince his father that love and responsibility *could* go hand in hand.

But Richard was getting ahead of himself. There was, of course, the not inconsequential matter of first persuading Kitty to accept him, and he was not at all certain he would succeed in that endeavour. She had never disguised the fact that she enjoyed his society but had never given him hope to . . . well, to hope that her affections were also engaged.

He couldn't blame her for that. She was probably just being kind, or liked to be with him because they shared a love of sketching and had the ability to make one another laugh.

In Richard's opinion, Kitty could do a very great deal better for herself than a man who could scarce utter a sentence without stammering. His speech impediment had been a cause for ridicule his entire life, shaping the course of it. Although it was now vastly improved, he wondered about his selfishness in asking the woman he loved to be a party to such derision, albeit exhibited less openly than had been the case when he had been a boy.

Be that as it may, Richard had to know what was in her heart but must not permit his father to guess at the true object of his affections until he'd contrived to speak privately with Kitty and declared himself. In spite of his own disregard for his family circumstances, having had time to reflect upon his father's disclosures, he could understand why a man with such a strong sense of familial pride would attempt to manipulate Richard's choice. He would not have taken Richard's refusal to oblige him seriously, thinking that a son whom he had always found it so easy to intimidate would not actually go against his wishes.

Unfortunately for the pater, he didn't understand the man Richard had become.

Having considered his brothers' and cousin's situations, he had to accept that in all probability, none of them *would* sire an heir. He felt almost sorry for his uncle and father, knowing how important the continuance of the title was to men of their stature. He was equally aware that Kitty, as Richard's wife, might very well be the lady who produced a future Earl of Cheshire.

And, of course, that changed everything.

Richard knew his heart's desire would not meet with parental approval; and would not have done, even if there wasn't so much riding on his choice. His father's disparaging remarks about Mrs. Darcy, a lady he was not even acquainted with, and her suitability as mistress of Pemberley, reinforced that opinion.

Richard halted the conveyance at the front steps, where a footman ran up to take the horses' heads. He alighted from the carriage, booted feet crunching on the pristine gravel, squared his shoulders and felt determination course through his veins. In spite of their numerous differences over the years, it was not Richard's deliberate intention to overset his father. Even so, he was quietly resolved to put his own felicity ahead of perceived duty. And to do so he would need to exercise guile and patience. Instead of spending every possible moment of his time here with Kitty, as had been his intention, he would need to play a game of cat and mouse to divert his father's attention away from his ultimate goal.

The pater knew he had set his heart on a particular lady and probably expected she would be at this party simply because Richard had made the mistake of showing too much enthusiasm about attending. But he didn't know her identity and that was the way it must remain, at least until his father had become accustomed to Kitty's sweet temper, amenable personality and ladylike qualities.

'The family and guests are dressing for dinner, Major,' Simpson, the butler, informed Richard when he admitted them to the house. 'If you would care to follow me, gentlemen, I will show you to your rooms and arrange for hot water to be sent up.'

'Thank you, Simpson.'

Richard shed his regimentals, washed the dust of the journey from his hands and face and changed into regular evening clothes. He would not be wearing a uniform again during this party. He was most definitely off duty. Was Kitty anxious about his arrival, he wondered as he tied his neckcloth, wondering what could be keeping him, or had she not even noticed his absence? Had another young man taken her fancy, causing her to forget all about him?

Such torturous thoughts ran through his head as he stepped along the corridor and tapped on his father's door.

'Are you ready, Father?'

'Perfectly so.'

The two of them made their way to the drawing room together. It was already crowded with superbly attired ladies and gentleman, the low buzz of polite conversations and muted laughter filling the air.

Mr. and Mrs. Darcy noticed them the moment they entered the room and broke away from their guests to greet them.

'Major Turner,' Mrs. Darcy said, bobbing a curtsey and extending her hand. 'I am so very glad you are here, and congratulations upon your promotion, which is well-deserved.'

'Your servant, ma'am,' Richard replied, bowing over her hand and then shaking Darcy's outstretched one. 'M-may I present m-my father, The Honourable Angus Turner.'

'It's good of you to include me, Darcy. Mrs. Darcy,' the pater said.

'We are happy to make your acquaintance,' Mrs. Darcy replied with great civility, Richard thought, given that the pater was making little effort to be agreeable. Mrs. Darcy must have noticed his critical gaze linger upon her but to her credit she didn't allow it to affect her.

'I a-apologise for our l-late arrival,' Richard said. 'The colonel d-detained me with last m-minute duties.'

'Ah, the travails of rank, Turner,' Darcy replied, slapping his shoulder.

'Quite so.'

'I think most of the people here are known to you, Turner,' Darcy said. 'But not perhaps to you, sir,' he added, turning Richard's father. 'Allow me to do the honours.'

Darcy swept the pater away, while Mrs. Darcy begged permission to introduce her mother and father and a fifth sister. Richard readily agreed and allowed Mrs. Darcy to lead him towards a stout lady, fussily gowned, speaking with Mrs. Wickham in exaggerated whispers. Richard's gaze had roved the room the moment he entered it and fell almost immediately upon Kitty, dressed in yellow silk, looking elegant and composed. Their gazes clashed for the briefest moment and Richard nodded to her. She responded in like manner, cool and distant, before returning her attention to Miss Darcy, with whom she was engaged in conversation.

'Mama,' Mrs. Darcy said. 'Here is Major Turner come to join us. Major, this is my mother, Mrs. Bennet, and my father,' she added, touching the shoulder of a white-haired gentleman with his back to them, 'Mr. Bennet.'

'Y-your servant, ma'am,' Richard said, bowing. 'Sir,' he added, shaking Mr. Bennet's hand.

'Oh, Major, I am so very glad to meet you,' Mrs. Bennet twittered. It was immediately apparent to Richard that she twittered a very great deal and had a lot to say for herself. It was quite a shock and he hoped she didn't carry on in such a way in front of his father, who could not stand women who put themselves forward. He considered them vulgar, and such behaviour, however well intentioned, would not help Richard's campaign. 'I have heard so much about your heroics.'

'E-exaggerated, I am s-sure, ma'am.'

'Oh no, I'm perfectly sure they are not. Doctor Sanford told me most particularly.'

'Sanford saved the day. I c-can't take any c-credit.'

'How do you do, Major,' Mrs. Wickham said, bobbing a curtsey.

'Mrs. Wickham.'

Before anything more could be said, Mrs. Darcy introduced her sister Mary. She was a slight girl, with a sallow complexion, a near-permanent look of disapproval and a serious mien. So very different from all of her sisters. Quiet and withdrawn, Richard struggled to make polite conversation with her, hoping all the time that Kitty would approach them. It would be a natural thing for her to do, given that Richard was engaged with her immediate family. To his intense disappointment, she did not. Nor did she look at him again. Richard knew she didn't since, despite his resolve not to single her out, he couldn't seem to help sending frequent oblique glances her way. But if Kitty noticed she gave no sign and acted as though he wasn't in the room.

Richard moved on and remembered himself to Mr. and Mrs. Gardiner, who greeted him with apparent pleasure. As he chatted with them, he was very pleased to see Colonel and Mrs. Fitzwilliam present, looking as radiantly happy as they had on their wedding day several months previously.

'I had no idea Halstead was such a bad apple,' Fitzwilliam said to Richard by way of greeting. 'It can't have been easy for you to condemn your own friend and it's to your credit that you performed your duty.'

'Especially since it ensured Georgiana met her heart's desire,' Mrs. Fitzwilliam added, nodding to Miss Darcy and Sanford, heads together, on the opposite side of the room.

'Y-yes, indeed,' Richard agreed. 'Some good came out of the unhappy affair.'

He paid his respects to Lady Catherine, her daughter and the rest of her entourage, which included Sir Marius and Mr. Asquith. Sir Marius had been acquainted with Lady Catherine when she was a young girl. Richard suspected they had formed an attachment which had been forbidden by one side's connections or the other. Sir Marius took himself off to the Indies but had recently returned a successful man and settled in Kent, close to Lady Catherine's estate. The lady herself seemed far less austere since that gentleman and re-entered her life. Richard was glad for them, as he was for Asquith whom, it transpired, was Sir Marius's son, born on the wrong side on the blankets. Sir Marius acknowledged him and Lady Catherine permitted him to court her precious daughter; although had not, as yet, given permission for the couple to marry.

Richard knew the particulars because this real-life drama had unfolded at Pemberley alongside the play they had performed together on a previous visit. A play that included Halstead in the cast at a time when Richard thought he had settled his interest upon Miss Darcy. He couldn't possibly have anticipated that person's real agenda.

Darcy was still introducing his father to the various guests. Richard's breath hitched when he noticed Kitty make her curtsey to the pater. She behaved appropriately but Richard's father didn't find any reason to speak more than a word or two to the woman destined to become his daughter-in-law before moving on to people who interested him more.

Having shaken Sanford's hand and spent several minutes remembering himself to Miss Bingley and her sister, Richard was finally at liberty to approach Kitty, who was now in conversation with Mrs. Wickham. She looked up at him when he approached, and other than a slight heightening of colour, she seemed perfectly composed.

'Miss Bennet,' he said. 'I hope I find you well.'

'Thank you, sir,' she replied coolly. 'I am in the best of health.'

Her detachment cut Richard to the quick. Did she really feel indifferent towards him or were her actions guided by his own, hitherto aloof, attitude? The thought that he might have hurt her feelings drove him to recklessness. He held her hand for longer — a lot longer — than was strictly necessary as he raised her from her curtsey and spontaneously offered her the ghost of a wink. She gasped and her cheeks flooded with colour, but there was no opportunity for private discourse between them before his attention was claimed by Asquith.

★ ★ ★

Kitty sensed the moment the major entered the drawing room, even though she had her back to the door. She had been in a plethora of anxiety all day, expecting his arrival at any moment. Looking forward to it.

Dreading it.

And now he was here, looking as suave and composed as always. Their gazes clashed and he nodded at her. She returned the gesture, maintaining a remote expression for fear of exciting her mother's interest. The major was bound to join her as soon as he had paid his respects to Lizzy and Mr. Darcy. They would then be at leisure to greet one another less formally.

To her intense disappointment he did not join her; nor did she notice him look at her again, other than fleetingly and without warmth in his expression. She watched him circulate, dying a little inside when Lizzy introduced him to their mother. Mama spoke in her usual loud voice, waving her arms about to emphasise her point. Kitty was glad there was too much noise in the room, and she was standing too far away, to hear what her mother was saying to the major. She was relieved when he moved on before Mama could really get into her stride.

She tensed, gripping Lydia's hand when Mr. Darcy headed towards them with the major's father at his side. He was a tall man with an erect posture, a rugged face that might once have been handsome but now bore the ravages of age. His hair was thin, heavily threaded with grey, his expression discouragingly aloof. He wore authority like a second skin and moved with the air of a gentleman unaccustomed to being gainsaid.

Kitty's hopes of engaging Major Turner's affections withered as she observed his austere father. No one could defy a man with such an iron will indefinitely, she mentally conceded; especially not over something as important as a son's choice of bride. She was aware that everything the major had done in his life to date had been with the sole purpose of impressing his father. Marrying a woman who did not meet with parental approval was hardly the best way to go about fulfilling that ambition: an ambition that in Kitty's view would be near impossible *to* achieve. Mr.

Turner was clearly a man who set his standards very high and was probably accustomed to having his way in everything to do with his family.

Was that why the major had contrived to bring his father with him to this party? Had he sensed Kitty's aspirations, even though the major had not said anything specifically about his intentions, and thought to let her down gently by this visual demonstration of the impossibility of the match? The notion angered Kitty, causing her to straighten a spine that was already rigidly upright as the gentlemen drew closer. She had not thought Major Turner quite as weak as all that, but it would explain why he had so far avoided approaching her.

Choking back a sob, Kitty's pride came to her rescue and she was determined not to allow her desolation to show.

'He thinks well of himself,' Kitty whispered to Lydia, her gaze still fixed on Mr. Turner.

'Too well,' Lydia replied. 'But don't be downhearted, Kitty. It's not him you need to impress.'

Is it not? 'I'm not out to impress anyone,' Kitty said with a defiant toss of her head.

When the introduction finally came, Mr. Turner gave Kitty a brief, disinterested look and had little to say to her or Lydia. Kitty thought he was the most terrifying person she had ever encountered: cold, aloof and barely civil. If marriage to the major would have required Kitty to spend time in this gentleman's presence, then perhaps it was just as well that the union wasn't predestined after all.

'He's coming,' Lydia said a short time after Mr. Darcy and Mr. Turner had moved on, nudging Kitty with her elbow to drag her out of her reverie.

'He has to,' Kitty replied, glancing up to see the major approaching them, furious when her heart did a strange little flip in her chest and she felt heat invade her face. Her heart had no business flopping about all over the place when she had quite made up her mind she and the major would not suit. 'He's spoken to everyone else in the room, including the odious Miss Bingley. At length, I might add. Although I'm sure he can speak to whomsoever he wishes for as long as he likes.' Kitty pursed her lips. 'It's nothing to me.'

'Is that how you really feel?'

'I once imagined there might be something between us, I will admit that much, but I can see now I was quite mistaken. Don't worry about me, Lydia. I shall not die of a broken heart.'

Saying it was one thing; enduring the debilitating pain of rejection was entirely another, but not for nothing was Kitty related to Lizzy and Jane. They were not the only ones who could stand on their dignity when looked upon as inappropriate. She drew on her pride and refused to allow the major to see just how profoundly his desertion had affected her.

'Miss Bennet,' he said in an urbane tone, taking her hand as she bobbed a curtsey.

'Major Turner. Congratulations upon your promotion.'

'Thank you.'

His manner was rigidly correct. But confusingly, he also held her hand for far too long and winked at her — the major actually winked! — before he released it and strolled away to converse with Mr. Asquith. Kitty was left feeling hot with confusion, but didn't have time to dwell upon the oddities of the major's behaviour since her attention was claimed by her mother's raised voice.

'I hope you have made my daughter Kitty's acquaintance, sir,' she said. 'She is the most obliging girl imaginable, and such a very fine artist. Her home is here at Pemberley with her sister. It pains me to be parted from her but I wouldn't be so selfish as to hold her back.'

'Oh, Lydia, we must do something!' Kitty caught a glimpse of Mr. Turner's astonished expression, for it was to that gentleman whom her mother's oration was directed, and inwardly quailed. 'I shall die of embarrassment, I just know it.'

'There is little we *can* do without making matters worse.'

Kitty sent her father a supplicating look but he merely shrugged. Simpson saved the day by announcing that dinner was served. Kitty studiously ignored her mother's exaggerated gestures designed to assure Kitty went into dinner on the major's arm. If the major wished to escort her, he could ask her himself. She refused to throw herself at him. But, clearly he did not wish to since he proffered his arm to Miss Bingley instead.

Her humiliation complete, Kitty attached herself to Mary and went in with her since there were more ladies than gentlemen present.

Matters didn't improve once the party was at table. Kitty was seated halfway down its length, with Mary on one side of her and Mr. Hurst on the other, neither of whom had much to say to her. With such dull dinner companions, Kitty couldn't avoid hearing her mother's constant outbursts, even with the conversations of the other twenty-three people at table to mask her remarks.

'Kitty is so much improved since she came to live here, would you not agree, Mr. Bingley?' she asked, breaking just about every social more by shouting the question down the length of the table. If that were not bad enough, the statement, far from extolling Kitty's virtues, made it sound as though she had been in some way deficient before her removal to Pemberley.

Kitty lowered her flaming face and concentrated on her fish. The major and Miss Bingley were seated together on the opposite side of the table, a few places up from Kitty. She noticed Miss Bingley's smirk and died a little more inside. As far as Kitty could tell, nothing much had changed with Caroline Bingley. She was still vindictive and held the Bennet family as a whole in intense dislike. She was just better at hiding her feelings since her efforts to dislodge Lizzy from her rightful place as mistress of Pemberley. If Kitty was any judge, Miss Bingley had not finished making mischief for them all, and she wondered if she ought to warn Lizzy to be on her guard. Not that there was anything Miss Bingley could do, but still . . .

The major glanced her way occasionally, but appeared to be enjoying his animated conversation with Miss Bingley so much that she was unsure if he had heard Mama's outburst. For that, at least, she was grateful, even though she was perfectly sure that Mr. Turner, seated on Lizzy's right-hand side, hadn't missed a word. His expression grew more severe in direct proportion to Mama's want of tact and he made little effort to disguise his contempt for her behaviour, for which Kitty couldn't really blame him.

'Is it this way for you at Longbourn, Mary?' Kitty asked. 'Does Mama take every opportunity to promote your talents?'

'My talents speak for themselves,' Mary replied portentously. 'We seldom attend a soirée where I am not invited to play. I have no wish to put myself forward, but I can't in all conscience disappoint our neighbours.'

Kitty refrained from rolling her eyes. 'I expect you're obliged to go about a lot more, now none of the rest of us are at home. I know how much Mama enjoys society, but Papa does not.'

'Oh, I don't mind making the sacrifice, just so long as I can still have my mornings to myself. Society has a claim upon us all and I would not spoil our mother's pleasure for any consideration.'

Whereas I could happily throttle her at this moment.

'Lizzy, Lizzy.' All conversation stopped as

Mama again shouted down the length of the table, tapping a spoon against the side of her glass to attract Lizzy's attention. An unnecessary gesture. Every person at the table was now looking at Mama with varying degrees of astonishment, condemnation or amusement. 'You must arrange an outdoor sketching party for the young people; indeed you must. I am sure Kitty and Major Turner will want to form a part of it. Kitty is such a talented artist, you know,' she added to the table in general, beaming with reflected glory.

It was all Kitty could do not to bang her forehead against the table; her mortification complete. Lizzy had once told her that years of marital bliss would not make up for all the embarrassment their mother had caused her in the days leading up to her wedding. Kitty had not understood, being too busy chasing officers with Lydia at the time to give their mother's habits more than a passing thought.

Now she understood what Lizzy had meant only too well.

Sympathy for her current discomfiture came from a most unexpected quarter.

'She means well, you know,' Mr. Hurst muttered gruffly; almost the first words he had spoken to her since they had taken their seats. 'Dare say she thinks she's being helpful.'

'Yes,' Kitty replied, too stunned to say anything more.

Eventually the meal drew to a close. She felt the major's gaze following her as he stood, along with the rest of the gentlemen, while the ladies withdrew. He's probably congratulating himself upon his narrow escape, Kitty thought, tears blurring her vision.

She didn't follow the rest of the ladies into the drawing room. A half-hour or more of Mama's banal chatter, or worse, continued speculation about the major's intentions, while they waited for the gentlemen to rejoin them, would be too much to endure. She would like to go to her chamber and enjoy a moment's solitude but to do so she would have to pass the open door to the dining room, where the gentlemen were doubtless already making inroads into Mr. Darcy's port. She didn't want to be seen escaping and have conclusions drawn about her weak character. She was no longer trying to make an impression upon anyone but her wretched pride still dictated her every action.

Unnoticed by the rest of the ladies, she slipped into the morning room and from there, through the French doors onto the terrace. Alone with her thoughts, she lifted her tear-strewn face up to the cool night air and wished herself a million miles away.

6

Richard took the decanter from Bingley, poured himself a measure and passed it on to his left. Now that the ladies had withdrawn, the conversation turned to masculine pursuits: shooting, horseflesh, a recommendation from Hurst for a new London tailor. Richard took little part in it, his mind full of the events of the past few hours and the havoc they had caused to his plans.

He had been wrong to assume that Mrs. Darcy and Mrs. Bingley owed their pretty manners and command of society's mores to parental guidance. Given their mother's vulgar display this evening, he could only commend her daughters for rising above her example. Mr. Bennet didn't escape Richard's censure. An easy going gentleman, he appeared to take a perverse sort of pleasure out of foolishness, as evidenced in his unwillingness or inability to stay his wife's indiscreet tongue. By allowing her such licence, she had made the worst possible impression upon his father. He suppressed a sigh. This was disastrous!

Kitty's oldest two sisters had made

splendid marriages, which said much for their individual characters and ability to enthral. Kitty had ensnared Richard in a similar fashion and he still firmly intended to take her for his wife but Mrs. Bennet's uncouth display had just made that ambition ten times more difficult for him to achieve.

As he settled down to savour the excellent port, Richard decided that if Darcy could defy the wishes of his relations and marry a lady with such an embarrassment for a mother, so too could he. Ignoring Kitty all the evening had been unnecessary. Her mother's loose tongue had alerted the pater to Richard's intentions and he knew he would hear all about it the moment the two of them were alone again.

So be it, he thought, starkly determined. Battle lines had been drawn and Richard excelled at combat strategy.

Dining with Miss Bingley had seemed like a good way to deflect his father's suspicions but Richard had not enjoyed the experience. Miss Bingley thought far too well of herself and had bombarded him with questions about his uncle, the earl. She clearly disliked Mrs. Darcy and her entire family. She didn't miss an opportunity to make a snide remark directed towards one or the other of them, but saved the majority of her disdain for Mrs.

Bennet and especially Mrs. Darcy. She appeared to think she was being witty by denigrating her hostess.

Richard thought she was impolite.

'Damned gout,' Hurst complained, struggling to find a more comfortable position. 'Don't suppose you can prescribe anything that will give me relief, Sanford. The bally quacks in London are next to useless, and charge me a fortune for doing nothing.'

'I dare say I can help,' Sanford replied affably. 'I'll take a look in the morning.'

'Admirable.'

The conversation turned to medicine, and Sanford explained some of his alternative methods. The subject interested Richard but he could see from his father's somewhat superior expression that he didn't share that view. The pater was nothing if not a traditionalist.

'Does your sister live with you all the time, Bingley?'

His father's question took Richard by surprise. Not only was it the first time he had opened his mouth since the ladies had left the room, but it was also a most unlikely question. Richard wondered what could have promoted it.

'Caroline divides her time between us and Hurst,' Bingley replied.

'You have an establishment in London, Hurst?'

'That I do, Turner. And a fine penny it costs me to maintain it, I don't mind telling you. You keep a London house yourself?'

'My brother, the earl, keeps a property in Sloane Square. It's at the family's disposal. There is no necessity to keep a separate establishment since I am not often in London.'

Richard hid a smile behind the cupped fingers of one hand. The admission would have cost his father a deal of pride. He *had* kept his own house in London and spent every season there, until straitened circumstances forced him to sell it. He had trusted Richard's brother Edmund with responsibility for the family's investments, with disastrous consequences, and any reminder of that fact still smarted. But in spite of being permanently short of blunt nowadays, he still looked down upon his wealthier, less well-born contemporaries. Money could be earned, he had told Richard on numerous occasions, but blue blood was a privilege that set one apart.

His grandfather had favoured Richard over all his other grandchildren in his will. Ergo, Richard was in a comfortable financial position. His father hadn't once suggested

110

that Richard use his inheritance for the good of the family as a whole but it occurred to him now that should he marry, he would probably be expected to take up residence at Gaston House, his father's rambling Cheshire home. Both of his brothers had remained in residence there after their marriages, but the prospect of doing so had not once occurred to Richard. He had not told his father of his intention to live elsewhere, so presumably he was depending upon Richard's fortune to keep the family property in good order — another pressing reason to persuade him to matrimony.

'Shall we rejoin the ladies?'

Darcy's suggestion recalled Richard to his social obligations. As soon as he reached the drawing room, Richard looked to see where Kitty was seated and knew she wasn't there, even before he failed to detect the distinct yellow of her gown. The crowded room seemed a very dull place without her in it. Miss Bingley, Mrs. Hurst and Mary Bennet were all quick to respond to Mrs. Darcy's request for some music. The entertainment started and the rest of the company settled down to listen. But there was still no sign of Kitty.

The desire to find her, to explain why he had behaved in the way that he had and spend a few precious moments alone in her company overcame all other considerations. Guided by a predisposition that defied common sense, Richard was quickly finding out that he couldn't rely upon the iron will and strict self-discipline he was famous for within the regiment when it came to affairs of the heart.

He glanced around the room, looking to see where his father was since he wouldn't put it past him to stop him leaving the room. To his utter astonishment he noticed him in animated conversation with Miss Bingley. He was actually laughing at something she had just said to him and paying no attention at all to Richard. Marsden would already have learned from gossip in the servants' hall that the Bingley fortune was accumulated through trade. Richard could imagine the derisive sniff such intelligence would earn from the pater, who would consider the entire family beneath his notice as a consequence. So his interest in Caroline Bingley made absolutely no sense.

With a careless shrug, Richard slipped unnoticed from the room. He found Kitty on the terrace, her back turned to the house, gloved hands leaning on the balustrade, her face turned up to the sky. She seemed totally absorbed by the display of stars overhead, or so he thought, until he noticed her shoulders were shaking. Dear God, she was crying. He couldn't bear it.

'Miss Bennet,' he said softly. 'Kitty.'

She whirled around. 'Oh . . . Major, I did not hear you.'

'I couldn't find you. Are you all right?' Stupid question. She patently was not all right. 'Can I fetch anything? A shawl? A glass of w-wine? I c-cannot bear to see you overset.'

'Why were you looking for me?'

'I need to speak with you privately.'

'And yet you have been at pains to avoid me.'

She lowered her gaze, as though regretting her outburst. It gave him hope. She whirled away from him again in a rustle of yellow silk, the elevation of her chin implying indignation she had every right to feel.

'Walk with me,' he said softly, proffering his arm.

She looked down at it for what seemed like an eternity, before placing a hand that wasn't quite steady upon it. He led her to the opposite end of the terrace, away from the drawing room windows and prying eyes.

'I have been unpardonably rude, but there's a reason for that.'

'You don't owe me any explanations.'

113

Richard stopped walking and they stood together, staring out at the gardens, the darkness alleviated by the flambeaux that lit the driveway and the blanket of stars that continued to put on a spectacular show. He took her gloved hand in his own and caressed her palm with the pad of his thumb. She gasped but didn't pull her hand away.

'I have been anticipating this party since receiving your sister's invitation to attend it,' he said, not once stuttering. 'Because it meant I would have the pleasure of seeing you again.'

Her mouth fell open, her eyes huge in the dull light as she turned them upon him with incredulity. 'But you — '

'Shush, I know.' He placed a finger against her lips. 'What you can't possibly know is that I came with the intention of proposing marriage to you.'

★ ★ ★

Kitty was sure she had misheard him. She had never shared Lizzy's view that the major's feelings for her mirrored hers for him, and his attitude that evening had reinforced her view. The pain of betrayal, even though he couldn't actually betray her because nothing had been agreed between them and she had simply assumed too much, was unbearable. If by admitting he had considered proposing he intended to relieve her bruised feelings by explaining why it was no longer possible, then she had no wish to hear it. She snatched her hand away, anger fuelling her determination to never reveal he was the cause of her earlier tears.

'Then I am glad common sense prevailed. We would never suit. But since we're on the subject, I have never heard of a gentleman actually informing a lady that he had decided against her.' She levelled a cool gaze upon his face. 'Not very gallantly done, Major.'

'N-no, you don't — '

'I dare say my mother's outspokenness frightened you off, which shows how shallow your imagined feelings for me must be. Since we are speaking candidly, I would advise you not to mistake friendship and shared interests in leisure activities for admiration.' She tossed her curls back from her face and continued to harangue him, aware that it gave away far more of her true feelings than if she had maintained a dignified silence, but unable to still her tongue. 'Mama's behaviour can be trying but, as my father is wont to say, if callow youths are put off by it, they're not worth knowing.'

'I am neither a youth, nor callow.'

'And *I* am not my mother, Major Turner. However, I imagine you're glad Mama happened to be here. She behaves the way she has tonight all the time, so you can congratulate yourself on your close escape.'

'Who said anything about escaping?'

She responded with an aloof stare, her heart hammering against her ribcage as he caressed her with eyes that burned with emotion. She found it impossible to look away and dared to wonder if she had somehow misinterpreted. A gentleman with no feelings invested would hardly look at a lady in such a manner.

'I beg your pardon,' she said offhandedly. 'You are talking in riddles, Major, and I am not clever enough to understand you.'

'I had not anticipated that my father would invite himself along, or why. But, of course, you know nothing of his real agenda, so it's little wonder you're confused.'

He began to talk in a low tone about his family, his uncle's concerns for the future of the earldom and his father's quite extraordinary demands of him in that regard. Kitty was conscious of her mouth falling open as sympathy for the major gripped her. Ye gods, to have such a father! Kitty's mother, embarrassing as she was, seemed like a paragon by example.

'How could he be so callous?' she asked, shaking her head. 'I have never heard anything half so . . . well, so feudal before.'

'It's not that unusual. Aristocratic families are very conscious about their position in society. My cousin will inherit the title upon my uncle's demise, but if neither he nor any of us produce male heirs then the title will die out. My uncle's Cheshire estate offers employment for a large number of the local populace. He feels responsible for their welfare and I do have a certain sympathy for the older generation's view.'

'But you told me once that your father tried to persuade into matrimony and you resisted.'

'He seemed to think I would put the future of the family ahead of my own aspirations, given the altered circumstances.' Richard firmed his jaw. 'He mistook the matter.'

'I see.' She shook her head. 'Well, actually, I do not. What do you intend to do?'

'I avoided you this evening because I knew the pater would be watching me. He assumes I have fixed my interest upon a lady in attendance, accounting for my refusal to oblige him. If he were to guess that lady's identity he would set about frightening her . . . ' He paused and fixed Kitty with an intent look. 'That is to say he would set about

117

frightening *you*, away. He can be very intimidating and I wouldn't have you subjected to his coercive methods if it can be avoided.'

Me? Kitty felt giddy with joy as the nature of his words struck home. Did they really mean what she hoped they might? Her mind was so muddled by his explanations, his intensity and fierce determination, that she could scarce cobble two coherent thoughts together.

'Yes, I am sure he can be,' Kitty replied dazedly.

'But, thanks to your mother, my secret is out and further caution seems pointless.'

Kitty felt heat invade her face. 'I can assure you that I did not put Mama up to it, if that's what you're thinking. I didn't even mention our friendship to her.'

'Hush now, actually I'm grateful to her. I should not have been able to endure another day of not speaking to you, or having Miss Bingley cling because she hankers after my family connections.'

Kitty offered him an arch smile, astonished she could think about Miss Bingley when her future with the major hung so precariously in the balance. She longed to ask him what his intentions were, but pride held her back. She felt tense, anxious, and would burst with impatience if he didn't tell her what was in his heart.

'I realise you could do a very great deal better than me,' he said. 'I'm not much to look at, come from a family that seems to be in permanent conflict with itself and can't string two sentences together without stammering.'

Her smile was wide and uncontrived. 'You don't stammer when you're with me.'

'Because you make me feel comfortable, sweet Kitty.' His fingers made light contact with her face. 'People make fun of me, which means you would be included in their derision. For myself, I don't mind too much, but I should mind very much indeed if you were ridiculed.'

'Sticks and stones . . . '

'But that's not the worst of it. My father is very strong-willed. He is very conscious of our position as a family and will go to great lengths to keep that position secure. He would not have put himself in the position of being beholden to me for any other reason and will not give up trying to have his way. Once he learns of my interest in you, he will try very hard to dissuade you from accepting me. If we defy him, he can be vindictive and will make trouble for us.'

'Major Turner,' Kitty said, losing patience.

'Are you asking me to marry you?'

'Yes, my love, but I need you to understand what you will be letting yourself in for before you give me an answer.'

Her smile already felt as though it was too wide for her face, but still it stretched wider. 'If I didn't know you better, I might think you were trying to dissuade me from accepting you.'

'Nothing could be further from the truth, but you do need to be aware — '

'Hush now.' It was her turn to place a finger against his lips. 'I don't care about your family, so long as we wouldn't have to live with them.'

'Absolutely not,' he replied firmly. 'One thing I can offer you is financial security.'

'I shall be very sorry indeed to spoil your father's plans but I can't persuade myself that we should squander our happiness in order to further his ambitions. He frightens me, and I know I'm not what he wants for you, but if you are serious in your proposal, then I accept with pleasure.'

The major's enticingly heated smile melted Kitty's vulnerable heart. She knew then that he really did love her and that their mutual feelings would overcome all the obstacles his father put in their path.

'Are you absolutely sure, my love? I would

not have you take me out of a sense of . . . well, sympathy.'

'I think I decided I wanted to marry you on the first day we were introduced here at Pemberley a year ago. I felt . . . oh, I don't know, a connection, a kindred spirit, something like that. Lizzy hated Mr. Darcy when they were first acquainted, but I have never felt anything but pleasure in your society.'

'I felt the same way about you, my love.' He pulled her into his arms and Kitty went willingly. 'Were it not for my father, and my duties, I would have spoken to you long before now.'

'Then we shall not let your father come between us. If I am secure in your love which,' she added with a tilt of her head and a castigating smile, 'you have not actually expressed in words, then I shall be strong. I have some of Lizzy's determination in me when there is something I very much want.' Her eyes were moist with tears, but this time they were tears of joy. 'And I very much want you, Major Turner.'

'Richard, you must call me Richard.' He held her a little closer and Kitty was conscious of the fast beating of her heart as their torsos collided. 'And as to my loving you; you ought to know that I have never felt such a deep, abiding love for another person in my entire life. My family look upon me as an object of derision and there has never been any love between us.' He smiled. 'My father considers overt displays of emotion to show weakness of character.'

'Then I feel very sorry for him. And your brothers sound odious. My sisters and I squabbled all the time, but I was secure in their affection and there was always lots of laughter at Longbourn.'

'Families such as ours are more common than you might imagine. You come from a close-knit clan and so cannot be expected to understand.'

'And yet my sisters and I have had to endure our mother's . . . well, you have seen her for yourself.'

'We could be happy on — '

'Could be?' She sent him a quizzical look. 'Are you having doubts already?'

'Not in the least, but I need to be sure you understand there *is* every possibility that you and I will produce a future heir to the earldom.'

'But surely your cousin will inherit, and then your brothers?'

'My cousin is next in line, but if he doesn't have a son, my uncle plans to make the first boy born to either myself or my brothers his heir. Neither of my brothers' wives is likely to oblige, which is why — '

'Why your father is so anxious for you to marry someone deemed suitable.' Kitty nodded against his chest.

'What perhaps you don't fully appreciate is that our son's upbringing would be interfered with every step of the way.'

Kitty stiffened in his arms. 'They are certainly welcome to try, but from what I have seen and heard of your own upbringing, I shall probably have very different ideas.'

'Kitty, my love, I shall not approach your father just yet. I need you to reflect upon what I have told you. Life in the Turner family is not for the faint-hearted. I need you to be absolutely sure — '

She stood on her toes and wrapped her arms around his neck. 'I *am* sure. I shall not change my mind, but I can quite see that we ought to keep our agreement private for the time being. I don't expect your father ever to like me, but we ought to give him the opportunity to become accustomed to the idea gradually.'

'I have no right to expect you to be so understanding.' He sighed. 'I want to kiss you so very badly.'

'Since we are unofficially engaged, I don't see why you should not.'

With a victorious grin, Richard swooped. He pulled Kitty closer, lowered his head and slanted his mouth over hers. Sparks flew between them, reinforcing Kitty's conviction that she and Richard had always been destined for one another. Something that felt so fundamentally right couldn't possibly be wrong. A fine tremor passed through Kitty's body as Richard deepened the kiss and his tongue invaded her mouth, velvety and smooth, further fuelling her passions. Floating on a surging tide of emotion, she willed time to stand still and for her first ever kiss to stretch into infinity.

But, of course, that wasn't possible and a small squeak of protest slipped past Kitty's lips when Richard released her.

'We ought to go back inside before we're missed, my love,' he said with transparent reluctance. 'Think about what I have said, speak with your sisters if that would help. I feel persuaded they will keep our secret. We shall talk again after Miss Darcy's betrothal party.'

'Three whole days,' Kitty protested.

'I shall not avoid you anymore and it will give the pater time to adjust.'

'Shall you actually tell him?'

Richard shuddered. 'I dare say he will want to talk to me. He is not the type to sit back and allow events to overtake him. But if he does, I will make my position clear. I would have told him before now since I'm certainly not ashamed of you, but I was unsure of your own feelings.'

Kitty gasped. 'How could you possibly think I didn't — '

Richard silenced her with another, all too brief, kiss. 'I hoped, but I couldn't be absolutely sure.'

'Your lack of self-confidence is truly shocking. However, I have decided to make you see yourself as the world sees you. As I see you. A gentleman of honour and integrity.'

'Now that I know you don't hate me,' said Richard. 'Now that you have given me hope, I shall know how to deal with my father.'

'I don't envy you that task,' Kitty replied, shuddering.

'Come, sweetheart, we ought to rejoin the others.'

'I shall do as you ask,' Kitty said as they walked together towards the open morning room doors and slipped through them, 'and not speak openly about our agreement. But I cannot do anything about my happy expression, which is bound to give me away.'

Richard laughed. 'That's a chance we shall just have to take.'

When they returned to the drawing room Miss Bingley's performance at the pianoforte had just come to an end. Kitty was astonished to see Richard's father leading the applause.

7

Wickham woke in the apartment he occupied above Gardiner's warehouse with a raging headache and the half-naked body of a woman sprawled across him. Even with her mouth open as she snored off the excesses of the previous night, her hair a tangled mess across Wickham's torso, Molly still looked ravishing.

And ravish her again Wickham would, just as soon as she was conscious.

She was one of Mrs. Younge's best girls; much in demand and a favourite of Wickham's. He had persuaded her to return to his lodgings with him the previous night; a private agreement between friends that would save him Mrs. Younge's share of her price. Flush he might be at the present time, but there was no point in throwing money away.

Wickham roused Molly with a sharp slap to her buttocks. She was awake in seconds and more than willing to satisfy his needs. Molly took pride in her occupation, was a natural at it and understood Wickham's eclectic requirements perfectly.

They lay together afterwards, Molly falling

asleep on his chest again, Wickham staring up at the bed's canopy and feeling invincible. At last his time had come and there would be no more of the warehouse drudgery he had been forced to endure for an entire year. Any doubts had been eradicated by his good fortune at cards the night before, which had resulted in him walking away from the table over ten pounds richer. The gods were finally smiling on him, even if his card game had been played in the squalid backroom of a Covent Garden tavern instead of in one of the fashionable clubs where gentlemen of his ilk mingled freely and small fortunes were won and lost at hazard. But even thoughts of his unfair exclusion from the hallowed halls of Brooke's could not dent his optimistic mood.

'Molly,' he said impulsively. 'I'm for the north today. How about accompanying me?'

'Oh, I don't know. What about your wife?'

Wickham grinned. 'I won't tell her if you don't.'

'I have a job here.'

'Mrs. Younge will hold it for you. Besides, if I'm successful in my business, I shall be leaving these shores permanently for more exotic locations. If you keep me entertained, then you can come along too.'

'Here, you're not going to do anything

illegal, are you?' Molly sent him a sceptical look. 'I don't want any part of it if you are.'

'Not in the least,' Wickham replied in a suave tone, annoyed that she didn't jump at the generous offer of his protection. 'I merely intend to reclaim what is lawfully mine.'

Molly bit her lip and he could see she was tempted. 'I'm still not sure.'

Wickham said nothing, really hoping she would agree. She really was a comely lass: beautiful, a skilled courtesan and better yet, she didn't take life too seriously. Lydia, on the other hand, never stopped nagging him about the debt he owed to her relations. What about the debt *his* relations owed to him? The devil take it, they wouldn't even acknowledge that Wickham *was* a relation. He firmed his jaw, determined that situation was about to change.

'All right then,' Molly agreed cheerfully. 'If your business doesn't come off then I can always make my own way.'

'You will never want for customers,' Wickham assured her, tempted to prove it to her. Again. But there was no time. 'Come along then, up with you. We need to catch the public coach.'

'What, no hired carriage?' she asked reprovingly.

'Not this time, but soon, I promise you.'

129

'I'll keep you to that, an' all.'

She stood beside him, magnificent in her nakedness, and once again Wickham slapped her backside. Molly liked it rough and didn't flinch.

'I thought you were in a hurry.'

'Unfortunately I am. We must call upon Mrs. Younge and let her know you will be away for a while.'

'Can I take some of these baubles?' she asked, searching through a box on the dresser that contained Lydia's ribbons and other odds and ends.

Wickham shrugged. He didn't plan to see Lydia again, or take responsibility for the brat she carried in her belly, so it mattered not to him what Molly helped herself to. 'Take whatever you like,' he replied.

'Even this?' She cavorted around the room, wearing nothing more than a black velvet choker with Lydia's favourite cameo brooch attached to it, and a seductive smile. She looked adorable and Wickham felt himself reacting to her provocative show. What the devil, there would be another coach later. He snaked an arm around her waist when she came within range and tumbled her onto the bed.

'You're insatiable,' she said without real conviction.

'Get used to it.'

By lunchtime they were settled side by side in the cramped coach, giggling like school children, not caring about the chastising looks they received from their fellow travellers. Molly's attire was a little risqué perhaps, but Wickham could see he was not the only gentleman in the conveyance to enjoy the view.

It was a shame about Lydia, he thought as the carriage trundled along and Molly's head lolled on his shoulder. She used to be such fun; game for anything, totally and completely enamoured of Wickham. But then her family poisoned her against him.

Well, his dear wife had chosen her family over him and she would live to regret that decision. She would soon be a deserted wife, branded incapable of holding onto a husband; whispered about and pitied, required to live in seclusion for the rest of her days. For someone as outgoing as Lydia, that would be a living hell, and one she richly deserved for her lack of loyalty. Damnation, a woman's first duty was to her husband! Why could she not see that?

This journey was being undertaken at almost the same time of year as Wickham's previous visit to Derbyshire, and by the same lowly means of transportation. But thanks to

Molly's company, he could tolerate his uncouth travelling companions without rancour. Two nights on the road with his obliging bedfellow to keep his mind off his complaints and then he would be ready to put his plan into action.

Unbeknown to her, Lydia had a small part to play in it. It was the only aspect of his strategy that made him feel uneasy since Lydia was nowhere near as easy to dupe as she had once been. Wickham had managed to convince himself she would do as she was told. Since he hadn't given her advance warning of his intention to be in Derbyshire himself, she would have no time to consider the consequences in the unlikely event of his plans failing.

But failure was not an option and Wickham refused to consider it. Instead he leaned back against the worn squabs and permitted himself a small smile. This time nothing would stop him from exacting revenge against Darcy and lining his own pockets into the bargain.

Absolutely nothing.

★ ★ ★

Lizzy was about early on the morning following the disastrous dinner at which her mother had embarrassed them all — Kitty most of all. Even Lady Catherine had been shocked into temporary silence by Mama's outspokenness, but had plenty to say on the subject once she got over her initial surprise. And, for once, Lizzy was in agreement with her. Oh lud! Had seeing two of her daughters advantageously married caused Mama to abandon what little restraint she had once exercised?

Will had laughed it off, assuring her that their guests had looked upon her mother's behaviour as eccentricity. But Lizzy couldn't shake off the image of Mr. Turner's aloof expression, and the manner in which he had looked disdainfully down his long nose as Mama rattled on. Far from helping, Mama had just made it ten times harder for Kitty to achieve her heart's desire. Even if Major Turner was sufficiently in love to overlook Mama's behaviour, his father would have strong objections to the match.

Such thoughts ran through Lizzy's head as she studied the day's menus. She was pleased when Jane joined her and quickly dispensed with her duties so she could give her sister her full attention.

'You are about early,' she said with a bright smile.

'With the house so full your time is not

your own and I suspect now is the only time we can be assured of privacy. I so enjoy our time together.'

'As do I.' Lizzy smiled at her favourite sister. 'How are you, Jane? How are things at Campton Park with Miss Bingley there?'

'It's difficult.' Jane sighed. 'I cannot pretend otherwise: not to you. Caroline seems distracted, although on the surface she's the same as ever and anyone who doesn't know her intimately would never realise anything untoward had happened. She has certainly never spoken to me of the event and acts as though it never took place.'

'Which is just as well.' Lizzy covered Jane's hand. 'Hopefully Caroline has come to her senses and will put her mind to finding a husband of her own, thus relieving you of her company sooner rather than later.'

'I asked her in a roundabout sort of way if she had met anyone interesting while she and Louisa were away, but she said not. I didn't like to pursue such a delicate subject for ... well for fear of her thinking I want rid of her, or because she might think I was alluding to events here. She must realise that I know but it doesn't seem to trouble her.'

Lizzy grinned mischievously at Jane. 'Caroline seemed much taken with Mr. Turner last night. It's a shame he isn't a little younger. I know you don't have the capacity to dislike anyone but I dislike them both and think they deserve one another.'

Jane smiled as she picked at a speck on her skirt. 'I am no longer quite as trusting as I once was, and can see Caroline for what she is. You were right about her all along.'

'Poor Jane. To be compelled to think ill of your husband's sister must be a torment.'

'Save your sympathy for Kitty,' Jane replied, sighing. 'Our mother gets worse. Whatever can the major have thought?'

'The same thing our husbands thought when their intentions were subjected to such coarse speculation, I dare say. I was hoping to speak with Kitty when the party broke up last night, to reassure her, but I couldn't find her anywhere.'

'I expect she escaped as soon as she possibly could.' Jane shuddered. 'I'm sure I would have done so in her position. I heard Lady Catherine describe Mama as a person of voluble opinion.'

Lizzy snorted. 'She's a fine one to talk. But still, at least I managed to keep the pair of them apart for most of the evening, thanks to Sir Marius's kindly intervention.'

'What did you make of Mr. Turner, apart from considering him a suitable paramour for Caroline?'

'I wasn't serious in that conjecture; it was merely wishful thinking. Only imagine, Jane,' Lizzy said, putting on a horrified expression. 'The Bingley fortune came from trade!'

Jane laughed. 'Yes, Mr. Turner would never sully himself to such a degree.'

'To answer your question, I disliked him on sight. He was barely civil to me. Will was furious and wanted to take him to task for his rudeness, but I managed to dissuade him. Mr. Turner has a very high opinion of himself and clearly thinks I have no place at Pemberley.' She flashed a wry smile. 'He and Lady Catherine can idle away the hours, comparing notes upon my unsuitability.'

'Oh, Lizzy!' Jane laughed. 'Lady Catherine is polite to you.'

'She has no choice if she wants to come to Pemberley.'

'Poor Kitty,' Jane said. 'She clearly likes the major very much.'

'Yes, but his father will make all sorts of trouble if the major offers for her.'

Jane nodded. 'Undoubtedly, but I have noticed that Kitty is showing more of your fighting spirit, Lizzy. If the major offers for her, I think she will find the courage to stand up to him.'

Their conversation was interrupted by the lady in question. Far from looking downcast, she wore a radiant smile. Lizzy and Jane exchanged a significant glance and turned together to greet their sister.

'Good morning, Kitty,' Lizzy said. 'You're about early. Could you not sleep?'

'No, I was too excited.'

Lizzy grinned. 'I wonder why.'

'Where did you disappear to for so long last night?' Jane asked, smiling.

'I was angry with the major for ignoring me during the early part of the evening. It was most uncivil of him.' Kitty tossed her head, defiance in her eyes. 'I know nothing had been agreed between us but we were definitely more to one another than idle acquaintances. If he had decided to cool our friendship then he ought to have had the manners to tell me directly to my face. However, he was either brave or foolish enough to come in search of me — I still cannot decide which. He found me on the terrace and I was the one to do the telling.'

'Come and sit down,' Lizzy said, patting the space on the sofa between her and Jane. 'I can see you are bursting with news. I can't imagine what it could be,' she teased. 'Can you, Jane?'

Jane bit her lip. 'I don't have the first idea.'

'It's not what you're both obviously thinking. Well, not precisely. I was never more shocked, and I'm sure you will feel the same way when you know it all.'

Lizzy was indeed totally surprised when Kitty related the particulars of her discussion with the major.

'I knew his father wished him to marry a woman of his choosing,' she said when Kitty ran out of words. 'But I didn't know why.'

'Well, now you do.' But Kitty, far from being cast down, seemed to glow. 'But you do not know it all yet. The major claims to be in love with me —— '

'Well, of course he is!' Jane cried, clutching Kitty's hand.

'He is quite determined to defy his father and marry me, and I have accepted him.'

'Oh, Kitty, I'm thrilled!' Lizzy hugged her sister. 'I am sure you will be very happy, in spite of his father.'

'Thank you, Lizzy, but I can't talk about it to anyone other than the two of you. I promised most particularly. The major needs time to deal with his father, but I want the entire world to be as happy as I am at this moment.'

'You ask a lot,' Jane said with a beaming smile.

'Richard insists I think about the implications before he accepts my answer.'

'He's right to be cautious,' Jane said. 'The dispute with his father will be brutal and he needs to be absolutely sure you're prepared to weather the storm before he commits you to it.'

'You could indeed produce a future Earl of Cheshire, if what you have been told about his other relations' inability to do so is factual. That's a huge responsibility,' Lizzy said, 'although our mother will be in seventh heaven.'

'Oh, please don't say a word to her! She will never keep it to herself.'

Jane patted Kitty's hand. 'We won't tell anyone. Certainly not Mama.'

'Oh, why does his father have to be so beastly?' Kitty grumbled, propping her chin on her clenched fist and scowling. 'This should be such a happy time for us, but between him and Mama it's more likely to be a nightmare.'

'I know,' Lizzy said. 'We could lock Mama and Mr. Turner in the summerhouse and not allow them out again until they agree to be friends.'

Jane laughed. 'They would starve to death first.'

'I know you will overcome Mr. Turner's objections when he realises how sweet and obliging you are, Kitty,' Lizzy said, hugging her sister again. 'He won't be able to help himself.'

Kitty laughed. 'I'm not such an optimist as to imagine that situation will ever arise, but I hope he will come to see how much we love one another and leave us in peace. Richard's family are not close and never talk about their feelings. It wouldn't surprise me if Mr. Turner sees mutual affection as a weakness of character.'

'Then I'm very sorry for him,' Lizzy replied briskly. 'Shall you live with them?'

'Heavens, no! Richard has sufficient funds to form his own establishment. It will not be as grand as yours, Jane, and nothing compared to Pemberley, but I shouldn't be good at running a big household so I won't mind about that.'

'It sounds as though you have everything agreed,' Jane said, squeezing Kitty's hand.

'Everything except Mr. Turner's approbation, which is unlikely to be forthcoming.'

Lizzy sent Kitty a bright smile. 'Cheer up. He has seen Mama at her worst and survived the experience. From now on it can only get better, especially since your major knows his own mind and won't be bullied.'

'Oh lud.' Kitty dropped her head into her hands and shook it from side to side. 'I still want to shrivel up and die of embarrassment when I consider Mama's exhibition. She sounded quite desperate to marry me off. It was mortifying.'

'Then don't think of it,' Lizzy replied briskly. 'Think instead of your agreeable interlude on the terrace with Major Turner.'

Kitty blushed. 'I have already thought far too much about that.'

'It is impossible for a newly-engaged woman to think too much about the nature of her beloved's proposal,' Jane assured her.

'Just as well,' Lizzy added, laughing. 'But as to Mama, I shall speak with our father today and insist that he reins her in.'

'Much good that will do,' Kitty replied glumly.

'She is less forthright when Papa absolutely insists upon her doing as she's told.'

'Now that I am secure of Richard's feelings for me and he knows I have given Mama no reason to drop such outrageous hints, I can stand it, I suppose.'

'Will you settle in the north, Kitty?' Jane asked.

'Oh, I don't know. We haven't had time to talk of specifics.'

'Of course you haven't,' Lizzy said, grinning. 'Your time has been far more agreeably engaged, and rightly so.'

'It would be nice if the three of us were

close,' Jane mused.

'Kitty,' Lizzy said after a brief pause in the conversation. 'Do you know what ails Lydia? I have never seen her in such low spirits before.'

'I was wondering the same thing,' Jane added. 'It is not like Lydia to fade into the background when in company. You know how she loves to shine at a party.'

'Well, I — '

'Is she increasing?' Lizzy asked bluntly.

Kitty looked uncomfortable. 'What makes you ask?'

'I recognise the signs. She is lethargic, and her eating habits are rather peculiar.'

'And she has been married for two years,' Jane added. 'So Lizzy's assumption is not an unreasonable one. If we're right, I do wonder why she hasn't told anyone her good news.'

'You're putting me in an awkward situation.' Kitty twisted her fingers together in her lap. 'She told me things in confidence — '

'Then you must respect that confidence,' Lizzy said.

'No, I'll tell you some of what she said because I'm worried about her and am unsure how to advise her.' Kitty paused, presumably to assimilate her thoughts. 'Wickham flew into a rage when she told him about the baby.'

'That doesn't surprise me,' Lizzy said, pursing her lips in disapproval. 'That man thinks of no one's comfort other than his own.'

'Lydia told me what he tried to do this time last year, Lizzy, and how he came to be employed by our uncle.'

'Ah, I thought she might have.'

'You should have told me yourself.' Kitty touched Lizzy's hand. 'I could have been a help to you. I'm quite responsible now, you know, and you should not shut me out.'

'I didn't want to worry you.'

'I didn't know until recently either,' Jane said evenly.

'And now you must put up with Miss Bingley's company. I know you liked her, Jane, and it must be hard for you to face what she did.'

'It *is* awkward,' Jane conceded. 'I shall never look at her in the same way again. Charles can't either.' Jane shook her head. 'Anyway, what has become apparent is that Wickham is an angry, resentful young man.'

'Whom Lydia is stuck with, for better or worse.' Lizzy sighed. 'I dare say he will get used to the idea of the baby in due time and, provided he behaves himself and attends to his duties, the Wickhams will eventually be able to make a decent living for themselves.

Our uncle will reward Wickham's efforts when the time is right. We all know how fair-minded and generous he can be.'

'When you think of the excitement and expectation with which our children were anticipated, Lizzy, it seems such a shame that Lydia can't take her turn to be the centre of attention at what ought to be such a happy time for her.'

'I will try and speak with her when I have a moment,' Lizzy replied. 'Perhaps between us, Jane, we can help her in some way.'

'I'm ready to do what I can,' Jane said without hesitation. 'Lydia's behaviour has improved beyond recognition and I so want her to be happy.'

★　★　★

Richard rose early, ready to take on the world because the deep, abiding love he felt for Kitty was actually returned. He was the luckiest man alive with every incentive to overcome all the pressure his father and uncle would inevitably apply to make him change his mind. If he had been a vindictive man, he would have gloried in this opportunity to revenge himself against a family who had looked upon him with derision for most of his life. Instead he was sorry that such a happy time would be blighted by his family's disapproval.

Only a happy time, he reminded himself, if Kitty didn't give in to pressure and have a change of heart. The thought brought his soaring spirits thumping back to earth. He was determined that if she decided against him it wouldn't be because his father had meddled in their affairs. Or through an unselfish gesture because she felt inadequate to join his family. Richard laughed aloud at such a ridiculous notion. Kitty was everything that was good and lovely, and his family ought to fall to its knees in gratitude if she agreed to join its ranks.

Three interminable days before Miss Darcy's betrothal party, after which he and Kitty would speak of the matter again. In the meantime, he must try to behave as normal. To that end, Darcy had spoken of a fishing expedition that morning. Richard would go down and volunteer to be a member of the party.

As he was about to leave his chamber, his father entered it without bothering to knock.

'Good morning, Father,' Richard said civilly. 'Are you planning to fish also?'

'I was rather more concerned with your own intended catch.'

'Darcy spoke of trout,' Richard replied,

deliberately misinterpreting.

'Don't be obtuse. You know very well to whom I refer.'

'You mistake the matter,' Richard replied remotely.

'Miss Bingley.'

'Miss Bingley?' Richard failed to keep the incredulity out of his voice.

'You are hopeless at dissembling,' his father replied, not unkindly. 'As soon as you took her into dinner last night, I realised which way the wind blew.'

Richard opened his mouth to object, then closed it again, unsure quite what to say. It would be ungentlemanly to perpetuate the myth, but then again, Richard had not said anything to generate his father's suspicions. The pater had simply assumed.

'I made it my business to speak with her, and had Marsden find out something about her family's circumstances.' Richard didn't doubt it. 'She has a decent dowry, but you must know where her family's money came from. It could be worse, I suppose. You could have taken a shine to the gal whose dreadful mother was extolling her virtues over dinner. That would be out of the question, of course.'

'Father,' Richard said, his temper getting the better of him. 'This conversation is not helpful. I have made my position plain. I shall marry whomsoever I wish, with or without your approval.'

'Miss Bingley, on the other hand, in spite of her lowly family connections, has ladylike qualities,' the pater said, ignoring Richard's interruption. 'She is keen to improve her circumstances by marrying well.'

Richard blinked. 'She told you that?'

'No, of course not, but I'm not a greenhorn. She has pretty manners and knows how to conduct herself in the presence of her betters. Not that there are many of those at this gathering, apart from myself and Lady Catherine.'

'Which insults your host,' Richard said coolly.

'Our host lost any right to my respect when he married so far beneath himself. Gentlemen of our stature have a duty to maintain the dignity of our positions instead of diminishing them. With privilege comes responsibility and it's deuced irresponsible to forget the fact because one is diverted by an averagely pretty face.' The pater fixed Richard with a hard look. 'I sincerely hope you have more sense than to follow Darcy's example.'

The pater appeared to think he had fixed his interest on Miss Bingley, and had given his lukewarm approval. He had made it equally plain he wouldn't approve of Kitty and a serious dispute between father and son would be inevitable when Richard made his intentions clear.

'I don't approve of Miss Bingley but am willing to give your infatuation time to run its course. Enjoy yourself, by all means. You have earned the right. Then we shall speak of the matter again.'

Having said as much, Richard's father swept from the room. Richard fell back onto his bed, shaking his head.

What the devil was he supposed to do now?

8

'It's awkward,' Richard said. 'In all conscience, I can't allow the pater's assumption to continue without setting him straight. The lady's reputation is at stake.'

Kitty, to whom this remark was addressed, screwed up her nose. 'I admire your principles, but if you were aware of the true nature of Miss Bingley's character you wouldn't be at such pains to protect her reputation.'

'You know her a great deal better than I do, and I won't ask you to what you refer, but I — '

'Hush, tonight is Georgie's ball. These last three days have been the longest of my life, pretending we don't have feelings for one another, aware of your father's disapproval each time he looks at me, which isn't very often, thankfully.'

'For me also, my love.'

'Let's look forward to dancing together tonight and let everything else take care of itself. We will talk of our own situation tomorrow. I've promised Lydia I will accompany her into Lambton in the morning.

She has business there on behalf of her husband that she doesn't wish anyone else to know about.'

Richard frowned. 'I don't like the idea of you going alone.'

'We shall be quite all right. I shall have one of Lizzy's coachmen drive us there and Lydia's business will only take a few minutes to transact.'

'I make no apology for wanting to protect you from the entire world.'

'And I shall permit you to do so.' Kitty grinned at the man she adored. 'When I deem it appropriate.'

'I can see that you don't intend to make my life easy.'

'Where would be the fun in that?'

Kitty and Richard were part of a sketching party supervised by Mr. Asquith. They had stolen away from the others for a brief moment. Richard had, to Kitty's delight, spent most of that time kissing her witless.

'Very well,' he said, capitulating. 'I shall look out for your return tomorrow and we will talk then. And, depending upon what answer you give to my proposal, I shall then speak with the pater.'

'I have not changed my mind.' She reached up to touch his face. 'Nor shall I.'

'That's because Father has not realised

you're the lady I adore. I ought to apologise for his incivility — '

'It is not your fault. And as to not recognising your interest in me, are you quite sure about that? When we snatched a moment together in the conservatory yesterday, I thought he caught sight of us from the garden.'

'If he did, make no mistake, I should have heard all about it by now.'

'Perhaps he's being devious.'

'What do you mean?'

'Well, by giving you leave to enjoy Miss Bingley's society, perhaps he hopes to remind you how impossible it would be to offer for me without disappointing your entire family.'

Richard snorted. 'Subtlety is not a trait my father knows anything about.'

'Your reaction to his proposals for your future has surprised him. He probably thinks gentle coercion is the best way to remind you of your obligations to the earl.'

'You are a gentleman's daughter and I have no reason to be ashamed of you.' Anger radiated from Richard's eyes as he stared at a point over her shoulder. 'Subtlety won't work any better than his usual bombastic style, as my father will soon discover for himself.'

'You have not been showing Miss Bingley any attention. That will make him suspicious.'

'I don't imagine Miss Bingley has any interest in me, and don't intend to let her think I admire her. I most emphatically do not and it would be ungentlemanly to excite her expectations. Besides, the pater has been monopolising her company.'

'He's probably trying to turn her against you,' Kitty said, grinning.

Richard sighed. 'What a fiasco.'

'One more day, my love,' she said, daringly standing on her toes and covering his lips with her own.

'May I claim the first waltz tonight?' he asked after he had turned her inexpert attempt at a kiss into something more passionate.

'With pleasure, but that will surely open your father's eyes.'

He smiled. 'So it will.'

'It will be a great relief to no longer pretend.'

'Steel yourself for unpleasantness once the pater understands my intentions.' He kissed each of her fingers in turn. 'I wish it did not have to be so, but — '

'As long as I know I can have you, I will not be afraid of your papa.'

'My brave, steadfast Kitty.' Sighing, he cupped her face with the fingers of one hand. 'Such strength of character. Such spirited determination. I don't deserve you; nor should I ask you to tolerate my unfeeling family's disdain.'

'You will protect me from their spite.'

'We're getting ahead of ourselves. I am quite determined to speak of this matter no more until tomorrow.' He sighed. 'We ought to return to the others. We have been gone too long and Asquith will wonder what has become of us.'

'I dare say he has a good idea,' Kitty replied with a capricious smile. 'Have you not noticed how frequently he and Anne de Bough find reason to separate themselves from the rest of us?'

'Then I'm very glad for them.' He pulled her into his arms. 'One more kiss, my love.'

Kitty was happy to oblige.

★ ★ ★

Lizzy had just finished dressing for the ball when Kitty tapped at her door and let herself in.

'You look radiant,' Lizzy said, smiling.

Kitty's gown was of figured deep pink silk, gathered with a ribbon beneath her breasts and showing more of her décolletage than normal. The gown had small capped sleeves, a spangled overskirt of silver sarsenet and a pretty, flounced hemline that whispered around her ankles. But not even the quality of her exquisite gown could compete with her glowing eyes.

'Remind me,' Lizzy said playfully. 'Which lady is the guest of honour tonight?'

'Georgie, of course,' Kitty replied, laughing. 'But I fully intend to tell Richard tomorrow that I've not had a change of heart and we will face his father's wrath together.'

'Does he still imagine Miss Bingley is the object of your major's desire?'

'Presumably so since he's told Richard he's relieved it isn't me who holds his interest.'

'How very impolite.'

'My thoughts precisely, but part of me doesn't blame him.' Kitty spread her hands. 'After the way Mama has been behaving.'

Lizzy shuddered. 'Quite so. Anyway, the major's disinclination to involve Miss Bingley does him credit, even though I wouldn't much care if her feelings were hurt.'

'I wonder at her nerve, showing her face here at Pemberley and behaving as though she never tried to cause mischief for you.'

'She probably still thinks she was doing my husband a favour.'

'Odious woman!'

'Well, my dear,' Lizzy said, standing. 'This evening is likely to prove interesting, to say the least. With so many additional guests expected for the dancing, and with Georgie and Doctor Sanford being the centre of attention, I give you leave to enjoy yourself with your major as much as you like and we will deal with the consequences tomorrow. Just remember you're not alone. I shall fight Mr. Turner tooth and nail to ensure your happiness.'

'Thank you, Lizzy. But now I had best go and see if Lydia is ready. I said we would go down together. Have you spoken to her yet?'

'No, I've barely had a spare moment.'

Lizzy felt guilty, even though she really had been run off her feet trying to keep the peace between her mother and Lady Catherine, preventing Mama from accosting Mr. Turner and ensuring the rest of her guests were suitably entertained. It had been exhausting and there was still this ball and three more days to go. Lydia had been so quiet that Lizzy had almost forgotten she was there.

'I shall make time for Lydia tomorrow.'

'I'll see you downstairs, Lizzy,' Kitty said, disappearing through the door to the corridor in a rustle of silk.

Lizzy hadn't been left alone for more than a minute or two before Will entered the room through the door that connected it to his.

'How are you bearing up, my love?' he

asked, kissing her brow.

'None of our guests have murdered one another,' Lizzy replied, smiling. 'Yet.'

Will laughed. 'That, I suppose, is as good a yardstick for success as any other.'

'Three more days and Mama will be gone.' She turned to Will and smiled. 'Does it make me very wicked to want to see the back of her?'

'She has been better behaved since that first night.'

'Papa and I both took her to task, which totally bewildered her. As far as she is concerned, it's a mother's duty to extol her children's virtues and she's convinced that the major won't find the courage to offer for Kitty without her encouragement.'

'It would not matter so much if Turner wasn't here.'

'Quite, and the damage was done that first night, giving Mr. Turner a legitimate reason to object to Kitty.'

'Nonsense!'

'You forget, Mama could become grand-mother to a future earl. Even I can see why that would not sit well with Mr. Turner.'

'She is grandmother to Marcus and that doesn't seem to have affected our son's prospects.'

Lizzy gave her husband a brief, cautious

hug, careful not to crush her gown. 'You always know exactly the right thing to say.'

'What else are husbands for?'

'Well,' Lizzy replied pensively. 'I dare say I can think of a use or two if I apply my mind to the subject.'

Will laughed. 'And I shall be at your complete service. Later.'

'What do you make of Miss Bingley's return to Pemberley?'

'She seems a little quieter, but otherwise unaltered.'

'In other words, she still hangs on your every word and has not given up hope of somehow securing your affections, in spite of Marcus and me standing in her path.'

'I have scarce exchanged a dozen words with her.'

'Which has not discouraged her. She will expect you to dance with her this evening.'

'Then she will be disappointed. She's here under sufferance, out of deference to Bingley and Jane, and for no other reason. I shall not dance with her or Mrs. Hurst.' Will smiled down at Lizzy and kissed the end of her nose. 'You, on the other hand, had best wear your most comfortable dancing slippers since I intend to show my guests just how much I adore my wife by dancing with her alone the entire night.'

Lizzy laughed. 'Mr. Turner will think that the most terrible form.'

'Turner is at liberty to leave Pemberley if he objects to my ways.' Will proffered his arm. 'But now we ought to go downstairs. It's almost time.'

'Lizzy, you're needed.' Kitty burst through the door. 'Lydia says she's not coming down.'

Lizzy smiled up at Will. 'I had best go and see what's wrong.'

'Can your mother not deal with it?' Will asked, irritation in his tone.

'You know Mama will make an almighty fuss if her favourite daughter is absent. It would be better if I saw to it.'

'Very well.' Will seemed exasperated, for which Lizzy couldn't altogether blame him. Thus far he had tolerated Mama's theatrics with commendable patience; patience that was clearly running thin. 'Try to join me before our guests appear.'

'Sorry,' Kitty said as she and Lizzy hurried along to Lydia's room.

'Why won't she come down?'

'She says she's not in a party mood.'

'Those are not words I ever expected to hear pass Lydia's lips. Perhaps she really is ailing.'

'She doesn't seem herself.'

'Lydia,' Lizzy said as soon as she walked

into her room. 'Are you feeling unwell? Oh, dear God, whatever's wrong?' Lydia was sitting on the window seat, knees pulled up to her chin, her face resting on them, tears coursing down it. 'Has something happened?'

'It's nothing.'

'The baby,' Lizzy said. 'I used to cry over nothing all the time.'

'You told her?' Lydia turned accusing eyes upon Kitty.

'She guessed.'

'I recognised the signs,' Lizzy said, taking Lydia's hand. 'But if you don't want Mama to guess also, you had best get dressed and come down.'

'No one will miss me.'

'You have an obligation, Lydia. Think of Kitty's happiness, if you cannot bring yourself to be pleased for Georgie, and come down for your sister's sake. I don't have time to talk to you about your difficulties now but I promise to make time tomorrow.'

'There's no point,' Lydia replied sullenly. 'There's nothing you can do. Please, Lizzy, I would much rather remain here.'

Lizzy and Kitty exchanged a glance. 'Very well, if you're absolutely sure. I'll have something sent up for you on a tray and try to come up later. What do you want me to tell Mama?'

'Oh, just say I have a headache. If she tries to come in, I shall pretend to be asleep.'

'Which will not prevent her.'

'I can deal with Mama.'

'That remains to be seen.' Lizzy stood again, aware that time was passing and Will would be getting even more impatient. 'I have to go down now. Are you sure you'll be all right?'

'Quite sure. I am just having a fit of the blue devils.'

Lizzy kissed her sister's brow. 'I'll have Nora pop in, in case you need anything. Your bell may not be answered otherwise, since everyone is dashing about below stairs. We'll talk properly tomorrow. Doctor Sanford might be able to give you something to ease the sickness.'

Lydia, looking wan and deeply unhappy, gave them a brief wave. Lizzy hated leaving her but had no choice in the matter. She encountered Nora in the corridor, gave her instructions regarding Lydia and then accompanied Kitty downstairs. Lydia had not lost the ability to make trouble at the most inconvenient times but on this occasion she was not doing so to draw attention to herself.

When Lizzy entered the drawing room most of the guests for dinner were already down. Mr. Turner and Lady Catherine, in

160

conversation together, naturally noticed her late arrival and scowled in unison. Lizzy didn't have the energy to care.

She found Will in conversation with Mr. Bingley and went to join them.

'Crisis averted?' he asked.

'She isn't coming down. She seems genuinely upset, Will. I'm worried about her.'

'If it's something medical, at least Sanford is here. Although as this is his betrothal party, I feel loath to call upon him unless absolutely necessary.'

'Let's hope it doesn't become necessary then.'

Lizzy glanced across the room to where Georgie and Doctor Sanford were in conversation with Colonel and Mrs. Fitzwilliam.

'Georgie looks radiant,' Lizzy said. 'This must be a very proud evening for you, Will. You deserve a lot of the credit for the way your sister has turned out.'

'As do you. Your influence has been the making of her.'

'Don't let Lady Catherine hear you say that,' Lizzy said, laughing. 'Nothing will convince her that I have not corrupted her niece's morals beyond recall simply by living beneath the same roof as her.'

Mr. Bingley laughed. 'You cannot mean what you say.'

'Oh, but I do. Lady Catherine is my fiercest critic and has still not completely forgiven Will for marrying me.'

'She seems remarkably restrained,' Mr. Bingley remarked. 'Which is not like Lady Catherine at all. She is nothing if not forthright in the expression of her views.'

'That's only because she knows I won't be bullied,' Lizzy replied. 'So few people have the courage to stand up to her that she's unsure how to act when she encounters one who does.'

'Lizzy, Lizzy, where are you? You're needed at once.'

Lizzy sighed as her mother's voice caused most conversations to stall and for everyone in the room to focus their attention upon her mother.

'What is it, Mama?' Lizzy asked, closing her eyes for an expressive moment.

'Lydia. I cannot find her anywhere. You must have your servants search the entire house. She must have had an accident, or worse, for she would not miss a party otherwise.' She fell into a chair and fanned her face with her hand. 'Oh, I cannot bear it. My poor nerves.'

'Lydia has a headache, Mama. She's remaining quietly in her room.'

'A headache?' Mrs. Bennet appeared

dumbfounded. 'Why did you not say so before? A doctor must be summoned at once, Mr. Darcy. Lydia doesn't complain any more than I do, but we are both slaves to sick headaches. They can last for days if we're not prescribed restorative tonics. In fact, now that you mention it, I can feel one coming on myself.' Mrs. Bennet clutched her brow and appeared on the point of swooning. She had the attention of the entire room, much to Lizzy's mortification, but no one seemed in any great hurry to comfort her. 'Really, Lizzy, I can't think why you haven't attended to the matter already. My poor child, I must go to her at once.'

'Lydia would be better left undisturbed, Mama.'

'Disturbed? How can you think I would disturb her? A child needs her mama at such a time.'

Lizzy thought perhaps it would not be such a bad idea if her mother did go upstairs and sit with Lydia. But it would be selfish to encourage that course of action just because Lizzy would prefer not to have her in her drawing room.

'Sleep is all she requires, Mama,' Lizzy said, pleased that the buzz of a dozen difference conversations had again resumed.

'Lydia pines for her dear Wickham,' Mrs.

Bennet said. 'That is what has brought on this headache and really, I feel his absence almost as much as she does. No wonder she's so dispirited. Really, Mr. Darcy, he ought to be here. I can't imagine why you neglected to include him in the invitation.'

Lizzy quailed when she observed the chilling cast to her husband's features. Will had made a great many allowances for Lizzy's sake, but he would never tolerate being taken so publicly to task. If only her mother knew just how generously Will had behaved towards Wickham, and what it had cost him to do so.

'That will do, Mrs. Bennet,' Will said in a quiet yet authoritative tone that immediately silenced Lizzy's mother.

'Well really,' she muttered beneath her breath. 'I'm sure I didn't mean to give offence.'

'Come along, Mama,' Lizzy said, suppressing a sigh. 'Dinner is about to be served.'

★   ★   ★

Kitty was delighted when, for the first time that week, Richard escorted her into dinner. She noticed Mr. Turner frown but she was too happy to care. Lizzy had Mr. Turner escort Miss Bingley but they were seated on the opposite side of the table, several places down, and Kitty didn't have to look at or speak to either of them.

'Georgie and Doctor Sanford look blissfully happy,' Kitty remarked wistfully.

'But it would be impossible for Sanford to *feel* happier than I do at this moment,' Richard replied so softly that only she could hear him.

'Your papa keeps frowning at us.'

Richard sent her an intimate smile. 'He's never happy unless he has something to frown about. Tell me instead what ails your sister.'

Kitty waved a hand, wishing she could tell Richard the truth, but now was neither the time nor the place. Besides, she had been sworn to secrecy. 'She has a lot on her mind,' she contented herself with saying.

'And I ought not to pry. It is just that I sense your concern and I don't want you to have anything more taxing on your mind this evening than enjoying yourself.'

'That I have every intention of doing.'

'Then I'm glad.' Richard paused. 'Wickham grew up here at Pemberley, I understand, and yet there is bad blood between him and Darcy.'

'Yes, and Mama is the only person in the room who doesn't sense the tension whenever she mentions his name. It isn't helpful but she will persist.'

'I don't believe Darcy suffers from my father's affliction and thinks himself above Wickham just because Wickham is his steward's son.'

'No, I am sure he does not.'

Richard changed the subject and they spoke of inconsequential matters for the rest of the meal. With Richard to entertain her, no sign of his stammer in evidence even when he addressed Anne de Bough, seated on his other side, Kitty couldn't recall a time when she had enjoyed herself more. She was aware of Mr. Turner, in the periphery of her vision, looking their way with increasing frequency. Richard kept making her laugh aloud with irreverent tales of his life in the military and some of the ridiculous rules and regulations he was called upon to enforce. Her laughter drew Mr. Turner's attention, but if Richard noticed, he seemed unconcerned.

The gentlemen didn't linger over their port and Kitty was encouraged when Richard joined her the moment he returned to the drawing room. The doors to the adjoining room had been thrown open while they had been at dinner to make enough space for dancing. Musicians were tuning their instruments in the gallery above.

Kitty and Richard watched Georgie and Doctor Sanford standing beside Lizzy and

Mr. Darcy as they greeted the arriving guests.

'I am so very pleased for Georgie,' Kitty said softly. 'She hated the idea of going to London and having a season, which is what Mr. Darcy had planned for her. He would have insisted upon going this last season, had not Lizzy been increasing. Georgie was pleased not to have to go through the rigmarole, for which I don't in the least blame her. Georgie is shy and would hate all the fuss, but I heard Lady Catherine take Mr. Darcy to task for depriving Georgie of the opportunity, which sounded rather two-faced to me, since Anne has never been to court.'

'Lady Catherine has very firm opinions about how things *ought* to be done, but doesn't always seem to follow her own advice.'

Kitty smiled. 'Yes, that's certainly true.'

'Should you have liked to be presented?'

'Me?' Kitty opened her eyes wide in astonishment. 'There was never any question of that. Our family is not nearly grand enough. Papa might be a gentleman but he doesn't have a position at court.'

The room became crowded, and over-warm now that the dancing had started. Kitty became separated from Richard. She danced the first two with Mr. Asquith, an experience she enjoyed, and then a quadrille with Mr.

Bingley who gently teased her about Richard. After that the first stanza of a lilting waltz, beautifully played on a solo violin, echoed through the room. To universal applause, Georgie and Doctor Sanford took to the floor. They circled it twice before Lizzy and Mr. Darcy joined them. Mr. Darcy's smile as he looked down at his wife with such total adoration in his eyes moved Kitty's heart. Miss Bingley, standing directly behind Kitty, obviously saw it too and a cross between an anguished cry and a growl slipped past her lips.

Kitty looked over her shoulder and sent her a castigating look, which Miss Bingley either didn't see or chose to ignore. It was as Kitty had feared. Miss Bingley was still obsessed with Mr. Darcy, which shouldn't matter to Kitty. There was nothing the interfering Miss Bingley could do to separate Lizzy from her husband, but Kitty's blood still ran cold when she observed the frozen expression of stark resolve upon the woman's face.

'Miss Bennet.' Richard moved in front of her and offered her a sweeping bow. 'May I have the pleasure?'

'The pleasure would be all mine, sir,' Kitty replied, aware that her smile was far too wide but unable to contain it. No one else had yet joined the two couples on the floor. If Kitty and Richard did so, it would send a definite message to his father. He had to be aware of that and so Kitty rose to the challenge.

As Richard pulled her into his arms and she fell into step with him, she was conscious of Mr. Turner, his lips compressed into a thin, hard line, drilling them with a ferocious scowl.

9

Molly's abiding good humour, her childish excitement at travelling beyond London and, most importantly, her dedication to his pleasures, kept Wickham in good spirits for the duration of the journey into Derbyshire. Until they drew closer to their destination, at which time her inventiveness could no longer distract him from the drastic measures he was being forced to take to secure justice for himself. As the scenery became progressively more familiar, so he became increasingly withdrawn. Molly had the good sense not to comment upon his short temper and contented herself with looking out of the carriage window.

Their arrival would coincide with the day of Georgiana's ball. Deliberately so. If he was identified, news of his presence was less likely to reach Darcy's ears when everybody at Pemberley was preoccupied with the preparations. Wickham scowled at the thought of Georgiana being engaged. Not because he admired her, but he did regret the loss of her twenty thousand pound fortune. Damn it, he had been so close to getting his hands upon it and revenging himself upon Darcy! As always, the fates had conspired to prevent that from happening.

He sighed, quietly fuming as he considered his run of bad luck, determined that his fortunes would finally take a turn for the better. He had laid his plans well, no one other than Lydia had a part in them, and he was satisfied he would prevail.

They left the public coach at Derby and Wickham hired a curricle to take them on to Lambton. They arrived late in the afternoon and took possession of the small cottage on the outskirts of the village that he had arranged through a friend to borrow. Molly wandered through the two slightly musty rooms without turning up her nose. She bounced on the lumpy mattress in the cramped bed chamber and grinned up at Wickham.

'Privacy at last,' she said, reaching for him.

But for once Wickham wasn't in the mood for a tumble. Thoughts of the preparations being made for the Pemberley ball, while creating the diversion he craved, also infuriated him. Damn it, he ought to have been invited! His exclusion nagged like toothache. He roughly pushed Molly's hands away, cursing Darcy to hell and back. Lydia would be at the centre of things, laughing and flirting as though *she* was the one who was entitled to be there instead of him. She was his wife and should have refused to go without him.

He brooded his way through the afternoon, rebuffing all of Molly's attempts to put him in a better frame of mind.

'Well, if this is how it's going to be, I might as well have stayed in London and earned money,' she said mulishly.

'Go for a walk and leave me be,' he replied sullenly.

She did so and remained away for over an hour. By the time she returned, Wickham had calmed down a little. Molly accepted his apology with her usual good humour and they shared the simple meal provided by the equally simple daughter of the owner of the cottage, whose discretion could be relied upon absolutely. No one would learn of Wickham's presence in Lambton from her lips, mainly because she had no idea who he was.

Lydia would come to this cottage tomorrow, as agreed, expecting to see Denny. He had best ensure Molly was out of the way since he needed Lydia's co-operation to help him gain access to Pemberley. Once she saw that he was here, and he convinced her he *would* get in with or without her help, she would have to support him. Her fear of his being caught and losing his position with her damned uncle as a consequence would overcome all her misgivings. She didn't need to know he had no intention of returning to that drudgery, no matter what the outcome of his latest scheme.

'Come along, Molly,' he said, leaping to his feet as afternoon turned to evening. It was foolish, he knew, but he simply had to be there, albeit on the outside looking in, to reinforce his determination. A visual reminder of all he was being deprived of thanks to Darcy's jealousy. 'I want to show you something.'

Wickham drove the curricle to Pemberley. He knew better than to approach via the main driveway and suffer the indignity of being turned away. But he didn't need to take such a direct approach. He knew every inch of the estate and turned onto a seldom used cart track that skirted Home Farm. Eventually they came within sight of the house itself. It looked magnificent in the twilight, every window on the ground floor blazing with light, lanterns lighting the terrace upon which he could see several couples taking the night air.

Wickham truly loved this place, felt an affinity with it, and was filled with regret for what might have been had matters turned out the way his mentor had intended. His plan this time would work: his reward for sitting for so many hours with old Mr. Darcy. Of being aware of his habits and knowing precisely where he kept the things most dear to him. But even though Wickham would benefit financially, Pemberley's doors would still be firmly closed to him. There was absolutely nothing he could do to alter that situation.

Unless . . . well, if Darcy were to die his son would inherit. His baby son whose mother was his own wife's sister. Just for a moment, Wickham was sorely tempted to bring that situation about, if only for the satisfaction of knowing the man he despised so comprehensively would be dead.

Reluctantly, he chased the thought away. If anything happened to Darcy then suspicion would immediately fall upon him. Besides, after the debacle with Miss Bingley, Lizzy no longer admired or trusted Wickham in the way she once had. It pained him to concede the point, but even if he took the ultimate chance — he had once tried to do away with Darcy during their childhood and had failed — there was no guarantee Lizzy would look kindly upon him when she became a widow.

No, his original plan would just have to serve.

Wickham halted the curricle, tied off the reins and concealed it beneath a stand of trees. Not that there was the remotest possibility of it being seen from the house, but Darcy had a small army of gamekeepers constantly on the lookout for poachers. It would be the ultimate humiliation if he was mistaken for a common thief.

'There,' he said to Molly, leading her to a position when she had a clear view of the extensive mansion. 'That is Pemberley, where I grew up.'

'It's very grand.' She sent him an appraising look. 'Did you really live in the house?'

'As good as.' He had no intention of diminishing his worth in Molly's eyes by telling her he had actually lived in the steward's cottage. 'The gentleman who owned it when I was a boy was the best man ever to draw breath. But his son is mean-spirited and resented the interest he took in me, which is why I am no longer welcome.'

'But your wife is? That seems rather odd.'

'Her sister is married to Darcy.'

'Well, I don't suppose the gentleman can refuse to entertain his wife's sister then. But

how can things have come to such a pass?'
Molly frowned. 'If Darcy merely resents you
and yet invites your wife, surely he could
endure your presence for a week also?'

'You would think so, but great men can do
whatever they please without a thought for
the feelings they hurt.'

'Why did you come here if it oversets you
so?'

'Because I can.' Wickham ground his jaw.
'If Darcy thinks he can cast me aside because
he's jealous of my popularity then he's in for
a surprise.'

'This is why you wanted to come north?'
Molly nodded towards the house. 'Your
expectations of wealth centre upon this
estate. Are you sure you know what you're
doing? I doubt you'll get inside, even on a
night like tonight, without being detected.'

Wickham didn't agree. Tonight, when the
servants were run off their feet and the house
was full of strangers, would have given him
the perfect cover. But even if he'd sprung for
a private carriage, he might not have arrived
in Derbyshire in time to put his plans into
place. A small voice inside his head told him
he would have been sure to, had he left
London on Gardiner's heels instead of
spending a night gambling, carousing and
then dallying with Molly. But, damn it, a man

had to have some recreation. No, he would get in right enough, under cover of darkness tomorrow night, and find the evidence he needed.

He knew exactly where to look for it.

The sound of voices, of music and laughter, reached them on the still night air.

'Would you care to dance, ma'am?' Wickham asked, suddenly full of optimism as his mood lightened and he offered Molly an exaggerated bow.

'Why, sir,' she replied, tossing her head and fluttering her lashes over an imaginary fan. 'I do believe that that would be just the thing.'

Wickham swept her into his arms and swirled her into a polka, kicking up leaves as their feet stumbled over the uneven ground. They were unable to stay upright, due to Wickham's determination to dance so fast, and fell breathlessly in a tangle of limbs and spontaneous laughter onto a pile of the dried leaves they had just disturbed. Wickham's laughter turned to desire when he glanced down and saw her flushed face and the light of anticipation in her eye. The idea of taking her here in Pemberley's grounds appealed to his sense of . . . well, he was not precisely sure what devilish impulse drove him. But Wickham knew he would see the act through in spite of the prospect of being caught by roaming keepers — or perhaps because of it.

'Now he wants to play,' Molly said, laughing as he dragged her bodice down. 'Laying a few ghosts to rest, are we?'

'Something of that nature.'

'Well, I've never done it in a wood before.'

Wickham took her harshly, temporarily exorcising the anger that had blighted his adult years, preventing him from making the success of his life that old Mr. Darcy had intended for him. As he found release, Wickham's mind was flooded with images of a dead Darcy and his grieving widow turning to Wickham for comfort in her hour of need.

Unlikely, but if a man couldn't dream, what else did he have left?

This was just the start of his new life, Wickham reminded himself. Within a day or two he would have Darcy precisely where he wanted him. Not dead, but forced to acknowledge Wickham was his blood relation, which would be the next best thing.

'Enjoy your evening, Georgiana,' he muttered. 'I bear you no ill-will.'

★　★　★

It seemed to Kitty that she had only been asleep for an hour or so when a persistent tapping at her door roused her.

'Go away,' she muttered, thumping her pillows into a more comfortable nest and turning over. She did not wish to be disturbed from her recollections of an evening spent almost exclusively with Richard. Today consequences would have to be faced but Richard had assured her he would handle any threats or insults his father hurled at him and . . .

'Kitty, Kitty, wake up!'

A hand shook her shoulder, Lydia's voice penetrated her sleep-addled brain and she reluctantly opened her eyes.

'Lydia, what is it? Has something happened?'

'No, silly, but you need to get up.'

'No I don't. I only just came to bed.'

'You can sleep later.' Lydia tugged the covers away, leaving Kitty shivering since her fire had dwindled. 'We have to go into Lambton, remember? To see Denny.'

Kitty sat up and blinked sleep from her eyes. 'Now? What time is it?'

'We have to go before anyone else gets up and wants to come with us.'

'They won't,' Kitty said with an expansive yawn and equally expansive stretch. 'It was almost dawn before we all got to bed.'

'Never mind that. Come on, Kitty, you promised. If you order a carriage, no one will dare to ask why you need it.'

'What's the urgency, Lydia?' Kitty asked, awake now.

'Denny won't be here for long. I don't want to miss him. Wickham told me most particularly to call early in the morning, before he has second thoughts about repaying the money he owes, which is a goodly sum. If I collect it, Wickham might look more kindly upon my situation.'

'Of course.' Kitty gave her sister a swift hug and climbed from her warm bed. 'I hadn't thought of that. Debtors will use any excuse to avoid making restitution. Help me get dressed and then and we can be gone at once.'

'You used to be able to dress yourself,' Lydia reminded her.

'I've got out of the habit.' Kitty grimaced. 'Does that make me sound terribly spoiled?'

'If I could afford the luxury of my own maid . . . but there's no point in harbouring such unrealistic thoughts.'

'How do you feel today?' Kitty asked, running a brush through her hair and tying it back with a ribbon before squashing a straw bonnet on her head at a jaunty angle. She felt jaunty, full of optimism, and nothing, not even Lydia's dilemma, could spoil her mood.

'There was nothing really the matter with

me. Just a fit of the blue devils.'

'Then I am glad you have recovered from them.' Kitty picked up her reticule. Knowing Lydia, once she had seen Denny she would notice something in one of the shops that she absolutely couldn't live without and probably had no money of her own. Kitty hoped rather than expected Denny to change that situation and wanted to tell Lydia it was a very strange arrangement anyway. If Denny wanted to repay his debt, surely a more convenient means of doing so could be contrived. Involving Wickham's wife in the collection was not seemly. But Lydia seemed determined and Kitty knew her sister well enough to accept that nothing would deter her when she had made up her mind on a specific course of action. 'Come along then. I'm now at your disposal.'

After such a late night, John Coachman was obviously surprised to see Miss Bennet and Mrs. Wickham up and about so early, wishing to be taken into Lambton. Asking no questions, he obligingly harnessed his horses and the sisters were soon trundling down the driveway in a comfortable carriage. No one inside the house had, as far as Kitty could ascertain, yet stirred. Nor would she expect them do so before noon, or even later. She and Lydia would be back by then and no one need know about their excursion, or the reason for it.

'You have not told me how things stand between you and your major, Kitty,' Lydia said as the carriage rattled along.

Grinning, Kitty told Lydia everything that had happened since the major's arrival. Lydia, at first struck dumb by the enormity of her revelations, contented herself with flinging her arms around Kitty.

'I am so very glad,' she said. 'I knew that's how it would be. Take no notice that I once told you the major wasn't handsome. He adores you and is in a position to keep you in comfort, which is far more important that outward appearances.' Lydia grimaced. 'I ought to know. I was influenced by Wickham's looks and charm, and see where that has landed me.'

'Is it so very bad?' Kitty asked sympathetically.

'It was all right, until . . . ' Lydia glanced at her waistline and said no more.

'Things will improve for you, Lydia. I'm sure of it. Wickham will come round to the idea of the baby. He will continue to do well working for our uncle and everything will seem brighter.'

'Oh, let's not talk about me,' Lydia said, flashes of her old, indomitable spirit briefly apparent. 'Tell me instead how you plan to persuade stuffy Mr. Turner that you will make an admirable mother for a future earl.' Lydia grinned. 'Only imagine what Mama will make of that.'

Kitty giggled. 'Oh, for the love of God, don't tell her! She has already made me squirm more than enough with her tactless hints.'

'I shall not say a word. I have become very good at keeping secrets.' Lydia grinned. 'Married life has taught me the importance of discretion. I know I used to be a terrible rattle-trap, but I tend to think before I speak nowadays. Well, usually.'

'Where are we going precisely?' Kitty asked as they reached the outskirts of Lambton. 'I need to give our coachman directions.'

'Oh, have him take us to the inn and wait for us in the mews. It's only a short walk but not a terribly respectable area of the village.'

'And yet Mr. Wickham expected you to go there alone?' Kitty frowned. 'I don't like the idea of that. I don't like the idea of the two of us going, come to that. Are you absolutely sure about this, Lydia?'

'Oh yes, this is not London. Ladies don't get accosted in broad daylight on the streets. We shall be perfectly all right, but I should be ashamed for Mr. Darcy's coachman to see where we're going. Besides, I promised not to say anything and the coachman is bound to talk.'

'Oh, Lydia, Mr. Darcy is not the ogre you make him out to be. He will not mind.'

'But I shall. I still have some pride, you know.'

Kitty patted her hand. 'Have it your way,' she said, feeling distinctly uncomfortable as they set off on foot, swept along by Lydia's indomitable will.

A short time later the sisters had made their way to a narrow street that Kitty had not previously been aware existed, lined by close-packed cottages in a poor state of repair. She felt suspicious stares being directed at them by a couple of surly youths, while children no older than three or four years danced around them, holding out grubby hands in expectation of largesse. Kitty resisted the urge to empty the contents of her reticule into those hands. It would start a riot and draw even more attention to them. She grasped Lydia's hand, more convinced than ever that her sister had come to the wrong place. They were overdressed for such an area, even in their plainest morning gowns and pelisses, and Kitty now regretted not insisting that their coachman accompany them. Denny could not be lodging here, surely? If he was, he was clearly down on his luck and in no position to repay Wickham.

'Are you sure this is right, Lydia?'

'Yes, Wickham gave me very precise instructions.'

How did he know? 'Even so, I don't feel comfortable. We ought to — '

'Don't make such a fuss, Kitty. It's just a bit further along, I think. I was told . . . arghh!'

'Lydia, what — '

Kitty's words were cut off when a hand was clapped over her mouth. Before she could react, she felt herself being lifted from the ground and thrown over a man's shoulder. At the same time Lydia was pushed violently to the ground and remained there, unmoving. Fear gave Kitty superhuman strength and she struggled like mad to go to her sister's aid. What if the baby had been damaged by the fall? What if Lydia had? Kitty absolutely had to get to her, but the arm holding her down was too strong for her to fight against and the hand over her mouth didn't budge, even when Kitty attempted to bite it. The youths were still in the street, staring at them, but doing nothing to help.

Before she had a chance to gather her wits Kitty was thrown into a carriage and driven away from Lydia at a cracking pace.

Lizzy sensed a presence looming over her, opened her eyes and stared up into the beloved face of her husband. He was fully dressed and had probably been going about his business for some hours. It would take more than a late night to keep him from his duties, but he had risen from her bed so stealthily that Lizzy had not stirred.

'Good morning,' she said, yawning. 'Is it still morning?'

'Yes, I didn't mean to wake you. I just needed to be sure you were all right. It was a very late night and you overdid it, trying to keep your relations happy.'

'You were with me all night to ensure I had everything I needed, which I did.' She smiled up at him. 'All I ever need is you.'

'And yet I have woken you. That is thoughtless of me.'

'I've had quite enough sleep.'

She patted the side of the bed, inviting him to sit.

'Is something wrong?' she asked. 'Has my mother done — '

'No, it isn't that.'

'Then what? Lydia?'

'She and Kitty went off to Lambton first thing this morning, so I've just been told.'

'Oh, then it sounds as though Lydia has recovered her spirits. She will be in search of new bonnets, no doubt.' Lizzy smiled. 'But it was thoughtless of her to drag poor Kitty out so early. It's all right for Lydia. She had a full night's sleep.'

'I expect Kitty is too happy to sleep, if what you've told me about the major's intentions is true. And stop worrying. If Turner has to choose between his family and Kitty then he will be guided by his feelings for your sister. There's no question he's a man desperately in love.' Will gently touched her face and tucked an escaped strand of hair behind her ear. 'I recognise in him the feelings I entertained for you before we were married.'

'Entertained?' Lizzy arched a brow. 'You no longer feel the same way?'

'Not in the least. I had not thought it possible, but my feelings for you have gained in intensity since our marriage. Every day I love you a little more.' Will shook his head, as though he couldn't quite believe it himself. 'You have a lot to answer for, Mrs. Darcy.'

She reached up to steal a kiss. 'I aim to please.'

A tap at the door saw them move apart. Lizzy's maid, Jessie, bustled in, looking worried.

'Excuse me, sir, ma'am, but there is such a fuss downstairs.'

'What's happened?' Lizzy asked, suspecting her mother, Lady Catherine or Mr. Turner to be responsible, although it was probably too early for either of the ladies to be about. Mr. Turner, on the other hand, was an early riser. He had been observed several times since his arrival at Pemberley walking in the grounds at first light.

'Well, ma'am, Mrs. Wickham and Miss Bennet went early into Lambton.'

Lizzy sat a little straighter, concerned now. 'What of it?'

'John Coachman has just returned. He was told to wait at the inn but he saw the ladies head off to a poor part of town and was worried about their welfare. So he followed them.' Jessie paused, her eyes bulging with her role as the imparter of what Lizzy feared would be bad tidings. 'Some rogue knocked Mrs. Wickham to the ground.'

Lizzy gasped and leapt from her bed. 'Did John bring her back with him?'

'Yes, ma'am. She's in her room. She's conscious but in some pain, I gather. I thought you would want to know.'

'Is Miss Bennet with her?'

'That's the thing, ma'am. John saw someone grab her and spirit her away. He

188

couldn't get to her in time to save her. He had to decide whether to rescue Mrs. Wickham or try and follow after Miss Bennet.' A tear slid down Jessie's face. 'Miss Bennet was taken off in a closed carriage and John couldn't follow on foot; especially not when he had Mrs. Wickham's plight to consider.'

Will touched Lizzy's shoulders, which were shaking. 'Are you all right? Stupid question; of course you're not.'

'I must go to Lydia and see if I can discover what they were doing in that part of the village, and why. Then perhaps we can work out who has taken Kitty.'

Will looked grim. 'Help your mistress to dress, Jessie.' Will kissed Lizzy's brow. 'I shall be downstairs, speaking with John. Let me know if you need me to rouse Sanford to attend to Lydia.'

10

After two hours Richard gave up chasing sleep and threw back the covers. He sat on the window seat instead, enjoying the absolute stillness of Pemberley as Darcy's guests slept late on the morning following the ball. His ever present sketch pad was open on his lap as Richard endeavoured to recreate the way Kitty had looked in her lovely ball gown. The sketch rapidly took shape, joining many other likenesses of the woman he adored.

Sketching helped him to assemble his thoughts and prepare for the ultimate confrontation with a father who could no longer doubt Richard's intentions. Perhaps he was aware that threats, bullying or direct orders would no longer have the desired effect and he was planning a less aggressive strategy. The thought made Richard smile. To his precise recollection his father had never used subtlety or compromise to get his way. Dictatorial authority and the assumption that his orders would be obeyed to the letter had always been his *modus operandi*.

Richard frowned as he struggled to get the

curve of Kitty's face exactly right. Matters would never be the same between him and his father again and despite everything, the thought of an estrangement saddened him. It didn't need to be that way. Kitty was a sweet, obliging girl who knew how to conduct herself in society and would not disgrace the family name. Richard loved her with unswerving passion but knew it would be a waste of breath to try and explain his feelings to his cold-hearted father who put duty above all considerations.

Sharp set, he put aside his sketch and decided to go in search of breakfast. Conscious of the fact that the servants had had a late night also, didn't bother to ring for hot water. He was a soldier, used to making do, and poured cold water from the ewer into the adjacent basin before splashing it over his face. Richard didn't travel with a valet and made short work of dressing himself. He then made his way downstairs. Sure enough, the dining room was devoid of other guests, but the sideboard was full of covered dishes and a footman, ineffectually stifling a yawn, was there to serve him with coffee.

He heaped his plate and took his place at the table, wondering when he could reasonably expect Kitty to put in an appearance. He dared to believe that she actually loved him

191

and would accept his proposal when he renewed it later today. That acceptance would come in spite of his family's connections and not because of them, which made her doubly worth fighting for.

His cogitations were interrupted by the appearance of his father.

'Morning, Pater,' Richard said, striving to remain calm.

'Good morning.'

His father also helped himself to a full plate and took a seat opposite Richard. They exchanged the odd word or two as they ate but his father made no mention of Kitty. Richard knew he owed that reprieve to the presence of the footman. Even his father would not take it upon himself to dismiss another man's servants but Richard knew he was on borrowed time.

And yet . . . and yet his father, whose moods were always evident from his expression, seemed remarkably unperturbed. It would be impossible to tell from his demeanour that he had anything more taxing on his mind than a decent breakfast. Far from feeling relieved, Richard's suspicions were now on high alert. The pater was up to something.

'What are you plans today?' his father asked.

'I shall wait and see what our host suggests,' Richard replied. 'Billiards, I would imagine. I don't suppose anyone will be up for anything more energetic.'

'I was considering a ride myself, if Darcy can spare me a mount.'

'His horses are at our disposal. You need only apply to his head groom and he will see you suitably mounted. Do you wish me to accompany you?'

'No need.'

Richard was astonished by his father's refusal. He must have known when he proposed a ride that Richard could not avoid offering his company, which would provide the older man with privacy in which to take Richard to task. His declination put Richard at a disadvantage. As a good military strategist, he felt uncomfortable when he couldn't anticipate the enemy's next move and prepare to counter it. What was he up to? Perhaps he intended to raise the subject with Kitty, hoping to bully or cajole her into capitulation. Richard firmed his jaw, determined to prevent that situation from arising.

'Something wrong?' his father asked nonchalantly, glancing up from his plate.

'Excuse me, Father. I have a letter to write.'

'Go ahead, my boy.' His father waved a

hand in dismissal. 'I shall see you later, no doubt.'

Richard did not doubt.

* * *

'Lydia, what on earth happened to you?'

'I don't . . . I'm not sure. It's all a blur. One minute we were walking, and then . . . and then, someone pushed me. I fell, and I . . . '

Lydia burst into tears. Lizzy, deeply concerned, sat beside her sister as Jessie helped her out of her clothing, which was dirty and torn. Her face was deathly pale, there was a graze on the side of her forehead and she was clearly in pain.

'Where does it hurt?'

'Everywhere,' Lydia replied as Lizzy and Jessie helped her into bed. 'My head, my shoulder where I fell, my belly . . . '

'Find Mr. Darcy and have him rouse Doctor Sanford,' Lizzy told Jessie, an urgent edge to her voice.

'Right away, ma'am.'

'Now, tell me what happened,' Lizzy said, tamping down her concerns for Kitty's welfare. Will would be quizzing John Coachman in that regard and there was nothing they could do to get her back until they had some idea of where she had been taken, and by whom. Lizzy had convinced herself that Kitty had been taken for a reason: a reason that wouldn't be furthered by hurting her — or worse. If she didn't believe that then she would go out of her mind with worry, and she was already worried enough about Lydia and her unborn child.

Lizzy didn't think Lydia was even aware Kitty had been abducted so there was little point in asking her if she saw her abductor. She was still groggy, had probably lost consciousness and hadn't asked why Kitty had not returned to Pemberley in the carriage with her.

'Why did you go to Lambton so early, Lydia, and what business did you have in such a rundown part of the village?'

'Denny,' Lydia mumbled.

'Denny? Wickham's friend?' Lizzy tensed. 'What is this to do with him?'

Lydia nodded. 'He owes Wickham money. I was to collect it.'

'Good heavens. Why didn't you mention it?'

'Wickham said not to tell . . . ashamed.'

The mention of Wickham's name caused Lizzy's concerns to intensify. Trouble followed that man more tenaciously than a devoted dog. 'What happened next? Who accosted you? Think, Lydia,' Lizzy said, gently shaking her uninjured shoulder when she closed her eyes and appeared to drift away. 'It could be important.'

'I don't know. I didn't see. It all happened so quickly.' She winced, clearly fighting pain. 'Ask Kitty.'

If only she could! Why would anyone want to abduct Kitty? If Wickham was somehow involved it could mean anything. But Wickham was hundreds of miles away in London. Perhaps Kitty had been taken in mistake for Lydia. The girls were of similar height and colouring, separated by little more than a year in age. She could have been taken by someone other than Denny who bore Wickham a grudge, Lizzy supposed. Someone who was owed money by Wickham and required a bargaining tool to persuade him to pay up.

Lizzy was being fanciful and she knew it. Apart from anything else, how could the miscreants have known Kitty and Lydia would be in Lambton at that precise time? The use of a carriage by the abductors implied forward planning. Dear God, poor Kitty must be terrified! Lizzy trembled when she considered what might even now be happening to her at the hands of her captors.

Perdition, they had to find her; and soon! If

Mama heard of this there would be pandemonium. Lizzy's head thumped and she felt like screaming with frustration. She was cursed. Every time she held a party at Pemberley, something untoward happened. If she and her family came through this particular episode unscathed she vowed never to entertain ever again.

'Did Wickham tell you to go at a particular time?'

'Hmm,' Lydia mumbled. 'Had to be today.'

Lizzy's worst fears were confirmed. Wickham *was* behind this; somehow. Finding Kitty was now imperative! Lizzy had been pleased at how readily he'd settled in her uncle's employ, but still harboured misgivings about his constancy. Wickham still bore her beloved Will a grudge. Lizzy had seen it in his eyes that day a year ago when he was sent away from Pemberley and it was made clear he would never be admitted to the estate again. Such resentment, such a burning desire for revenge, could not be extinguished with the offer of what Wickham would considered a position that was beneath his dignity.

Enough of Wickham! Kitty was all that mattered and there was not a moment to lose. Her reputation, to say nothing of her happiness with Major Turner, hung precariously in the balance. The major would have a hard enough time going against his father's wishes. If Kitty was in any way compromised, perhaps he would decide against fighting for her and toe the family line instead. The major had told her once that everything he had done in his adult life had been with the sole purpose of impressing his father. He was now being offered that opportunity. Given what he had seen of Mrs. Bennet over the past few days, Lizzy wouldn't blame him if he was having second thoughts. And now Kitty's disappearance had come about because she had been careless enough to venture into a poor part of the village unescorted. Was that the behaviour one would expect of a possible earl's mother?

Such thoughts tumbled through Lizzy's brain while she held her sister's hand and impatiently waited for Doctor Sanford to join them. Thank goodness he had stayed at Pemberley last night. Lizzy didn't like the look of Lydia's pallor, or the manner in which she kept clutching her stomach and groaning; how she seemed incapable of stringing a coherent sentence together.

It was Jane who entered the room a short time later, in company with Doctor Sanford.

'I encountered Jessie and she told me what has happened,' Jane said, looking as anxious as Lizzy felt. 'How is Lydia?'

'In pain.'

'Let me see if I can ease her discomfort.' Doctor Sanford placed on the floor the medical bag he never strayed from home without. Even, it seemed, on the day of his betrothal party.

'She's increasing,' Lizzy explained. 'She was knocked to the ground and is now complaining about stomach pains.'

'Do you think she will she lose the baby?' Jane asked in a low, anxious voice.

'Let's not assume the worst just yet,' Doctor Sanford said in a competent voice that helped to calm Lizzy's skittish nerves.

Lizzy took Jane aside while Doctor Sanford examined Lydia.

'What of Kitty?' Jane asked, clutching Lizzy's hand.

'We have to find her, and at once. Mr. Darcy is speaking with our coachman about what he saw. Then we shall decide what to do.'

'Thank goodness your coachman decided to follow after the girls.' Jane frowned. 'But who could possibly want to take Kitty?'

'She's known to live here and ventured into a poor part of the village without male protection. Some ne'er-do-well might have seized the opportunity to take her, hoping for a reward for her return.'

'And just happened to have a carriage to

hand?' Jane shook her head. 'It seems improbable.'

Lizzy agreed but didn't overset Jane by mentioning Wickham's possible involvement. 'My husband might know more by now. Stay with Lydia, Jane, while I find out. I shall be back directly.'

Lizzy slipped down the stairs and found Will in the library with the major. Both gentlemen wore grim expressions.

'How is Lydia?' Will asked.

'In pain. Doctor Sanford and Jane are with her. Have you found out what happened?'

'John tells me the ladies had him drive them to the inn and left instructions for him to wait for them there. He saw them walk to the edge of the village and knowing it wasn't a suitable area for ladies to venture into alone, he wisely followed them.'

'Did he see what happened?'

'Only what we've already heard.' Will's expression was forbidding. 'This is directed at me. Someone wishes to hurt me by abducting Kitty. It has to have been carefully planned, and they must have known the girls would be in that part of the village.' He shook his head. 'But how?'

'We ought to be out looking,' the major said, pacing the length of the room in agitation.

Lizzy couldn't postpone telling Will what she had learned. 'They went at Lydia's request,' she said softly. 'Denny was supposed to be there. He . . . er, he owes Wickham money — '

'Wickham!' Will thumped his thigh with his clenched fist, deep lines etching themselves in his forehead as he frowned. 'I ought to have known. Will I never be free of the accursed man?'

'Wickham asked Lydia to go to a cottage this morning and collect the money from Denny. He was only going to be there for a short time so it had to be today.'

Will's expression mirrored Lizzy's scepticism. 'What are the chances of Denny being here at this particular time, just when we happen to be entertaining and Wickham's wife is amongst our guests? He has no connection to the district and no reason that I know of to dally in a small village the size of Lambton.' Will shook his head, fury radiating from his eyes. Pushed beyond the limit of his endurance by Wickham's continued interference in Derbyshire, Lizzy had never seen him half so angry before. 'Wickham's behind this somehow. I'd stake my fortune on the fact.'

'But he's in London, is he not?' the major asked, looking justifiably confused.

Will curled his upper lip disdainfully. 'You don't know the man, Turner, and underestimate his cunning. He will go to the ends of the earth to get even with me.'

'How w-will taking Miss Bennet achieve t-that ambition?'

'I ought to return to Lydia. I'm concerned she might lose the baby.' Lizzy frowned. 'At least Mama will not rise until this afternoon. How we can keep this from her, I can't begin to imagine, but at least she need not know of it before then.'

'Look after Lydia,' Will said, touching her shoulder, the coppery glitter of rage briefly leaving his eye. 'We'll worry about the rest of the household later. Simpson!' Their butler, aware of a crisis brewing, had stationed himself outside the door in anticipation of being needed. He entered the room immediately and awaited Will's orders. 'Send several men to the area where Mrs. Wickham was attacked. Offer a reward for information regarding anyone unusual seen in the vicinity. I am particularly interested in anyone who has taken occupation of a cottage there in the past few days.'

'I shall see to it at once, sir.'

'Oh, and Simpson.'

'Sir?'

'John Coachman tells me Miss Bennet was

taken off in a closed curricle. Check at the livery yard. See if it was hired locally and if so, by whom. Not that I expect that person to have left his real name, but at least you might get a description.'

Simpson acknowledged Will's orders with a stately inclination of his head and left to carry them out.

'If they are in a curricle, they can't go that far,' the major said, seeming slightly mollified. 'Unless they have a larger carriage close by, of course.'

'My suspicion is that they will keep her somewhere locally,' Will said. 'If Wickham has arranged her abduction, he will want to extract money from me in return for her safe delivery.'

'And he won't harm her,' Lizzy said, trying to convince herself as much as anyone else. Wickham, when he had tried to compromise Lizzy a year previously, had seemed perfectly willing to harm her if she opposed him, but she saw little profit in reminding Will of that unpalatable fact.

'No he won't harm her.' Will scowled at the flames dancing in the grate. 'We'll find her before he has the chance and then it will be time to settle this matter between us once and for all.'

'Don't do anything rash,' Lizzy said,

frightened by the controlled rage she detected in his expression.

'I have done all manner of things for that rogue that went against the grain, for your sake,' he said softly. 'But enough.'

'Yes, I understand the time has come. But let's get Kitty safely home first.'

'Of course. That is my primary concern.'

Lizzy was about to leave the room when her uncle Gardiner entered it, a letter in his hand.

'Ah, there you are. Good morning, my dear. Major, Mr. Darcy.' He waved the letter in the air. 'Distressing tidings, I fear.'

'Let me guess,' Will said, compressing his lips together into a tight line. 'Wickham has left London.'

'Good heavens, however did you know that?'

⋆　⋆　⋆

Kitty must have passed out. When she opened her eyes again she was disorientated and it took her a moment to recall what had happened to her. Fear washed through her as it all came flooding back, making her feel nauseous, and she regretted opening her eyes. Even so, she knew it was important to take stock.

She appeared to be in a fast-moving curricle that felt as if it was traversing a rutted track. She tried the door handle. It was locked, which added to her fear, although how she could have alighted without breaking her neck when she was being driven so fast she could not have said. But she would have tried. The major planned to renew his address today and she fully intended to be there and accept him.

She didn't have time to be abducted!

The shades were pulled down and she was unable to let them up, either because her hands were shaking too much or because they had been fixed in position to prevent anyone looking inside. She was scared out of her wits but unharmed; and she would remain so if she had any say in the matter.

She sat up straighter and considered her dilemma. Calm deliberation always offered up solutions to impossible situations, she reminded herself. Oh God, Lydia! She had been knocked to the ground. Fear for her own situation was replaced with a far greater concern for her sister's. She could lose her baby, or even her life. She was alone, injured and unprotected in a poor part of the village. She recalled the unsavoury youths loitering in the street. She could well imagine them robbing Lydia of any valuables, but whether they would help her was less certain. If only she could believe that Denny was in that cottage, awaiting Lydia's arrival.

But she was certain now that Denny was nowhere near Lambton. She had always thought it a strange method of repaying a debt; a ruse concocted by someone who wished her sister harm. Denny would not rescue Lydia, and no one would rescue Kitty, either.

She was on her own.

Anger at such thoughts gradually overcame part of her fear. Put simply, she was incensed at the manner in which she had been treated. Kitty tried to imagine why anyone would want to abduct her. How she wished now that she had paid more attention to her disquiet when she and Lydia had entered that horrible street. She had known, just known, that something unpleasant would happen, but could not have anticipated quite *how* unpleasant.

Wickham had to be responsible, Kitty decided. He and Denny were the only people who knew they would be there and Wickham had somehow planned this to get even with Mr. Darcy. He would probably demand money for her safe return, through an intermediary, of course. He was safely in London and could not be held responsible.

How very clever of him.

But Kitty was quite clever, too. She was no longer the silly girl Wickham had known back in Hertfordshire who thought of nothing but flirting and chasing officers. A year of living at Pemberley had improved her mind. She modelled herself more on Lizzy than Lydia nowadays, which Wickham would discover to his detriment if she could somehow escape from her captors.

She thought it important to try and gauge how long she was in the curricle before she arrived wherever she was being taken. That might help her to pinpoint her location. They were still on an uneven track, which probably meant they were keeping clear of the only road into Lambton. Presumably then she was not being taken far from Pemberley. Good! She knew the surrounding area well; probably better than her captors if they weren't from the locality. That might work to her advantage.

The curricle rattled to a halt, heralding the return of her anxiety. It was all very well being brave when she was left alone, but what would happen now?

'Close your eyes,' said a rough voice outside the door. 'If you look at me it will be the worse for you.'

Kitty was happy to oblige, having no wish

to see the odious man's face. She would do precisely as she was told, pretend to be helpless and terrified, which required little pretence, and wait for them to lower their guard. The door opened, someone fastened a blindfold over her eyes and rough hands pulled her from the curricle.

11

Wickham had sent Molly out with some money to spend in the local haberdasher's; a task that would keep her occupied for a considerable time. He would go and find her when he had conducted his business with Lydia. His wife had damned well better not have overslept and keep him waiting. She knew he was not a patient man.

He strode four paces across the small parlour: the maximum movement the restricted space permitted a man of his size, and then four paces back again, glancing out of the window with growing impatience. Over an hour had passed, and Wickham was at the end of his patience by the time he noticed Lydia's approach. A string of execrable oaths slipped past his lips when he observed Kitty with her.

Wickham thumped the wall with his clenched fist, a red mist of anger blurring his vision. Lydia might be persuaded to keep his presence here a secret and offer him the help he needed to get inside Pemberley, but Kitty would never agree. She was Lizzy's devotee and her mind had probably been unfairly poisoned against him. What the devil was he supposed to do now?

Before he could decide he was astonished to see a burly individual appear from between the close-packed hovels. He pushed Lydia hard and she fell to the ground with an anguished cry. What the devil! Wickham sighed, resigned to the fact that he would have to rescue his wife from this desperate opportunist before she or Kitty were badly hurt.

But it soon became apparent that their purpose was abduction. Kitty was thrown over the brute's shoulder and spirited away in a curricle that appeared out of nowhere, driven by another shady-looking character. By the time Wickham galvanised himself into action, Kitty was long gone and Darcy's coachman appeared to help Lydia. That settled it. Wickham wouldn't have to show himself. He felt rather pleased with himself for briefly putting his wife's welfare ahead of his own plans. Fortuitously, such a noble gesture had proved unnecessary.

He fell to contemplating this latest string of events; another obstacle in his fight for justice and recognition, but one which he would not permit to deter him. First, he must collect Molly and move somewhere else. The moment Darcy heard what had happened he would have people flooding this area to look for strangers. If he was found here, awkward questions would be asked and he would be accused of abducting Kitty and harming his own wife, even though he hadn't done it. But he was supposed to be in London, couldn't explain his true purpose in being here, and no one would believe his denial.

One thing was now clear. Lydia would be no help to him in getting inside Pemberley. As usual he was on his own. Still, in one respect the business with Kitty would work to his advantage. Everyone would be preoccupied with looking for her — Darcy most of all — and access to Pemberley would be that much easier to achieve as a consequence.

Wickham gathered up the few belongings he had brought with him, which didn't take him long. Molly's were scattered all over the bedroom. Collecting them up delayed him for several minutes. It wouldn't do to leave behind any clues as to his identity; or hers. Satisfied he had found everything, he packed their things into two valises, pulled his hat low over his eyes and left the cottage. He tried not to resent the fact that he had paid an extortionate amount to rent it for a week but had only occupied it for one night.

Setbacks were inevitable, he reminded himself, even though he was furious with his wife for occasioning this particular one at such a crucial time. He felt a moment's guilt for insisting Lydia come without male protection. She ought to have been safe enough in broad daylight; especially if she had done as she was told and come alone. Kitty's presence changed everything. She was well known around these parts as Mrs. Darcy's sister and so profiting from her rash venture into the poorer part of the village would be hard for opportunist numbskulls to resist.

Wickham could not possibly have foreseen the attack and so was entitled to feel disgruntled. He reclaimed his curricle from the livery yard, thinking about what he ought to do next. Abandoning his plans was not an option. He had well and truly burned his bridges with Gardiner — not that he would go back to such lowly employment even if he could — and so it was simply a matter of adapting to his changed circumstances.

He found Molly at the haberdasher's, involved in a heated negotiation over a length of silk. Molly looked set to argue when Wickham told her they needed to leave at once. One look at his countenance and she brought the negotiations to a speedy conclusion.

Wickham helped her into the curricle, by which time word had spread and a small crowd had gathered to gawp at the finely dressed lady who wasn't all she should be. Well, of course Molly would stand out like a jewel in a pig sty when compared to the colourless folk of Lambton. Had circumstances been different, he would have enjoyed showing her off. As it was, her flamboyance had drawn unwelcome attention to them both. They would have to move somewhere even more remote for a day or two, Wickham thought as he drove from the village at a cracking pace.

And he knew just the place.

* * *

'How is she?' Lizzy asked, slipping back into Lydia's room.

Jane shook her head. 'Doctor Sanford fears for the baby,' she said softly. 'It's so very sad.'

'I've given her something to make her sleep,' the doctor said. 'If she remains very still and doesn't become agitated, matters might still have a happy outcome.'

'If anyone can ensure her wellbeing it's you, Doctor Sanford,' Lizzy said, brushing the hair away from her sleeping sister's pale forehead.

'Don't get your hopes up, ladies.' He packed up his bag. 'There's nothing more I can do for her at the moment. Have someone sit beside her and if there's any change in her condition, send for me. I can't stress firmly enough that she must not, under any circumstances, become agitated.'

'Thank you,' Lizzy and Jane said in unison.

'I shall find Darcy and see what I can do to help find Miss Bennet.'

'Jane,' Lizzy said, grasping her sister's hand when they were alone. 'I know you want to stay with Lydia. I do, too, but we cannot. I shall have Jessie sit with her.'

'Why can we not? Surely she needs her sisters near her at such at time?'

'We don't want Mama to hear about Kitty or Lydia. Or Lady Catherine, for that matter.' Lizzy wrinkled her nose. 'And remember what Doctor Sanford just said. Lydia must not become agitated. Mama will have hysterics if she sees her favourite daughter in this condition, which will make everything ten times worse.'

'Yes, I suppose you're right. What would you have me do instead?'

'I would prefer it if Mr. Turner didn't have to know about Kitty, but I don't see how that can be avoided.'

'You're concerned for Kitty's reputation? Her abduction would give Mr. Turner a genuine reason to object to the union since

Kitty . . . ' Jane gulped. 'Since there is a very real possibility that Kitty might be compromised.'

Lizzy nodded grimly. 'Precisely.'

'And wouldn't that suit the odious Mr. Turner very well.' Jane stood a little taller, a rare glower distorting her lovely features. 'Could be responsible for the abduction, do you suppose?'

'The thought had occurred to me. He looks down on us all and I wouldn't put anything past him when it comes to the protection of his family's reputation. But still, I don't see how he could have managed it.' Lizzy frowned as she thought it through. 'He had no prior knowledge of Lydia and Kitty's visit to Lambton. None of us knew of their plans, so he couldn't have hired miscreants to do the abducting, to say nothing of the curricle she was spirited away in.'

'I suppose not, but that doesn't mean he won't be delighted when he hears about it.'

'It will make his day; detestable man! But still, I think it more likely that some opportunist saw her in that part of the village and took her in the hope of financial reward.'

'You think someone will pretend to have found her by accident? Why would we believe that?'

Lizzy shrugged. 'Because all we care about

215

is having her restored to us unharmed.'

Jane nodded. 'Yes, perhaps.' But she didn't sound any more convinced than Lizzy felt.

'I have to believe that will be the case or I shall lose my wits.' Lizzy tugged distractedly at a stray curl. She had simply tied her hair back in her haste to get to Lydia and already it was escaping from its ribbon. 'Kitty is strong and she's sensible but — '

'But what can she do to defend herself?' Jane's complexion paled. 'She must be terrified.'

Lizzy nodded glumly. 'This ought to have been the happiest day of her life, and instead . . . '

'We absolutely have to find her!' Jane cried. 'I couldn't bear it if her entire future was ruined through no fault of her own.'

'I thought Kitty had more sense nowadays than to blindly follow Lydia's example in the way she used to when we were all still at Longbourn.'

'Lydia has been out of sorts. Kitty was just trying to help our sister, and didn't think about the consequences.' Jane spread her hands. 'She probably didn't know which part of the village Lydia planned to visit until it was too late to do anything about it.'

'Yes, I expect you're right.' Lizzy could see just how badly affected Jane was by Kitty's plight and didn't wish to add to her distress by revealing the extent of her own anxiety. 'And her life will not be ruined if I have any say in the matter.' Lizzy rang the bell. 'I need your help, Jane,' she said while she waited for Jessie to respond.

'Anything. What do you need me to do?'

'I had planned an excursion to Dovedale for the ladies this afternoon and I need that to go ahead so Mama doesn't get suspicious.'

'And you want me to go along and keep Mama distracted?'

'Yes, if you wouldn't mind.'

'I don't mind. But what of Papa?'

'We can't avoid involving him. I dare say my husband will set the gentlemen various areas to search once he has a better idea where Kitty might have been taken.'

'Charles will want to help.'

'I shall tell Mr. Asquith what's happened and ask him and Sir Marius to escort the ladies.' Lizzy paced the length of the room as she articulated her plans. 'They will keep Lady Catherine occupied between them.'

'Very well, but what if you have not found Kitty by the time we return?'

'I honestly don't know, Jane.' Lizzy shook her head. 'Let's pray that situation doesn't arise. It cannot,' she added, quietly.

'Leave Mama to me and you collude with

Mr. Darcy regarding Kitty's safe return.'

Lizzy kissed Jane, and then Lydia, and slipped back downstairs. Mr. Bingley had joined the other gentlemen in Will's library.

'How is she?' Will asked.

Lizzy shook her head. 'Doctor Sanford has given her something to make her sleep but isn't hopeful about saving the baby. He said he was coming down to join you.' She looked around, expecting him to appear out of nowhere. 'I dare say he's gone to tell Georgie what's happened, which is something I should have thought of myself.'

'You can't be all things to all people, Lizzy. Let others take some responsibility.' Will led her to a chair and forced her into it. 'I'm very sorry about Lydia but Sanford will do all he can.'

'Quite,' Lizzy replied, sighing.

'Now, your uncle was just telling us the contents of his clerk's express. Wickham, it seems, left his position on the same day that Mr. Gardiner left London, helping himself to the contents of the cashbox he kept for incidentals.'

'That long?' Lizzy asked. 'Then he has been away from his post for over a week. Why have we only just heard about it?'

'Simcock has been with me for years,' Mr. Gardiner replied. 'I could tell he was not best pleased when I brought Wickham in over his head, but Wickham is family and so he did his best to help him learn the complexities of our business. But Wickham, I now understand from Simcock's letter, didn't take kindly to being told how to conduct himself by someone whom he considered beneath him. I wish I had known, but Wickham took care to hide his disdain for Simcock from me.'

'We know how devious Wickham can be,' Lizzy said in a dismal tone.

'I should have kept a closer eye on the situation.' Uncle Gardiner looked suddenly older than his years, and considerably worn down. 'Anyway, he goes on to say that when Wickham went off without saying when he would be back, Simcock simply thought he was taking advantage of my absence to kick up his heels.'

'With your money?' Lizzy asked.

'He left a vowel in its place, which gave the impression to someone who doesn't know him well that he intended to repay the sum.'

'How much did he take?' Mr. Bingley asked.

'About twenty pounds.'

'As long as he didn't gamble it all away, that would keep him for a while,' Lizzy mused. 'But I fail to see what he hopes to gain from such dereliction of duty. He knows we had all grown tired of helping him and that this was his very last chance.'

'Simcock didn't wish to further sour relations between himself and Wickham and so waited several days, expecting him to return. When he failed to do so, he finally took the decision to advise me of the situation. I am so very sorry,' Uncle Gardiner added, looking directly at Will. 'I ought to have anticipated something of this nature. He had become very withdrawn as our departure for Pemberley grew closer. Any reminder of his exclusion roused him to anger.'

'He still feels he has a right to be here.' Lizzy shook her head in dazed disbelief. 'After everything that has happened. His arrogance beggars belief.'

'Do you imagine he has followed us to the north?' Uncle Gardiner asked.

'I'll wager fifty guineas that he's not ten miles from Pemberley as we speak,' Will replied in a venomous tone.

'But why?' Lizzy asked in bewilderment. 'What does he hope to achieve? He knows he won't be allowed anywhere near the house.'

'Could he have taken Miss B-bennet and caused his own wife's injury?' Major Turner asked, looking horrified by his own suggestion.

'I would not discount the possibility,' Will replied curtly.

'Then heaven h-help him when I g-get my hands on him.'

'I don't pretend to understand what's in Wickham's mind,' Will said quietly, flexing his jaw. 'But I do know he will have come here with the specific intention of upsetting my family.' He dropped a hand on Lizzy's shoulder. 'But in that endeavour he will not succeed. I have had quite enough of his interference and this time matters will be settled between us once and for all.'

★ ★ ★

Kitty let out a convincing cry of distress as she swooned against the chest of the brute who bodily lifted her from the curricle. He smelled like a man unacquainted with soap and water and was wearing a rough sort of coat with wooden buttons. Its coarse texture was abrasive against her cheek and an aroma she associated with cattle clung to it.

There were two of them. They didn't speak at first but she sensed the second man walking beside the one carrying her. She also felt his fetid breath fall against her face as she allowed her body to go limp and continued to act like a wilting violet. In actual fact, her senses had never been on higher alert but she had grown up with a mother who swooned whenever the mood took her and so knew precisely how to behave.

'Right out of it, so she is,' the one carrying her muttered. 'And a dead weight too.'

Well, really! She heard the clatter of their boots on an outdoor wooden staircase and the man carrying her grunted as he ascended them.

'Are you sure we got the right one?'

'Yeah, this is her.'

'Nice-looking piece,' one of them said.

'We'll have our fun later. That's part of the deal.'

Dear God, what does that mean?

Kitty was unable to control the tremor that coursed through her as she accepted she had been abducted to order rather than by chance and knew what they intended to do to her. She would not be returned to Pemberley in exchange for a ransom. That had clearly never been the plan. But what was less clear was why they needed to go to such lengths to have their . . . well, their pleasures, and why it had to be her. She briefly considered that Mr. Turner might be responsible but as quickly dismissed the notion. He would not go that far; even if he'd had the opportunity to make the arrangements. As to the men who had taken her, if they were caught they would hang. She was a maiden but there was no shortage of less well-connected innocents in the district if that was their aim, so it was simply not worth the trouble or risk they had taken to abduct her.

There had to be another explanation, but Kitty was too terrified to think coherently. It had just occurred to her that when they finished with her she couldn't be permitted to live, or her body found. They had abducted Mr. Darcy's sister-in-law and must know he would use his power and influence to tirelessly hunt them down if the finger of suspicion pointed their way.

'See, the prospect excites her,' the brute carrying her said, laughing at his own wit when he noticed the apprehensive shivers she was unable to control.

'With a bit of luck she'll fight us every inch of the way. I do like a gal with a bit of spirit.'

'Unlike yer wife.'

'Yeah, well . . . '

Kitty heard a door open and she was carried up more stairs, this time inside the building. Then a series of doors opened and she felt herself being thrown onto an uncomfortable bed. Someone grasped one of her wrists and tied it to what Kitty assumed must be the bedhead.

'Now listen 'ere, young lass,' one of the men said, his voice gruff, muffled, as though he was holding something over his mouth to disguise its true tenor. 'I knows you can hear me, so stop pretending. You're gonna stay here for a while, and not give any trouble.' Something cold and sharp pierced the skin on her neck. Kitty, who had fully intended to maintain a dignified silence, cried out. 'And you're not to make a sound, neither. Not that it will make any difference if you do. There's no one here to take no notice.' He chuckled. 'They're used to women screaming in this establishment. Now, nod if you understand.'

Kitty was too terrified to do anything other than nod, conscious of scalding tears trickling from beneath the blindfold.

'Right. When you hear the door close behind us you can remove the blindfold. If you do so before we've gone and see our faces, we shall have to be rid of you. Do you get my drift?' The cold steel again touched her neck and she nodded vigorously before it could draw blood. 'If one of us wants to come into the room, we'll knock, which is your signal to slip this hood over your head.' He took her unfettered wrist and closed her fingers over a rough sack. 'Oh, and don't try to untie your wrist. You'll never manage it. Those knots are far too well tied for a little slip of a thing like you to deal with. Now, be a good girl and this will all soon be over.'

'What . . . what do you want with me?'

Both men chuckled. 'You'll know soon enough.'

'Mr. Darcy will pay a goodly sum for my return.'

'We're loyal to our employer, thanks all the same.'

Kitty heard them leave and wrenched off the blindfold with her free hand. She blinked to clear the tears from her vision and took stock of her situation. She was probably in an attic room of some sort, small and cramped; perhaps at an inn but definitely not in Lambton. They had travelled too far for that. She could hear voices and laughter coming from several stories below her. She shuffled awkwardly across the narrow bed, her movement hampered by trembling limbs and her fettered wrist, until she was within range of a small, grimy window set high in the sloping ceiling. All she could see through it was the tops of trees and it was immediately obvious that she would break her neck if she tried to escape through it, even supposing she could get the warped window open.

Kitty shuffled back and leaned against the headboard, her despair absolute. No one would ever find her here; wherever here was.

Gradually her fear gave way to a slow, burning anger. Her future was supposed to be with Richard and she simply refused to allow these brutes to rob her of that pleasure. Help was unlikely to be forthcoming so she would just have to help herself. And the first thing to do was to release her wrist. They were planning to kill her anyway — eventually — she was quite sure of that and perhaps it would be better to die because she defied them rather than . . . well, what they intended to do to her.

She examined the knots and her heart sank. The rope was thin, and cut into her wrist whenever she pulled on it, tightening the knots. Her gaolers were right. She would never succeed in undoing them with her fingers. She needed something to work beneath them to loosen them; something sharp. But what were the chances of finding such an implement in her prison cell?

Such thoughts fled her mind when she heard several sets of boots on the boarded floor outside; more than the two who had brought her up here. Not already, please! Her heart hammered against her rib cage as fear again replaced her temporary defiance. It was hopeless.

'You're aware of your orders?'

Although speaking softly, presumably so

she wouldn't overhear, the newcomer definitely possessed a voice of authority. He must be the man in whose employment her captors were content.

'Wait until it's quiet. Well after dark, then you can do what you like with her, short of killing her.'

Kitty's relief was short lived. Death would be preferable to what they had planned for her. But she was distracted by that voice. It sounded vaguely familiar. She shuffled as close to the door as she could, ignoring the strain on her wrist, and pressed her ear to the wall. She had heard that voice somewhere before. And recently. But even though her virtue, to say nothing of her happiness very likely depended upon it, she couldn't recall where it had been.

12

Richard, fraught with anxiety, was unable to understand why the entire male population of Pemberley was not already out, scouring the countryside for signs of Kitty. The soldier in him conceded it would be a waste of energy until they had some indication of the direction the curricle had taken. Derbyshire was vast and there were a thousand and one places where she could be hidden from view; impossible to find unless they knew where to start looking.

But that was little consolation to a man so violently in love and he felt an overwhelming need to scream with frustration. Instead he clasped his hands behind his back, strode the length of the room and back again, refusing to accept that his Kitty was lost to him. Richard would tear the county apart with his bare hands if necessary, rescue her before she was harmed and then deal with the perpetrators of this outrage. He was prepared to face his father's wrath, and that of his uncle, the earl, in order to have his heart's desire. The ne'er-do-wells who had the audacity to separate him from Miss Bennet would soon discover just how unwise they had been to arouse his anger.

'It is almost time for luncheon,' Darcy said.

Luncheon? Richard looked at his host askance, probably failing to hide his shock.

'We need to keep up appearances until we're in a position to act,' Darcy said, slapping Richard's shoulder as though he understood his anguish. He probably did. Kitty was his wife's sister and this abduction was an affront to his authority in the locality. He clearly considered Wickham was responsible and Richard burned to ask for particulars of a dispute so serious that a man might resort to such a cowardly act.

But he could not ask.

'We need to consider Kitty's reputation,' Darcy said, having just apprised an astonished Colonel Fitzwilliam of the situation. 'I would prefer as few of the ladies as possible to know about it. Hopefully we will find Kitty quickly and then they need never know.'

'Jane and Georgie are aware,' Mrs. Darcy said. 'But I can see no reason to upset Mary, and definitely not my mother.'

'Mrs. Gardiner also knows,' Mr. Gardiner said. 'She will help to distract the other ladies, should they ask awkward questions.'

'Good,' Mrs. Darcy said, explaining about an afternoon's excursion to Dovedale.

'I shall not tell my sisters or Hurst,' Bingley said, sharing a speaking look with the Darcys.

'That would definitely be for the best,' Mrs. Darcy said.

'You keep a first-rate stable, Darcy. The countryside is quite superb and I had a good . . . ' Richard's father's words trailed off as he stood in the doorway, probably noticing their sombre expressions and sensing the brittle tension. Dressed for riding, his normally pristine boots were covered with dust and splatters of mud, as were his buckskin breeches. Marsden, who prided himself upon the pater's appearance, would be mortified. 'Is something wrong?'

Darcy glanced at Richard, who gave an imperceptible nod. Richard watched his father's reaction closely when Darcy explained what had happened. He didn't see how his father could have arranged for Kitty's abduction but the possibility that he might have done so couldn't be entirely discounted. It would explain his lack of reaction to Richard's attentions to Kitty the previous night and would certainly suit his plans for Richard if Kitty was no longer . . . no, he absolutely refused to believe in anything other than a positive outcome.

'This is extraordinary,' the pater said, glancing for a prolonged moment at Richard with genuine-seeming shock. 'Taken in broad daylight, you say, when everyone around these parts must be aware the lady is related to you, Darcy.' He shook his head. 'I cannot imagine why anyone would do anything so foolhardy. What is being done to find her?'

Before Darcy could respond, Simpson entered the room.

'What news, Simpson?' Darcy asked curtly.

'A curricle was hired from the livery yard in Kympton, sir,' he said. 'The man who hired it was a stranger. All other transactions can be accounted for, both at Kympton and Lambton, so unless the carriage we seek was hired elsewhere, it has to be the one.'

'Does the man who hired it have a name?' Darcy asked.

'He said his name was Watson, sir, but I doubt if that's the truth. He told the groom he would need the curricle for a week and paid in advance. But the oddity is that he left it at the yard with instructions for it to be readied for him at a moment's notice.'

'Presumably that notice came this morning?' Bingley said.

'Yes, sir.'

Richard shook his head, unable to make any sense of what he had just heard. He looked around the rest of the faces in the room and they all seemed equally in the dark.

'Was the groom able to describe the man?' Mrs. Darcy asked.

'Yes, ma'am. He was tall, dark-haired and dressed as though middle-classed. He spoke little and his voice was deep and reasonably cultured, but not upper class.' Simpson paused. 'The groom would know him if he saw him again.'

From which Richard surmised it was not Wickham, but then it would have been surprising if it had been. If Wickham was behind this, he wouldn't be working alone and wouldn't show himself publicly in an area where he was so well known.

'Did anyone see which direction the curricle took once Miss Bennet was in it?' Darcy asked, finally getting to the question that Richard most wanted to hear an answer to.

'It went across a cart track that could lead to the Derby road, or back to Kympton, sir. But if it did go back to Kympton, it's not been returned to the livery yard.'

Darcy shared a glance around the gentlemen. 'If she's been taken to Derby we might never find her,' he said grimly. 'But I doubt they would try to drive that far in a curricle. Putting a captive woman into another vehicle would draw attention since Kitty wouldn't go willingly.'

'Unless they have drugged her,' Mrs. Darcy muttered beneath her breath.

'Let's hope that isn't the case.' Darcy rested a reassuring hand upon his wife's shoulder. 'My feeling is that she's still in the vicinity and we ought to start the search in the area of Kympton.'

'I don't suppose they will risk holding her in the village itself,' Bingley said. 'The possibility of her being seen and recognised is too great. But there are so many small farms and out of the way houses surrounding Kympton that it's hard to know where to start looking.'

'Send some men to Kympton immediately, Simpson, and have them offer large rewards for any information about that curricle,' Darcy said. 'Immediately after luncheon, we will see the ladies off on their excursion and then divide the area up and start searching ourselves.'

'I could start n-now,' Richard said.

'Patience, Turner,' Darcy said. 'Speed is not always the best answer. By the time luncheon is over, we will know more.'

'There is something else, sir,' Simpson said, clearing his throat. 'Mr. Wickham is definitely in the vicinity. A gentleman had taken the cottage to which Mrs. Wickham had been directed and was seen leaving it in a hurry after Miss Bennet was abducted. He was recognised as Wickham.'

'Ye gods,' Darcy muttered *sotto voce*.

'He was with a woman, sir,' Simpson added gravely.

Mrs. Darcy gasped. 'He had the nerve to travel here with a woman who is not his wife?'

'She was at the haberdasher's at the time of the abduction, ma'am, and made quite an exhibition of herself.' Simpson studied his clasped hands. 'I'm given to understand she's not all she ought to be.'

A light skirt, Richard thought disdainfully.

'Poor, poor Lydia,' Mrs. Darcy muttered.

'The cottage was searched in the hope of finding something that would point to their destination,' Simpson said. 'Nothing was found other than this, concealed beneath the mattress.'

Richard watched as Simpson passed a velvet collar to Mrs. Darcy with a handsome cameo attached to it.

'That belongs to Lydia! It was a gift from our parents on her fifteenth birthday and she loved it above all things.' Mrs. Darcy choked on words that were hard to distinguish as tears tumbled down her cheeks. 'How could Wickham be so insensitive?'

The gong for luncheon sounded.

'Come, gentlemen,' Darcy said as he

waited for his wife to wipe her eyes and blow her nose before helping her to her feet. 'By the time the meal is over, I feel sure we will have a better idea where to look. If my name is mentioned, accompanied by financial reward, anyone who knows anything will talk, you just mark my words.'

Richard stood back and let everyone else leave the room ahead of him. As he anticipated would be the case, his father waited with him. A stickler for manners, for once he didn't seem to care that he was about to sit at table with ladies present in mud-splattered breeches.

'I saw the way you looked at me just now,' the pater said. 'And you are right to assume I don't approve of your fixation with Miss Bennet, but I hope you don't imagine this is my work.'

'I c-certainly h-hope it i-is n-not.' Dear God, his speech always deteriorated when he was angry or upset.

'But you don't deny the thought crossed your mind.' His father's accusatory scowl gave way to a reluctant nod. 'Well, I suppose I can't blame you for that.'

'I gave you every opportunity t-to voice y-your opposition to my choice t-this morning b-but you d-didn't d-do so. It s-seemed odd.'

'Damn it, boy, it's just infatuation! After the difficult time you've had recently, I wouldn't deny you the pleasure of a mild flirtation.'

It was Richard's turn to scowl. 'C-choose your w-words with c-care, sir.'

'You would not forget yourself so far as to marry the girl, especially not with a mother . . . ' Perhaps something about the forbidding nature of Richard's expression caused his father to cut short his litany of objections and replace them with a conciliatory smile. 'However, that is a conversation for another day.'

From which Richard surmised that even if . . . no, when, Kitty was found unharmed, his father would still be opposed to their union. But he must by now realise that Richard had inherited his stubborn character, which would serve as a good incentive for the pater to somehow arrange the abduction in the hope of preventing an alliance that was anathema to him. He wondered where he had ridden to that morning, and for what reason, but didn't ask. If he had overseen Kitty's capture, he was hardly likely to admit it.

'I don't approve of the girl, or her foolish mother, but I don't wish her any ill.' The pater clapped Richard's shoulder. 'I will do everything I can to help find her and see her safely returned to the bosom of her family. On that score you have my solemn word.'

★ ★ ★

Lizzy's head was reeling and she was sure her eyes must be blotchy from all the crying she had done. But if she looked frightful, no one at luncheon was ill-mannered enough to mention the fact. The meal was a subdued affair. Half the ladies present were blissfully unaware of the traumatic events of the morning but either picked up on the preoccupation of those who *did* know, or were still half asleep following their late night.

'Goodness,' Mama said, covering an expansive yawn with her hand. 'I declare I had forgotten quite how tiring balls can be. And now I have one of my headaches.'

'You ought to have remained in your room, Mama. I could have had your luncheon sent up on a tray.'

'Thank you, Lizzy, but I have not forgotten my obligations to society and am well able to tolerate a headache without complaining.'

'Shall you be well enough for the excursion to Dovedale?' Jane asked, sharing an anxious glance with Lizzy.

'Oh, I do hope you will, dear Mrs. Bennet,' Georgiana said earnestly. 'I so look forward to showing you the view. I can assure you it's quite spectacular.'

'A headache is a trifling ailment,' Lady Catherine decreed. 'I myself never have them. It's simply a matter of self-discipline.'

'How can self-discipline prevent one from having a headache, Lady Catherine, if one's head is determined to ache?' Mama asked. 'I am slavishly disciplined but that does not prevent me from having headaches.'

Lizzy sensed the dispute between her mother and Lady Catherine that had been simmering for days was about to escalate. What a time to choose! It would result in one or the other of them taking offence and refusing to go on the excursion. If either of them remained behind it would be a disaster since it would be impossible to conceal the truth from them. Lizzy sent Mr. Asquith an imploring glance.

'You, Lady Catherine,' he said in his usual charming manner, offering her a smile that contained exactly the right combination of deference and assertiveness, 'are blessed with a strong constitution. It is one of the things I most admire about you. But if Mrs. Bennet is not so fortunate and suffers with her nerves, I expect it would account for her succumbing to sick headaches.'

'Well, I suppose you're right about that,

Mr. Asquith,' Lady Catherine replied, looking down her nose and then the length of the table at the lady under discussion. If Mama was offended by her nemesis's superior attitude, she gave no sign, happy, no doubt, to have found vindication for a weakness she claimed never to talk about but seldom spoke of anything else. Mr. Asquith really was an exquisite judge of human nature, and thanks to his charm and quick thinking it appeared the crisis had been averted. At least for now.

'We ought to find it in our hearts to sympathise,' he added, sending Lizzy the ghost of a wink, 'since I don't suppose Mrs. Bennet can help being of a nervous disposition and no amount of self-discipline will alter that situation.'

'Certainly I can't help it.' Mama appeared delighted to have found a sympathetic ear. 'I cannot think what made me mention it. I seldom trouble others with particulars of my poor nerves.'

Lady Catherine helped herself to a chicken leg and snorted. 'By all means, we sympathise,' she said, sounding as though she did no such thing.

Lizzy sent Mr. Asquith a grateful smile, aware that no one else in the room, not even Will, could speak to Lady Catherine in such a manner and not be taken to task for it. She turned her attention towards her father, who was toying with his food, not contributing to the conversation or enjoying his wife's stupidity. He had been told about Kitty and was clearly deeply upset.

Well, of course he was!

Her father was not a demonstrative man. The last and only previous occasion upon which Lizzy had seen him so distracted had been when they learned of Lydia's elopement with Wickham and could not be sure the couple were actually married. Had it not been for her beloved Will, that situation would not have come about and the Bennet family as a whole would have had a very grim future to look forward to. But Papa didn't know that and still thought Uncle Gardiner deserved the credit.

Lizzy wanted to reassure her father, but even if she could have found the words she wouldn't have voiced them. She couldn't bring herself to make empty promises when she knew they could not realistically antici-pate a happy outcome to this sorry affair. She pushed her own food around the plate, fear for her sister's welfare gripping her insides like a vice. Poor Kitty! Despite the improve-ments in her conduct, she was not strong, or especially quick-thinking and would be too terrified to try and escape her captors. They simply had to find her, and they had to do so this afternoon, before the light failed.

She glanced at Major Turner across the table and felt as badly for him as she did for herself. He had shown remarkable strength of character in going against the express wishes of his austere father and uncle and following his heart, only for this unimaginable occurrence to interfere with his plans. His expression was one of frozen inaccessibility, as though he had sealed off his feelings somewhere secure and was forcing himself to contemplate the search for Kitty with detached, military-like precision.

Lizzy gave herself a mental shake and returned her attention to the rest of her guests, grateful to her mother and Lady Catherine, who between them were making enough noise to disguise everyone else's preoccupation.

'Lizzy, Lizzy!'

'Yes, Mama.'

'Why are Lydia and Kitty not at luncheon?'

A deathly silence greeted this question, but if her mother noticed it, she paid it no heed. Caroline Bingley most certainly did notice and appeared very glad to see Lizzy discomposed by it. What was in the hateful woman's mind now? Was she simply pleased to see Mama behaving with her usual disregard for the proprieties or were more sinister forces at play? Could it be that Caroline had something to do with Kitty's disappearance? Lizzy didn't see how that could possibly be, but was convinced she hadn't finished causing mischief for her and Will. And behold, mischief of the most despicable variety had indeed been caused.

Coincidence? Or was Lizzy allowing her dislike and suspicions cloud her judgement?

She pushed such thoughts to the back of her mind. For now. She had not absolved Miss Bingley from involvement but Mama expected a response to her question. Before she could formulate one, it was Doctor Sanford spoke up.

'Mrs. Wickham is suffering from a slight fever, ma'am.'

'You ought to have said so at once.' Mama pushed back her chair. 'I must go to her.'

'No, ma'am. I would advise against such action since it's very likely contagious.'

'Contagious!' Lady Catherine looked appalled. 'Are we all in danger of contracting it?'

'Not in the least, Lady Catherine,' Doctor Sanford replied smoothly. 'Just so long as she remains isolated, there is no danger whatsoever.'

'Hmm.' Lady Catherine fixed Mama with a deadly glower, as though she held her personally responsible. 'I only hope you know what you're talking about.'

'He does, Lady Catherine,' Georgiana said with a smile of total adoration for her intended.

'With your delicate constitution, ma'am,' Doctor Sanford said, turning towards Mama, 'we cannot risk exposing you to infection. It would only make your headache worse and you would then be of no help at all to your daughter.'

'Well yes, there is that, but I cannot think about myself at such a time. I put my daughters' interests ahead of my own. Have I not always done so, Mr. Bennet? I never allow my nerves to stop me doing anything at all.'

'You suffer with your nerves, Mrs. Bennet?' Papa fixed his wife with an astonished look. 'All these years and I had not realised.'

'You see,' Mama said, oblivious to Papa's sarcasm and beaming as though vindicated.

'Miss Bennet complained of similar symptoms this morning and so I have taken the liberty of sequestering the two patients together,' Doctor Sanford went on to say.

'Kitty, too.' Mama's gaze drifted to Major Turner. 'Only imagine that, Major. She seemed very well indeed last night, did she not? Everyone said she had never looked better. I am sure you must have noticed.'

The major uttered something unintelligible.

'Your daughters have one another's society to keep their spirits up. I anticipate that by this time tomorrow they will be past the worst and in a position to receive visitors.'

Lizzy could only pray that would prove to be the case.

★ ★ ★

Molly was fast becoming an irritation. Her flirtatious chatter that had proved to be so distracting on the journey to Derbyshire was now wearing Wickham down. He needed peace and quiet in which to plan his next move while everyone at Pemberley was engaged in the search for Kitty. All Molly wanted to do was rattle on about the silk she had purchased, how envious Mrs. Younge's other girls would be when the saw the beautiful gown she intended to make for herself, and endless other trivia. She was starting to sound just like Lydia. Or at least how Lydia used to sound before she changed.

Wickham slowed the horse to a walk and drove down a rutted track in Pemberley woods that was barely wide enough to accommodate the curricle. Overhanging branches scratched the side of the conveyance and the horse's

244

flanks. Twice the miserable beast stopped stock still and Wickham had to alight and persuade it forward by grabbing its bridle and giving it a hefty tug. His own clothing suffered as a consequence and he hadn't thought to bring anything better with him. He wouldn't be fit to be seen when the time came to confront Darcy, which would set him at an even greater disadvantage. Wickham recalled what ammunition was likely be in his possession when that confrontation took place and consoled himself with the thought that Darcy would be too distracted to worry about Wickham's appearance.

Eventually they came to the clearing he remembered well and the cottage situated in its centre.

'This is cosy,' Molly said, looking at it from her perch on the curricle's seat. 'Are we to stay here?'

'Just for tonight,' Wickham replied, hoping against hope that Sanford's dog wasn't inside. Hopefully not since Sanford would have spent last night at Pemberley and seldom went anywhere without the beast, according to Lydia's correspondence with her sister. Besides, if it was there it would have heard the curricle and been barking its head off by now. The dog could have been left at Sanford's main house, a short distance away, which was being renovated in readiness for his marriage to Georgiana. If he was, he could appear at the cottage at any time since it was Sanford's temporary abode.

That was a chance Wickham would just have to take. If Lydia had survived her fall, she would be making an almighty fuss about her injuries, or be worrying about the brat in her belly, and Sanford would remain at Pemberley to take care of her. Either that or assist in the search for Kitty, so Wickham was sure he would not return here tonight. That would give him an opportunity to get into Pemberley today, find what he was looking for and vacate this cottage before his occupation of it was detected.

Wickham tried the door and, to his relief, it opened. He had rightly assumed that Sanford wouldn't bother to lock it since few people could access this remote spot unless they knew Pemberley as well as Wickham did. Besides, Sanford was respected in the area, dispensing medical advice to those who couldn't afford to pay for it without expectation of recompense, and no one would attempt to steal from him.

'Come along, my dear.'

She followed him into the cottage, which was small but clean as a whistle and comfortably furnished. There was even a pantry stocked with food, which was just as well since Wickham hadn't given such nugatory concerns a passing thought. There was also some decent-looking single malt but Wickham resisted the urge to take a shot to steady his nerves. He would need to keep his wits about him; for now.

'Who lives here?' Molly asked, running her finger along the spines of the books neatly arranged on shelves beside a large desk.

'An old friend. We played together as boys.'

'What if he comes home?'

'He's at Pemberley.'

'Pemberley, Pemberley, is that all you ever think about?'

Molly was definitely starting to sound like Lydia. 'I have been ill-used. Is it any wonder I am so obsessed; if obsessed I am?'

'There are other ways to fill the time besides constantly thinking about Pemberley.' She sent him a salacious smile. 'There's a very comfortable-looking bed through that door and if I can't make you forget all about ill-usage then I shall enter a different profession.'

'I don't doubt you could do it, Molly, but it will have to wait until later. Help yourself to anything you want. I have to go out now and will be quite a while.'

'Aw, can I come? I hate being alone.'

'No, be a good girl for just a little longer,' he said, giving her backside a hefty pat, 'and I promise you we shall soon be living the good life.'

She threw herself into a chair and treated him to a full inventory of pouts. 'It's so quiet here. It gives me the creeps. Give me the noise and bustle of a big city any day.'

Wickham left Molly to her complaining and slipped from the cottage. He unharnessed the horse and hobbled him in the centre of a patch of grass, which would just have to do for his supper. Wickham had no intention of showing himself at Sanford's stables further up the track, visible from his main house, to obtain hay and feed for the disobliging animal. He strode back along the path he, Darcy, Fitzwilliam and Sanford had used many times during their youth when they engaged in their energetic, highly competitive games. Now, none of those gentlemen would give Wickham the time of day because Darcy had disowned him and they all followed his lead.

But all that was about to change.

He positioned himself a short distance from Pemberley, protected from detection by the trunk of a sturdy oak tree, and waited. The family would be at luncheon about now. His stomach rumbled, reminding him that he'd had no time to eat that day. Had the gentlemen already gone off to look for Kitty? In Darcy's position, Wickham would first try to ascertain which direction she had been taken in before attempting it. The Derbyshire peaks were extensive, hard to traverse in places unless you were a local, and if Kitty had been hidden away in one of the inaccessible locations she might never be found.

Yes, Darcy would still be trying to establish who had taken her, and where.

His patience was rewarded a short time later when he observed most of the ladies setting off in a series of carriages. A planned excursion, or a hasty arrangement to get them out of the way? Wickham neither knew nor cared. He was more interested in the intentions of the gentlemen, who were waving the ladies off. He was not left in ignorance for long. As soon as the ladies' carriages had disappeared down the driveway, the gentlemen headed for the stables and left Pemberley at a canter.

Wickham waited another ten minutes, then used the trees as cover to get as close to the house as possible. He was left with a distance of about two hundred yards of open lawn between himself and the terrace to cover. His gaze carefully scoured the myriad windows but saw no movement behind any of them. A lot of footmen had joined the search party and the staff remaining behind would be below stairs at this hour, covering the duties of those who had joined the search.

Wickham would never have a better opportunity.

He dashed across the lawn and reached the terrace without being challenged. The French doors to Darcy's library were very familiar and Wickham made straight for them, hoping they wouldn't be locked. He turned the handle and grunted with satisfaction when they swung open on silent hinges.

He slipped into a room he had never thought to enter again: a treasure trove of the Darcy family history that would prove beyond question he was a part of that family.

13

The musty room wasn't particularly cold but Kitty couldn't stop shivering. There was a threadbare blanket on the bed and she pulled it awkwardly around her shoulders, her movements hampered by her fettered wrist. This miniscule storeroom had obviously not been used for a long time. It might even be partitioned off from a larger room, she thought, which would account for the number of doors that her captors had carried her through.

Her prison was thick with dust that made Kitty sneeze, it smelled of mould and cobwebs hung from the ceiling like gossamer lace. She was unable to contain a shriek when she heard the scrabbling of tiny feet coming from somewhere close by. Then she laughed at her foolishness. Given her precarious situation, a few mice were the least of her problems.

What was she supposed to do now? Time hung heavily on her hands, and yet appeared to pass at an alarming rate, as evidenced by the rapidly changing shadows that penetrated the grimy window. When it was dark, those men would be back and they would . . . No, they would not! Kitty would kill herself before she allowed it. Except she had no weapon with which to do so, and was unsure if she would find the courage to use it on herself even if she did. She thought of her beloved major and decided she had far too much to live for.

There had to be a less drastic way to save herself. She fell to gloomy contemplation, but no ingenious solutions sprang to mind. What would Lizzy do? Kitty was convinced her sister wouldn't simply sit back and allow herself to become a victim. Which was all very well, in theory, but there was absolutely nothing in this room she could use to defend herself with. She knew, because she had searched every nook and cranny. Without a weapon, how could she get the better of the burly individuals determined to rob her of her virtue?

Tears of self-pity trickled down her face as she considered hurling herself through the window once her wrist had been released. But she would fall to a painful death and wasn't cut out to be a martyr. Kitty tried not to blame Lydia for insisting upon going into Lambton, or herself for agreeing to the excursion when she sensed there was something not quite right about it. Wickham had told Lydia to go for what had always seemed an improbable reason to Kitty. Could Wickham be behind her abduction? Most likely not since had expressly told Lydia to keep her engagement with Denny alone. Besides, he was in London and would have no reason to abduct Kitty even if he was not.

She was unaware how long it had been since she'd been left alone. Certainly not long enough for any insightful solutions to come to her. The sound of a light tread on the stairs warned her that her solitude was about to be intruded upon. Renewed fear spiralled through her when a male voice called out to her.

'Cover your head. I'm coming in.'

Kitty reached for the sack and pulled it over her head, wrinkling her nose at the unpleasant odour. She would remember the voices she heard earlier for the rest of her days, however many were left to her, and this young man's was definitely not one of them. How many brutes did it take to abduct one helpless female, she wondered, renewed indignation knocking aside her fear.

She heard an outer door open and close, something heavy being pushed aside, and then the door to her prison opened. She had been right to suppose this room was part of a larger space, its entrance concealed from general view. She had been too terrified to hear the heavy object being moved when she was put in here initially but any fledgling hopes of being found withered now she knew of its existence. No one would think to look behind whatever obscured the doorway. Except, if she heard the slightest sound that could even remotely herald her rescue, she would scream like a banshee.

'I brought you something to eat and drink,' the lad's voice said.

Kitty would like to have thrown it at him. They planned to have their way with her but wanted to make sure she had sustenance beforehand and presumably expected her to be grateful.

'Thank you,' Kitty said, her voice muffled by the sack.

'I'll leave it here.'

'Do you know who I am?' she asked, sensing that the young man's nervousness.

'Not my place to ask.'

'My sister is Mrs. Darcy.' A sharp intake of breath. 'You know who Mr. Darcy is?'

'Everyone around these parts knows the Darcys.'

Around these parts. Kitty was right to think she was still be fairly close to Pemberley.

'I don't know why I'm here, but whoever took me made a mistake. Mr. Darcy will leave no stone unturned until he finds me, dead or alive — '

'No one's gonna kill you, miss, far as I know.'

'It doesn't matter. Abducting a lady of quality will be enough to see them hang, so whatever they have planned for me, they can't let me live to tell the tale.' Another startled grunt. 'Mr. Darcy has the influence to ensure my abductors keep a date with the hangman, no matter how long it takes him to hunt them down. He will never give up looking and they will never be safe.'

'I have to go now. I have to get back to work.'

'On the farm?'

'How did you know that?'

Because I can smell it on your clothing, just like I smelt it on the other brutes. 'You could be spared more easily than the grown men because they will be doing the harrowing, I expect. But they wanted to make sure I hadn't escaped, or called for help. Is that why they sent you?'

A sniff was her only response.

'What's your name? Oh, silly me, of course you can't tell me. You criminals have to remain anonymous.'

'I ain't no criminal. I just brought you food. Didn't have to do that.'

'I shall call you Edmund. Is that all right?'

Each time Kitty opened her mouth to speak she ingested specks of dust and dirt from the sack that made her throat dry, causing her to cough. It seemed inconsequential, other than that it was vital she maintain the ability to communicate because she sensed she had her young friend's full attention. He had spoken of the need to leave her again but had so far not moved a muscle. If she could frighten him just a little more, who's to say he wouldn't help her escape? With no other hope open to her, she pursued this one thin opportunity with all the vigour of a woman . . . well, fighting for her life.

'You are a criminal, I'm afraid, even though I can sense you don't want to be. But, you see, I'm being held here against my will and you're acting as my gaoler.'

'I'm just doing what I'm told. They'll beat me else.'

'Edmund, if you help me to get back to Pemberley, I shall tell Mr. Darcy that you saved me. He will reward you handsomely and give you a position as well, most likely.'

'At Pemberley?'

'Yes, of course at Pemberley. Do you like horses? He always has a need for reliable grooms.'

'How did you know I like horses?'

Because all young men are fascinated by horses. Even so, Kitty was delighted to have got it right. It made her feel as though she had wrested back some small control over her situation.

'If you help me, your life will be a great deal better, Edmund, and no one will ever beat you again. You have my promise on that score.'

'I dunno.' Kitty's heart sank. She was sure he had been close to capitulation, but something held him back. Perhaps he was related to her actual abductors. 'They ain't gonna hurt you, miss. They promised me they was not.'

'I heard them talking with the man who employed them.' Kitty resisted the urge to ask who that was. Even if the lad knew, he would never tell her. She still hadn't been able to place the voice that had sounded vaguely familiar. Not that it mattered, but if she was to die, or worse, she would like to know who had ordered her demise, and why. 'Do you know what they intend to do to me?'

'No, I didn't ask.'

'They are going to take my virtue.'

A hiss of breath. 'They wouldn't do that.'

'Then why am I here? And not just one of them, but both.'

'No, no, you've got it all wrong.' She heard

him stand up and move towards the door, taking her fledgling hopes with him. 'I have to go.'

★   ★   ★

Lizzy fretted the afternoon away, feeling helpless and sick with worry about Kitty. She racked her brains, trying to think who could be responsible for taking her, but no obvious answers came to mind, other than Wickham. He had thrown away his final chance of respectable employment with her uncle, was not embracing the prospect of fatherhood, and had come to Derbyshire with a specific purpose in mind. Lizzy couldn't begin to imagine what that purpose must be. He was not a simpleton and could not seriously imagine that Will would reward him for Kitty's return and not seek revenge once she was safe.

Will would pay whatever Wickham demanded, of course, but as soon as Kitty was restored to them, he would hunt Wickham down and tear him apart with his bare hands. He had not said as much, but Lizzy knew it was true. Will's patience with Wickham had been exhausted and when he said he planned to settle matters between them once and for all, Lizzy knew he meant it. The stark determination in his expression, the burning anger that darkened his eyes, left her in no doubt. He had put up with so much from a man he despised for her sake, and whatever Will offered him, it was never enough to satisfy Wickham's avaricious needs. That individual was now hell-bent on revenge and Lizzy knew better than to imagine he would fight fair. A tremor of fear ran through her because Will didn't know how to fight any other way.

Perhaps Wickham planned to return Kitty and immediately leave these shores once he'd been rewarded. Part of Lizzy hoped that would be the case, preventing a final showdown between him and Will. But she also knew that Will would not be able to put Wickham behind him if the confrontation didn't take place. His pride, honour and self-respect were at stake.

'Men,' she muttered aloud. 'Why must they be so stubborn?'

'Lizzy, what did you say?'

'Lydia, you're awake.'

Lizzy had spent the afternoon sitting beside her sister's bed. Her condition remained unchanged, but her life wasn't in immediate danger and so Lizzy had encouraged Doctor Sanford to join the search for Kitty since he knew the area so well. She wondered now if that had been wise. She would have liked him to be there when Lydia awoke.

'What time is it?'

'How do you feel?'

'Everything hurts. Is the baby all right?'

'Yes, try not to worry. You need to rest.'

'Where is everyone?'

'Do you remember what happened?'

'Not really.' Lydia wrinkled her brow and Lizzy watched anxiously as a kaleidoscope of emotions flickered across her countenance. Perhaps she ought not to have asked since recollection might well set Lydia's recovery back. 'We were in Lambton . . . Denny was supposed to be there, but . . . ' She shook her head. 'We were attacked, and I don't remember anything more. How did we get back here?'

'Fortunately our coachman followed you.'

'Who attacked us? Why?'

'John didn't see. He was more concerned about you, and rightly so.'

'Oh, and Kitty, is she — '

'Are you hungry?' Lizzy asked, cutting across Lydia's question. Doctor Sanford had left orders that under no circumstances should Lydia be told anything that would make her agitated. 'I'll ring and have something sent up. The ladies have all gone on an excursion to Dovedale,' she added, implying that Kitty was amongst their number. 'Mama wanted to remain behind but we haven't told her what happened. She thinks you have a fever that is contagious.'

Lydia was quiet for a moment or two before saying, 'That's probably best.'

Lizzy rang the bell. Jessie answered it and Lizzy ordered a light meal to be sent up for Lydia. Eating it tired her and her eyelids dropped again almost as soon as she was finished. Grateful that her sister had not asked more probing questions, and increasingly worried because she was still weak and in so much pain, Lizzy left Jessie to sit with her and retired to her own chamber; exhausted by the strain of pretence and her even greater concern over Kitty's wellbeing. Her bed looked tempting but sleep was out of the question.

She stared through the window and thought she saw a movement on the treeline but it was gone again before she could be sure. The sky had darkened and rain threatened. That was the last thing they needed. Everything that could hamper the search clearly would and Lizzy quietly despaired, feeling impotent, torn apart by her inability to do something, anything, to bring Kitty safely home.

Facts had to be faced, she decided with a

weary sigh. Even if Kitty was returned to them, a shadow would hang over her reputation, giving Mr. Turner a legitimate excuse to forbid the match between Kitty and his son. He would have done that anyway but the major, she hoped, was sufficiently in love to put his own feelings ahead of familial responsibilities. But with all the expectations that now rested upon the shoulders of Major Turner's wife, there could be no skeletons in her cupboard; even Lizzy could see that.

Would the major still hold out for the woman he loved, aware that what had happened was not her fault? Lizzy didn't know enough about his strength of character to be able to decide, but was not optimistic. He had fallen for Kitty a year ago when they first met here at Pemberley and Lizzy suspected it was only fear of what his father would have to say on the matter that had prevented him from offering for her long before now. Finally on the verge of achieving her heart's desire, this terrible thing had happened.

Poor Kitty! It seemed so very unfair.

Lizzy's thoughts oscillated between Wickham, Mr. Turner and the despised Miss Bingley, wondering which of them might be responsible for Kitty's plight; or if any of them were. Her dislike of all three could be clouding her judgement, but with regard to Miss Bingley, there had been a smug satisfaction in her demeanour during luncheon which Lizzy hadn't imagined. Mr. Turner could not have orchestrated the abduction — at least not working alone. But he and Miss Bingley had spent a considerable amount of time in one another's company these past few days. That had surprised Lizzy, until it occurred to her now that Mr. Turner might have an ulterior motive in seeking her out. If he had somehow heard rumours of her dislike of Lizzy and her family, who was to say what he might have persuaded her to do? She was spiteful, vindictive and still totally obsessed with Will.

Knowing she could never have him, perhaps she had decided to assuage her wounded pride by destroying his family's reputation instead. She wouldn't hesitate if flattered by Mr. Turner into being his accomplice. If only Lizzy could decide how Caroline Bingley could have learned of her sister's planned excursion to Lambton in time to make the necessary arrangements, she would be convinced she had discovered the culprits' identities.

Lizzy was unsure how long she remained standing at the window, lost in thought. It was the sound of wheels on gravel that galvanised her. The ladies were returned from Dovedale already. Lizzy plastered a smile on her face and went to greet them.

★   ★   ★

Wickham knew precisely where to find the journals he wished to peruse. They had always been housed in a large breakfront cabinet in Darcy's library and would not have been moved. He was grateful to Lizzy for informing Lydia during the course of their correspondence that Darcy and Georgiana had read a few of old Darcy's diaries and found reference to an event years ago involving Sanford's father in his role as local magistrate. It reminded Wickham of something he ought never to have forgotten. Old Darcy recorded every small detail pertinent to life at Pemberley, no matter how insignificant. Wickham was convinced he would have committed his feelings for Wickham's mother to those pages, safe in the knowledge that they were for his eyes only during the course of his lifetime, perhaps not stopping to consider who might read them after his demise.

Or had he become such a meticulous diarist for precisely that reason?

Whatever his motivation, such a scrupulous

man couldn't possibly have failed to record the true nature of his relationship to Wickham. Over the next few hours Wickham planned to uncover incontrovertible proof that he was old Darcy's son; albeit born on the wrong side of the blanket. An event of such importance would not have gone unrecorded by a man for whom no domestic crisis was too small to escape his pen.

Wickham had convinced himself that Darcy would have expressed his intentions for his secret son's wellbeing after his demise, just as he had professed them without the necessity for words during his lifetime. He had made no secret of the fact that he favoured Wickham, going so far as to ensure he and Darcy enjoyed the same education: a gentleman's education. There could be no reason for such expense unless he intended for Wickham to live the life of the gentleman he was born to be.

Darcy had probably received written instructions from his father to that effect but would have destroyed them in a fit of jealous pique without adhering to them. All Wickham had to do was to find the appropriate journal entries. Time was of the essence since Wickham understood Darcy hadn't touched the diaries, until he and Georgiana looked for the information Sanford required. He now intended to read them all when he could find the time. Wickham absolutely had to get there first and confront Darcy with the evidence. Darcy would then have to do the right thing by him, otherwise Wickham would take recourse to legal action. That would mean keeping the pertinent diaries safe from Darcy before he could destroy them as well. If he could manage that, Wickham was confident Darcy would settle with him privately rather than have his precious name and reputation dragged through the mire.

He felt rather discouraged at first when he noticed just how many journals there actually were, but took solace from the fact that their numbers made it more rather than less likely that he would find the references he sought, eventually. The rewards — justice at last — and seeing Darcy humiliated when he was forced to acknowledge Wickham's rights, would be well worth the effort. He chuckled to himself as he contemplated the possibility of changing his name to George Darcy.

The spacious room held reminders of his old mentor and happier times. Ornaments, books and mementos occupied the same places they always had. How many hours had he sat here, making old Darcy smile, while his acknowledged son simply glowered and made no contribution to the conversation?

The journals were stored in date order. Tamping down his impatience, Wickham forced himself to act methodically and reached for one that covered the period about a year before he was born. But before starting to read it, he first needed to be sure he could escape in the unlikely event of being disturbed. All the gentlemen were out and the servants had no occasion to enter the room, but Wickham had not risked his all, only to have his plans scuppered through carelessness. There was plenty of furniture he could easily conceal himself behind if necessary. Darcy must attend to his duties as host when he returned and couldn't spend time dallying in his private domain. But if he did happen to come in here, Wickham would simply hide behind the long clock situated in one corner, where it had always stood. He experimented and found there was just room for him to squeeze behind it. No one would find him there, especially since they had no occasion to suppose he was in the district, much less on the premises.

Wickham took a chair close to his impromptu hiding place, ready to dive behind the clock at a moment's notice, and opened the first journal. He would hear anyone approaching the room long before they opened the door and so took a moment to savour the luxury of opulent surroundings he had once taken for granted. He would now be master of Pemberley had Darcy been obliging enough to drown in the lake when, as young men on leave from university, Wickham had gone to considerable trouble to bring that situation about. With no other sons, Wickham would have been old Darcy's obvious choice as heir.

But, of course, Darcy had refused to drown.

Wickham flipped through the pages of the journal open on his lap, taken back in time by the sight of the elegant hand, and disciplined himself not to allow his mind to wander. He could do nothing to change the past, but could and most certainly would fight to carve out the future for himself that was due to him.

Time passed and, frustratingly, Wickham found nothing significant that expressed beyond question old Darcy's feelings for Wickham's mother. Wickham's birth received a passing mention; nothing more. Wickham closed that journal and took out the next one, discouraged but by no means ready to give up. Darcy had been very aware of his position. Perhaps, after all, he *had* considered the consequences if anyone read his journals after his death: his wife, for instance. He had often wondered about the precise nature of Darcy's relationship with the woman he'd married. He didn't think it had been a love match. They had seemed remote with one another, polite but passionless and very mindful of their status as principal landowners in Derbyshire, just as they should be. Old Darcy's feelings for and intentions towards Wickham were probably worded more obliquely than Wickham had at first supposed, which meant he would have to read more slowly, absorbing every word, looking for hidden clues and double meanings.

The task he had set himself would not be as easily accomplished as he had at first supposed. He wouldn't mind that, but for the fact that darkness was falling, the gentlemen would soon return, with or without Kitty, and he couldn't risk staying here indefinitely.

He smiled when he read a passage relating to him, Wickham. He had only been five years old but had apparently bloodied the nose of one of the boys from the village. He had had his backside tanned for the misdemeanour but old Darcy had found the situation diverting and admired Wickham's spirit.

'Well, of course he did,' Wickham told the quiet room. 'He took a paternal interest in my development for a reason.'

Wickham stiffened when he heard activity. The ladies had returned from their excursion already and Lizzy's melodious voice asked how it had gone. He relaxed. None of the ladies would come to this room and would most likely take tea together before going to their chambers to recover before changing for dinner. Even so, he would have to leave soon.

An hour must have elapsed since the return of the ladies and, in spite of applying himself, Wickham was discouraged not to have found anything of significance. Then he heard the sound of booted feet on the terrace outside the window and noticed it was almost full dark now. He had been so preoccupied that he hadn't realised how difficult it had become to read in the diminishing light. The search party was back, and from the few words he caught, they had not found Kitty.

A short time later, Wickham heard footsteps approaching the door to the library and only just had time to dive behind the clock before Darcy threw the door open. He was not alone.

'Tell me the truth,' he heard Lizzy say. 'Is there any hope?'

Darcy sighed and the rustle of clothing he heard made Wickham suspect he had pulled Lizzy into his arms. 'I cannot lie to you, my love. The situation looks grim.'

'Wickham has her then?'

Damnation, they did know he was here and would never accept he was innocent of Kitty's abduction. Just for a moment, Wickham experienced true fear. When it came to the protection of his family Darcy, with all his influence, was not a man to cross. He had learned that first-hand when he almost succeeded in eloping with Georgiana. Perhaps he ought to leave Derbyshire, return to London, invent a convincing reason for his absence and deny ever having been north of Watford.

That would be the sensible course of action, but Wickham couldn't bring himself to do it. He couldn't go back to that wretched warehouse; he would prefer to take his chances here. Slowly a plan formed inside his head. He could do worse than ask some of his less reputable connections in the locality who had taken Kitty, and why. Someone had to know and they would tell him things they'd never reveal to Darcy. He could then liberate her and turn himself into the hero of hour by ensuring her safe delivery.

Except Darcy would think he had arranged the entire thing. Kitty would be able to say she hadn't set eyes on him since being taken but, if he really was abductor turned rescuer, Wickham would have to be a complete numbskull to allow himself to be seen by her ahead of time.

'If Wickham took her, I don't comprehend what he hopes to gain from it.'

'It is not one of his better thought out schemes, I'll grant you. But we know he was out of sorts because he wasn't invited to this party, and baulked at the idea of fatherhood. Perhaps that made him take leave of his senses. How is Lydia, by the way?'

'I'm terribly worried about her, Will. She is so pale, so listless. She says everything hurts and can't seem to remain awake for long.'

'She hasn't lost the baby?'

'No, but it might still happen.'

'It might be for the best,' Darcy said softly.

'Will, how can you say such a thing? It is not the baby's fault if it has such a man for a father.'

'I'm sorry, my love. Of course we must think of the baby. Sanford has just gone up to check on Lydia and will remain at Pemberley until she is well, and until Kitty is found.'

'That's comforting. But what are we going to do? I can't keep Mama and others in ignorance indefinitely.' Wickham heard the woman he still prized above all others sob. That need he felt to comfort her, despite the danger to himself, surprised Wickham. Through no fault of his own, he had been forced to put his own interests ahead of those of anyone else and live on his wits. But there was something about Lizzy that caused his sense of self-preservation to desert him.

'Don't cry, sweetheart. It will be all right.'

'No, it won't be.' Lizzy's voice was muffled, probably because she was resting her face against Darcy's chest; damn him! 'Even if Kitty is restored to us, her reputation will be destroyed and she will lose her major.'

'You don't give Turner much credit for his strength of character. Not even his father will talk him out of matrimony with the woman who's stolen his heart. Take it from one who knows.'

'Even if she has been compromised?'

'No one around these parts, not even Wickham, would be foolhardy enough to compromise my wife's sister.'

There was a brief pause. Wickham chanced a glance around the side of the clock and observed Darcy passionately kissing his wife. Well, well, Darcy showing passion, he thought. Who would credit it?

'Kitty must be terrified,' Lizzy said when Darcy broke the kiss, causing Wickham to abruptly return to his hiding place. 'She isn't strong. It would be better if it had been me.'

'Don't you dare say such a thing! I still have nightmares when I think of Wickham entrapping you in the summerhouse.'

'He would not have harmed me. He merely wanted you to think the worst.'

'Which shows how little he understands the depths of our feelings for one another.'

'True.'

'I will confess to surprise at his having returned to Derbyshire. I just wish I knew what he hoped to gain from it.'

You soon will, brother dear. You soon will.

'I will deal with Wickham once we've found Kitty. And we will find her. I still have men out looking, and others leaning hard on all the people most likely to be in the know. I still anticipate her being returned to Pemberley today.'

Lizzy gasped. 'Do you really? You wouldn't say that just to comfort me?'

'You know me better than that. And once she is returned, then will be the time to confront Wickham. Whatever he's here to achieve, it has to be to do with me and I have had quite enough of his interference in my affairs.'

'I hope he didn't come north with the deliberate intention of taking Kitty hostage. I wouldn't like to think him capable of such behaviour, if only for Lydia's sake.'

'Lydia would be better off without him.'

'I can't think of anything more shaming

than being a deserted wife. But to be stuck with a husband who could give his wife's favourite jewellery to his mistress . . . well, words fail me.'

Damnation, Wickham thought, the blasted cameo. He must have left it at the cottage and Darcy's men found it. How could he have been so careless?

'To brazenly bring his mistress to within a few miles of the house where his wife is being entertained surprises even me, who has a very low opinion of his character,' Darcy remarked, a disapproving edge to his voice. 'But I still fail to see how he could have taken Kitty when he specifically told Lydia to go to that cottage alone, presumably so he could further whatever plans he was making by forcing her to help him.'

'In front of his mistress?'

'We know she was at the haberdasher's at the time, spending Wickham's, or should we say, your uncle's money.'

'Yes, it can't have been Wickham. We know he left the village in a big hurry when his wife was attacked. If he had orchestrated that attack, he would have been better prepared.'

Lizzy sighed. 'I wonder where he is now.'

Closer than you imagine.

'Come along. Let's go upstairs and check on our son. Then you must rest before dinner. You look worn out.'

'I can't possibly.'

Darcy chuckled. 'Oh yes you can. And I shall be there to ensure that you do.'

'Will!' Lizzy laughed, sounding shocked.

'You're my wife.' Wickham thought his ears must be deceiving him when he realised Darcy was teasing Lizzy with sexual innuendo. 'It's my duty to ensure your well-being.'

'And we both know what a slave to duty you can be.'

The door closed behind the Darcys and a flirtatious conversation that Wickham found offensive and inappropriate. Kitty was missing and all Darcy could think about was tumbling with his wife. Feeling vindicated in his dislike of the man, Wickham listened to their retreating footsteps and stayed where he was until he was sure they wouldn't return. He then emerged from his hiding place. What to do now? They had not lit a lamp and the room was almost completely dark; certainly too dark for him to read. Besides, it would be too dangerous *and* Molly would be wondering what had become of him. He heartily wished now that he had left her in London.

Still Wickham lingered in the library, fraught with indecision. He would never have a better opportunity to look through the journals and was determined not to give up the search for evidence. It was simply a matter of narrowing it down. He had read all the earlier diaries and had been about to go on to the ones written just before Darcy's death, which would be when he was most likely to have put his affairs in order. He looked along the shelves and found three that interested him. He would just have to take them with him and hope they weren't missed. He removed them and slid them inside his coat. He then covered the space they had left by moving the rest of the journals along the shelf, leaving slight gaps between them that had not been there before. But with the glass doors closed, it barely showed.

Wickham trusted to luck that with everyone so preoccupied about Kitty and Lydia, the absence of the books would not be noticed for a day. He would read them carefully tonight in the comfort of Sanford's cottage, secure in the knowledge that Sanford himself was remaining at Pemberley. By morning he would have found the information he needed. With the journals in his possession, he could then copy out the relevant passages and lodge the originals safely with a solicitor so Darcy couldn't destroy the evidence.

With a lightness of step, Wickham slipped quietly through the French doors and closed them behind him. It was funny how things had a habit of turning out for the best, he thought, if one was prepared to be patient.

14

Fat raindrops bounced off the window of Kitty's prison, bringing darkness with them. Time was running out and she was no nearer to devising a means of escape. She had been told not to make a sound, but desperation made her disobey that command. She screamed until her throat felt raw, but if anyone heard her, no one came to her aid. Her family would be frantic, looking for her everywhere. She'd heard it said it was possible, in desperate situations, to communicate one's presence by concentrating upon one's location. That was all well and good, but Kitty had no idea where she actually was.

'Oh, please,' she muttered, whispering now rather than allowing her voice to rattle the dusty rafters. 'Please!'

She huddled on her musty bed, arms wrapped around her raised knees, and sobbed. It was useless. No one was going to help her and there was nothing she could do to help herself. She had long since given up on Edmund returning to rescue her. She had drunk the water he brought her to ease the soreness of her throat after all the shouting she had done, but the bread and cheese remained untouched. She wondered how long it would be before the mice she had heard earlier found the courage to come and help themselves to the cheese.

Kitty's heart stalled when she heard footsteps on the boards as someone ran up the stairs. This was it, she thought despondently. She was too cowardly to do away with herself and would have to suffer whatever indignities were visited upon her. She could swoon, of course, and might be able to cause enough of a distraction to escape, but somehow she doubted it.

She was astonished when the door flew open without her first being asked to cover her head. Her captors not wanting her to see their faces had given her a desperate sort of hope that she might somehow survive this ordeal. Presumably they'd had a change of heart and she was to die after all. Could telling Edmund who she was have made matters worse for her? Kitty's brain was too addled for her to be able to decide.

A young man with a shock of brown curls and ruddy cheeks, dressed in muddy, threadbare clothes, stood on the threshold.

'Edmund?' she asked in confusion.

He produced a knife and cut through the

bonds on her wrist. 'Quick! We have to leave at once.'

Kitty tried to stand but her legs gave way. On the second attempt they supported her. She wasn't sure what was going on, but this young man intended to help her and that was all that counted.

'Why are you doing this?' she asked.

'I asked them what they intended to do to you.' He scowled. 'You were right, and I can't let that happen. My Ma, God rest her soul, would turn in her grave if she thought I was a party to such iniquities.'

'Thank you, Edmund. You won't regret this.' Kitty's fear gave way to a frenetic energy. The other men had said they would come back after dark. It was dark now and they could come at any moment. Or Edmund might be missed. Either way, there was clearly not a moment to lose.

Kitty draped the smelly blanket over her head and held it close around her torso. 'Why did they take me?' she asked, aware it wasn't the time for questions but a burning desire to know who was behind her abduction superseded all other considerations. 'Who are they working for?'

'I don't know, but they were paid a handsome price. They're laughing about it. They think they're such big men.' He shook his head, then checked the window and seemed satisfied that no one was outside. 'Quick, there's no time to lose.'

Kitty didn't need telling twice. She followed close behind him as they left the tiny room. Edmund paused to push a heavy chest back across its entrance, hiding the doorway from view, before running ahead of her down the internal flight of rickety stairs. He held up a hand to halt her when they reached the bottom and checked the dim corridor. There was no one loitering there, but Kitty heard the sound of voices and laughter coming from a room close by.

'The taproom's below us,' he whispered in answer to her unasked question. 'We need to use the outside stairs now.'

Outside, fresh air, freedom — Kitty couldn't wait, even though she knew the danger was far from past.

'Where are we?' she asked.

'Kympton.'

So, she had been held in the inn at Kympton all along. How audacious!

They slipped out of the back door and down the stairs into a secluded courtyard where an ancient cob was tethered. Kitty assumed the farm where Edmund worked was some distance away and the cob was his means of riding over to check on her. It would also be

Kitty's salvation and she had never seen a finer-looking beast. Edmund leapt onto its broad back with athletic ease, then held down a hand and pulled Kitty up behind him. He couldn't be more than fourteen but was surprisingly strong, presumably thanks to hard physical labour in the fields from an early age. In no mood to worry about her ankles showing when her skirts rode up, Kitty hugged Edmund's waist with both arms and buried her face against his back.

'You have to keep your promise and look out for me,' he said, doubt in his voice as he urged the cob forward. It obliged with a frustratingly slow, plodding gait. 'I can't come back here; not ever.'

'I know that, Edmund, but you have no reason to worry. Just take me back to Pemberley and your future will be secure. I give you my absolute word.'

'My name's not Edmund. It's Jed. Jed Bains.'

'I am very pleased to meet you, Jed,' Kitty replied, her voice ringing with sincerity. She pulled the blanket more tightly over her straw bonnet in a futile effort to keep the rain off. Not that she really cared about getting wet. Never had rain on her upturned face felt more welcome. 'Do you have family here at Kympton?'

'No, me Ma passed away two years ago. Old Spencer took me on as a general dog's body on his farm.'

'Which is where the men who took me work?'

Jed didn't answer. Men were riding down the street at speed and he turned the cob down an alleyway to avoid meeting them. Kitty shared his anxiety. Presumably he and the cob were both well known in Kympton and questions would be asked if Jed was seen riding along with a woman up behind. When the road was clear again, Jed swung the cob onto another track. It was pitch dark and raining harder than ever but Jed appeared to know where he was going, as did the cob, and Kitty didn't distract him with needless chatter.

She was soaked to the skin and frozen to the core by the time they reached the outskirts of Pemberley Park. Kitty revived at the sight of the house she had given up hope of ever entering again; at least not unscathed.

'We're here, Jed! This is Pemberley.'

'Aye. Just remember your promise, miss.'

'Oh, I will remember, Jed. You can be sure of that.'

They got close to the house and Jed slid from the cob's back and helped Kitty down. He then turned the cob, slapped its quarters and it plodded off the way it had come.

'What are you doing?'

'I ain't no horse thief. That 'un'll find its way back home and by the time they miss me, I'll be secure 'ere.'

'That you will, Jed. Come, this way.'

In her anxiety to be home, it only just occurred to Kitty that she could hardly present herself at the front door, soaked to the skin. Hopefully not everyone in the household knew she had been abducted and she would much prefer to keep it that way. She led Jed round the side of the house, hoping that at this hour Lizzy would be in the small parlour she liked to sit in immediately before dinner. She peered through the window and her heart lifted when she saw her sister and Mr. Darcy there, alone.

'Lizzy!' She rapped on the window. 'Lizzy, quick, open the door.'

Lizzy and Mr. Darcy both turned to see who was trying to attract their attention. Their eyes widened at the sight of her and Mr. Darcy immediately dashed across the room to throw open the doors. Kitty sped through them, straight into her sister's arms.

'Kitty, oh Kitty, we have been beside ourselves. Are you all right? What happened?'

'Who's this?' Mr. Darcy asked, taking Jed's arm in a firm grasp.

'Don't hurt him! He helped me to escape. Without Jed, I would . . . I would have been — '

Kitty burst into tears and her words became unintelligible.

★   ★   ★

Lizzy felt giddy as tears of her own, tears of relief that her prayers had been answered, misted her eyes. She hugged Kitty until she had her emotions under control, her gaze clashing with Will's as she did so. He sent her a tender look of understanding that made her insides melt. He had taken Kitty's abduction as a personal affront and Lizzy would not like to be in the abductors' shoes when he caught up with them. She knew he would not take the law into his own hands, but he did hold considerable sway with the local magistrate. The rogues who'd had the audacity to snatch Kitty from a public street in broad daylight would soon regret their actions.

Lizzy relieved Kitty of the ratty blanket covering her head and helped her to remove her sodden bonnet and pelisse. Her hair fell down in a soggy, tangled mass and her gown was torn, dirty and damp. Lizzy moved her to a chair beside the fire, rubbing her hands between her own until they warmed and a little colour returned to her cheeks. Will moved to the fire as well, still holding onto the lad who had brought Kitty home, but no longer scowling at him. The boy seemed over-awed by his surroundings, shuffled his feet awkwardly and didn't open his mouth.

'Tell us what happened, if you can,' Lizzy said when she gauged Kitty was in sufficient command of herself again to speak. 'Did they harm you?'

'They were going to . . . going to, well, you know.'

'Oh, Kitty, I'm so sorry you have been put through this.' Lizzy again hugged her sister. 'But we will find the men responsible and they will be severely punished. Take some comfort from that thought.'

'Where were you held?' Will asked, looking thunderous as he absorbed the enormity of Kitty's words.

'In a hidden attic room at the inn in Kympton. They tied one of my wrists to the bed,' she said, rubbing the wrist in question. Lizzy noticed that it was chafed red raw. 'They were going to come back later, and do things. I heard them outside the door, laughing and boasting about it. I couldn't escape. I tried so very hard but it was hopeless. I couldn't free my wrist.' Fresh tears trickled down her face. 'If I hadn't persuaded

Jed to help me, I . . . '

'Don't distress yourself, my dear. You're safe now.'

'I shall have words with that landlord,' Will said, grinding his jaw. 'I have often suspected him of turning a blind eye to nefarious wrongdoings but have not been able to prove it. This time he's gone too far.'

Will turned to Jed and questioned him in a gentle voice. Gradually the story spilled out. He was an orphan, working on a Kympton farm. Two of the farmer's sons had been approached by a gent and paid a goodly sum to abduct Kitty, take her virtue but not kill her.

'Are you sure it was Miss Bennet they were told to abduct?'

'Aye, sir. They got word this morning, were told when and where she would be, and dropped everything to attend to it.'

'Wait a moment. Where precisely did they say she would be?' Will asked before Lizzy could. If they could discover how anyone could possibly have been in possession of such information, they might be closer to identifying the person responsible.

'They were told Miss Bennet and her sister were going into Lambton in one of your carriages, sir. They were to follow the ladies when they left the conveyance and capture

Miss Bennet when they could.'

'One man must have followed on with the curricle while the other did the abducting,' Will mused. 'Which would explain why only one man was seen by my coachman.'

'It doesn't take more than one villain to capture a helpless female,' Lizzy said, wrinkling her nose in disgust.

'Carry on, Jed. What else can you tell us?' Will asked.

'You're right about the curricle, sir. They were told there would be one waiting for them on the outskirts of Lambton. The man who hired them drove it there and then disappeared.' Lizzy's thoughts turned to Mr. Turner, who had been out riding alone that morning, but she still failed to understand how he could have known about the girls' excursion in time to make such elaborate plans. 'I knew nothing about it until they told me to take her some food this afternoon. They said they were holding her for ransom but Miss Bennet told me what they really intended to do. I didn't believe her at first, but I asked them about it and . . . well . . . ' Jed again examined his boots and blushed scarlet. 'They asked me if I wanted to, begging your pardon, miss, take a turn.'

'And yet you realised it was wrong and helped her to escape.' Lizzy smiled at Jed.

'That was an incredibly brave thing to do.'

Clearly emboldened by Lizzy's praise, Jed explained how he had managed to do that. 'I knew I couldn't let it happen. My Ma was a good Christian woman. I might be poor but I know the difference between right and wrong. She taught me that and I couldn't have lived with myself if anything untoward had happened to Miss Bennet. So I pretended to think it was a lark, so they wouldn't suspect me, like. Then I slipped away while they was doing the harrowing, borrowed the old horse and managed to get Miss Bennet away.'

'Definitely brave,' Lizzy said, smiling at the lad.

'Do you know who hired the men to capture Miss Bennet?' Will asked.

'No, sir. They never said, but I did catch a glimpse of him when he first approached them, although they don't know that.'

'Have you ever seen him before?' Lizzy asked.

'No, ma'am, but I'd know him again. At least I think I would.'

'All right,' Will said. 'Best not mention to anyone that you saw the man.'

'Why?' Kitty asked, lifting her head and focusing her gaze on Will.

Lizzy knew the answer but suspected he would not explain it to Kitty for fear of oversetting her further. The probability was that someone within this household was behind the abduction; unless it really was Wickham all along. Again Turner and Miss Bingley sprang to mind, but Lizzy still couldn't see how they had achieved it.

'Jed will need to speak with the magistrate about it, once the farmer's sons are taken in charge. Best to keep quiet until then.'

'Oh.' Kitty shrugged. 'All right.'

'He may not have to say anything,' Lizzy added, seeing that Jed was frightened by the prospect. 'Once they arrest the Spencer boys they will most likely reveal their employer's identity, always supposing they know it, if only to make things easier for themselves.'

'What of their father, Jed?' Lizzy asked. 'Does he know his sons did something so wicked without trying to stop them?'

'He's old and housebound, ma'am. His sons run the farm, and run wild, begging your pardon for saying so. They struggle to make the farm pay so I expect they saw this as easy money.'

'They will take off the moment they realise Kitty has escaped,' Lizzy said. 'They know who she is and what fate awaits them if they're caught.'

'Yes, I expect they will try to,' Will replied. 'But I will send someone for the constable directly. Hopefully it won't be too late.'

'Jed can't go back, Mr. Darcy,' Kitty said frantically. 'I've told him you will find a position for him here. He's very good with horses.'

'You can depend upon it, Jed, and need have no fear.' Will slapped the boy's shoulders. 'No one will dare to touch you when they know you are in my employ.'

The tension left Jed's rigid body and he nodded his thanks. 'I won't let you down, sir.'

'You have already proven yourself a dozen times over,' Lizzy told him.

'Now then, the guests will be down soon. Not everyone knows what happened to you, Kitty, and I would prefer to keep it that way,' Will said. 'I suggest you go up, have a bath and recover in your room.'

'We will, of course, tell Major Turner of your safe return,' Lizzy added, smiling. 'He's been in a terrible taking. He wanted to continue searching for you long after darkness fell. Will practically had to drag him back here. Mama thinks you have a contagious fever and that Lydia is suffering from a similar affliction.'

'How is Lydia?'

'She took a nasty tumble,' Lizzy replied. 'She's in bed and Doctor Sanford is looking after her. I shall have him check on you as well, just to put all our minds are rest. Your poor wrist will require a dressing.'

'And you, young man,' Will added, his hand still on Jed's shoulder, 'will go with Marshall, my head groom. He'll find you clean and dry clothing, a decent meal and give you a billet above the stables.'

'Thank you, sir.'

'No, thank you, Jed. We will never be able to repay you for what you did,' Lizzy said.

Will rang the bell, Simpson responded and expressed surprised pleasure at seeing Kitty relatively unharmed. In short order, Kitty was conducted upstairs by Jessie, Jed had been taken under Marshall's wing and two of Will's most reliable men had been sent to rouse the constable in the hope of capturing Spencer's sons before they fled the area.

Will pulled Lizzy into his arms when they were alone. 'I am so very relieved that Kitty had the sense to befriend a young man of conscience and morals.'

Lizzy nodded against his chest. 'It could have turned out very differently otherwise. It makes me tremble to think what a narrow escape she had. Who would want to do that to her, Will, and why? Take her virtue, I mean, but not kill her? What was their purpose?'

'I have no idea but you can take my word for it that I shall not rest until I discover the answer.'

'I have never seen you half so angry before, not even when — '

'Shush, don't upset yourself.' Will tightened his arms around her, dropped his head and covered her lips with his own.

'Do you really have no idea who could have done this?' she asked, feeling rather breathless when Will broke the kiss.

'Someone who knew Spencer's sons would jump at the opportunity to make money without having the sense to worry about the consequences.'

'Because Kitty is my sister?'

'I would like to think the magistrate would look equally severely upon the abduction of any young lady, no matter what her background; as would I.'

'Of course.'

'But,' Will added, his voice tight with controlled anger. 'It takes a special type of stupidity, arrogance or desperation, I have yet to decide which, to abduct any relation of mine and not anticipate dire repercussions.'

'You know the Spencer sons to be dishonest?'

'Nothing has ever been proved but there have been suspicions. They are bullies, unpopular in Kympton, and people are afraid of them.'

'Is that why they were able to conceal Kitty

at the inn without the landlord protesting?'

'Very likely, but that landlord is not much better than the Spencers when it comes to making a dishonest shilling. Even so, I'm satisfied he didn't know she was being held in his establishment. I spoke with him myself this afternoon while we were searching, and he assured me he knew nothing of a young lady being held against her will. I'm confident that, for once, he spoke truthfully when he denied all knowledge of Kitty's whereabouts. He's too frightened of me to knowingly have anything to do with it. We looked at all the rooms on the first floor, just to be thorough, and there was no sign of Kitty.'

'Because she was in the attics, which you did not search?'

'We did search them.' Lizzy regretted raising the subject when her husband's eyes darkened with anger. 'Not me personally, but Kitty just told us the room she was in is hidden from prying eyes. She would have been taken up by an outside staircase to first floor at the back of the premises, where no one would have seen her arrival. The Spencers could easily have done that but don't have the wits, or any reason, to be the orchestrators of this particular crime.'

'Wickham,' Lizzy said musingly. 'He would know of the Spencers if they're established in the area. They are just the sort of people he would associate with, and he *does* have the arrogance and wits to try something of this nature.'

'My thoughts precisely,' Will replied, setting his jaw in a rigid line.

'Presumably so he could return Kitty unharmed, but . . . ah, I see.' Lizzy fell into momentary contemplation. 'Kitty would have to remain untouched in order for him to be the hero on the hour. And how could Wickham possibly suppose you wouldn't think he orchestrated the abduction in order to redeem himself in your eyes? It's so very transparent. He's in Derbyshire when he isn't supposed to be *and* happened to find and rescue Kitty when a whole posse of gentlemen from Pemberley failed in that endeavour. He knows you don't believe a word he says at the best of times and would certainly not do so on this occasion.'

'Wickham is so anxious to either revenge himself upon me, or to somehow find a foothold back into Pemberley, that he's becoming desperate. Besides, we only have Kitty's word for it that her captors intended to take her virtue.' Will's brows snapped together in a straight line across his forehead, demonstrating just how intently he disliked having the problem of Wickham foisted upon him. Yet again.

'I think it strange that they didn't enter the room to check on her, but spoke about their intentions in a location where she was bound to hear them.' Lizzy sighed. 'Perhaps that was part of the plan. Kitty was supposed to really believe she would be compromised, and then Wickham would ride to the rescue, making his intervention seem more plausible.'

'That's one possibility,' Will conceded, rubbing his chin in thoughtful contemplation. 'Or the abductors could have decided to molest her against their employer's instructions and wanted her to know what fate was in store for her, just to increase her anxiety. If she knew she wasn't to die, she might prove more obliging. And don't forget, their only precise order appears to have been to keep her alive.'

'But what of Jed? They told him they intended to take Kitty's virtue.'

'Again, we don't know if they were exceeding their instructions, or teasing the lad because they thought . . . well, it doesn't matter what they thought.'

'I can well imagine. There is no need to worry about my sensibilities. They thought the young man asked what they intended to do because the idea excited him and he wished to be a part of it.'

'Such is the nature of disreputable men everywhere, my love.'

'I dare say.' Lizzy sucked in a shuddering breath. 'I assume you would prefer it for Spencer's sons to have exceeded their order rather than consider the logical alternative.'

'That Turner is the only person with a compelling reason to want Kitty to be compromised?' Will grimaced. 'I don't much care for the man's society but cannot imagine that he would stoop so low, even if he could have made the arrangements.'

Lizzy returned to the circle of Will's arms and rested her head on his shoulder. 'Would you like me to ask Kitty if she's sure about what she heard?'

'Yes, but don't overset her.'

'I certainly won't do that.'

'Why has Wickham travelled to the north?' Lizzy asked after a brief pause. 'There's nothing he can do to harm you or your reputation and must realise that my uncle will have run out of patience with him. That, in turn, means he will no longer have a means of making a living.'

'Whatever his reasons, I dare say we shall hear about them sooner rather than later.' Will kissed the top of her head. 'But let's enjoy having Kitty back and not spoil the moment by thinking about Wickham.'

'Yes, by all means, let us do that.'

'And much as I would love to remain here with just you for company, my love, I ought to put the major out of his misery and let the other gentlemen involved in the search know the happy news. Perhaps you would provide the ladies with the same service. There's just enough time to spread the glad tidings before everyone comes down for dinner.'

'Of course. Jane will be so relieved. In fact it's cruel of me to have kept her in ignorance for so long. As for myself, I'm just delighted that Mama didn't have to know.'

Will rolled his eyes. 'I think it safe to say we're all relieved on that score.'

15

Richard paced the length of his chamber, alternately fuming and then giving way to abject despair. He fumed because he'd seen no reason to call off the search for Kitty simply because it was dark. Damn it, she would be frightened half out of her wits and nightfall would make her plight seem ten times worse. Darcy had orchestrated a systematic examination of all the buildings in and around Kympton, and asked questions of everyone in authority. He was treated with respect bordering on awe and it seemed that no one would dare to lie to him.

But somebody clearly had. Someone had to know where Kitty was but had been paid well to keep silent on the point.

Thoughts of her suffering God alone knew what indignities brought on the despair — despair and disgust at his inability to protect the woman he loved. Despite his best endeavours to assess the situation dispassionately, as a soldier should, his feelings for Kitty made that an impossible ambition to achieve, reducing his thought process to a chaotic, jumbled mass of contradictory theories. Who would have reason to abduct Kitty in the first place, and had sufficient blunt and authority to overcome local respect for Darcy; to say nothing about fear of repercussions?

There was only one logical answer, but in spite of his differences with his father, Richard hesitated to point an accusatory finger in his direction. Richard had kept him within his sights the entire time they had been searching and he had done nothing to excite Richard's suspicions.

Damn it, where was she!

Richard had suggested calling in members of his regiment to scour the area beyond Kympton but Darcy chose not to, arguing that Kitty's identity would then become known — something they had thus far managed to avoid — and her reputation would suffer irreparable damage.

Perdition, Richard should have insisted upon military intervention! He didn't give two figs if Kitty's reputation was compromised. This was not her fault and he would still marry her no matter what indignities she suffered at the hands of her captors. Well, he decided, grimacing, if at first light Darcy was still reluctant, Richard would call in reinforcements himself.

But for now he was expected to dress for

dinner, go downstairs, make polite conversation and act as though nothing was wrong. Disgusted, he threw aside the second neckcloth he had failed to tie properly and attempted a third. He *would* go down, if only to keep up appearances and deflect any awkward questions Kitty's mother might ask, but it would be one of the hardest things he had ever had to do.

A part of him seriously considered crying off on some pretence and going out alone to continue with the search. The only thing that prevented him was lack of geographical knowledge. Without an experienced guide, and in the pitch dark, his horse could easily turn a fetlock on the rutted ground; or worse. Common sense told him he had no choice but to exercise patience, but to a man of action, a man so desperately in love, that was asking a very great deal.

His thoughts were interrupted by a knock at his door. It was most likely his father, whom he had no wish to speak with. He might genuinely wish to find Kitty but Richard would prefer not to receive sympathy that wasn't heartfelt.

When Richard didn't answer the door, it opened and Darcy put his head round it. The burden of responsibility had left his expression and he was smiling, damn him!

'She's back,' he said without preamble.

'What!' Richard blinked rather foolishly, slow to absorb Darcy's words. 'When? How? Is she hurt?' He crossed the rooms and grasped Darcy's shoulders. 'Who — '

Darcy held up his hand to halt Richard's flow of questions and gave an obviously abbreviated account of her ordeal. Richard fell into a chair, relief washing through him when Darcy assured him she was unharmed, although he wouldn't be satisfied on that point until he saw her with his own eyes.

'Some of my men have ridden over to rouse the constable. If they make haste, they might just succeed in arresting the Spencers before they realise Kitty has gone and try to abscond themselves.'

'You ought to have let me go.'

Darcy chuckled. 'We need them alive, so we can discover who put them up to it.'

'Ah, I had not considered that.' The desire for retribution flowed through Richard's veins like liquid venom and, had Darcy permitted him to go after the snivelling cowards, he might well not have been able to prevent himself from tearing them limb from limb with his bare hands. To abduct a helpless female for monetary gain was quite simply beyond the pale. 'Have you any idea who it might be?'

'No, but Jed, the lad who helped Kitty to escape, says he would recognise the man again.' Darcy paused. 'I have not made that knowledge public.'

Richard nodded, his expression grim. Darcy was telling him in a roundabout fashion, that if his father *was* behind the abduction, then Jed would notice him sooner or later.

'I am as anxious as you are to know why this iniquity happened, but for now I rejoice in Miss Bennet's safe deliverance.'

'As do I. She is in her chamber, recovering, and obviously won't come down tonight.' Darcy smiled. 'Sorry, Turner.'

'Don't give it another thought. Knowing she is well and safe is all that signifies.'

Suddenly dressing for dinner no longer seemed such a chore. Richard applied himself to the task as soon as Darcy left him, tying his latest neckcloth in a perfect mathematical without once making a wrong turn.

* * *

Wickham made his way swiftly back to Sanford's cottage, taking care to keep well within the shelter of the trees once he had successfully negotiated the area of open lawn without being challenged. The weight of old

Darcy's journals, secreted inside his coat to protect them from the pouring rain, was a comforting burden. He had convinced himself that the information he sought would be somewhere inside of them.

It absolutely had to be.

Kitty had not been found. The fools obviously didn't know where to look, or the right people to ask. Wickham was sure he would be able to find her but saw no profit in being diverted from his reason for being here. The reason held tight against his body as rain penetrated the leafy canopy above his head, plastering his hair to his head since he'd forgotten to wear a hat, slipping down his collar and soaking his back. He cared nothing about a little discomfort; just so long as the precious journals remained dry.

The moment he entered Sanford's cottage he knew Molly would make trouble. He could sense her bad mood, even before she opened her mouth to voice her complaints. It was cold and dark inside the place, she told him. Wickham resisted the temptation to ask her why she hadn't bothered to light a lamp. A fire was out of the question, since the smoke might attract attention, but a lamp could do no harm.

'I thought you'd deserted me,' she said

petulantly from her position in a chair beside the unlit fire.

'I told you I would be a while.' He found the tinder box and lit the lamp himself. 'What is there to eat? I'm sharp set.'

'Why are you asking me? I didn't come with you in the expectation of being your cook and housekeeper. You promised me there would be diversions, entertainments.' She threw up her hands. 'I wish I hadn't left London. The other girls will take my regulars and I might not get them back.'

'You won't need to go back to all that,' Wickham assured her, even though the prospect of taking her with him when he embarked upon his new life no longer seemed quite so appealing. 'But you must be patient for a day or two longer, then we will be at leisure to enjoy ourselves.'

'It's not as though I have a lot of choice in the matter.'

Sighing, Wickham carefully removed the journals, which were only slightly damp, and placed them on the table. He threw his coat aside, scooped Molly bodily from the chair, sat in it himself and settled her back on his lap.

'I shall just have to find something else to eat then.'

She giggled, smiling and flirtatious now

that his attention was all for her, and nuzzled his neck. 'That's more like it.'

Wickham resented the time and trouble it would take him to restore Molly's good humour. He would much prefer to eat a good meal which, he supposed, it had been optimistic of him to expect her to prepare, drink some of Sanford's whisky and settle down to read the journals. But keeping Molly sweet for just one more night, rather than risk her making her way back to Lambton and shouting about Wickham's activities, would not be so very arduous. He would have to find whatever old Darcy had written about him tonight, even if it required sitting up all night. Sanford might return home at any time, Darcy might miss the journals, and Molly would never be content to stay here for longer than that anyway.

★　★　★

Nora made a terrible fuss of her mistress. Her eyes still puffy with tears, she told Kitty repeatedly that she had given up hope of ever seeing her again.

'I'm sure I don't know what the world's coming to, miss, when a young lady can't even walk down the street without being molested. I was only saying as much below stairs earlier.'

'You mustn't repeat any of the particulars,' Kitty said, having revealed very few to Nora for that precise reason. Mr. Darcy had been most insistent in that respect.

'Oh, miss, I would never say a word.' Nora's eyes were agog. 'On my life, I swear it.'

'My Mama knows nothing about it, and I would keep it that way.'

'You can rely upon me, miss.'

Kitty gratefully climbed into the bath Nora had prepared for her, closing her eyes as the warm water seeped into her bones and she gradually felt herself relax. What a day it had been! She could still hardly believe she had managed to escape, albeit with Jed's help, and refused to consider what terrors she would have had to endure if he had not had such a strong moral upbringing.

How she wished she could see Major Turner and set his mind at rest. He would know by now that she was safe and well. Jane, her aunt and Georgie had all been to see her; to hug her and tell her how worried they had been. Georgie also told her that she had never seen the major half so angry, or determined, before. She went on to say that she wouldn't like to be in the shoes of the men who took her when the major got his hands on them.

In his usual calm, capable fashion, Doctor Sanford had applied soothing ointment to her sore wrist and protected the abrasions with a bandage, assuring her that she would be as good as new in a day or two. When she asked after Lydia she thought she saw a shadow of uncertainty pass through his eyes. He told her there was no change, she was still very tired and in some pain, and he had given her something to keep her calm. She mostly slept, which was the best thing for her, and knew nothing of Kitty's ordeal. Kitty took that to mean she ought not to visit her, at least not that evening.

She remained in the bath until the water turned cool, then allowed Nora to brush out her hair and generally fuss over her. She picked at the food that was sent up for her, unable to eat very much in spite of the fact that she'd not had anything all day. She heard the distant sound of voices coming from below. Everyone would be at dinner and she wished she could be there too. She was tired but too buoyed with relief to sleep. Besides, if she closed her eyes, all the events of the day would come flooding back; she just knew they would.

And she wanted to see Major Turner.

'Nora,' she said, motioning for her to take her tray away. 'Bring out my yellow silk, if you please, and help me to dress. I shall go down when dinner is over.'

'Oh, miss, do you think you should?'

'Certainly I should. And I shall.'

Perfectly coiffured, poised and just a little excited, Kitty paused on the threshold to the drawing room, as yet unobserved by its occupants. She heard her mother's voice rise above the general conversation as she loudly disputed some insignificant point with Lady Catherine. Kitty suppressed a smile. She recalled the one occasion upon which Lady Catherine had called at Longbourn. None of them had known anything of Mr. Darcy's interest in Lizzy at the time and were unable to account for the honour of her ladyship's visit. Mama had been so overwhelmed that she scarcely uttered two words. But now that two of her daughters were so advantageously married, she appeared to believe that elevated her to the same social status as Lady Catherine — an attitude which that lady clearly took exception to.

Her gaze fell upon her beloved major, who was in conversation with Mr. Bingley. Perhaps he sensed her presence, or felt her watching him, since he was the first person to notice her. His smile when he did so was spontaneous and completely uncontrived. He excused himself from Mr. Bingley and in three strides was at her side. He took her hand and kissed the back of it, his eyes burning with emotion as he held her gaze.

'My dear, I rejoice to see you looking so well, so lovely.'

'Thank you,' she replied, speaking low. 'I am unharmed and wanted you to know it. I thought you might be anxious, you see.'

'Anxious! I was out of my mind with worry, but still, you should not have come down on my account.'

She smiled. 'I'm stronger than I look.'

'Most young ladies would take a week to recover from such a terrible ordeal.'

'Most young ladies wouldn't have an engagement to keep.' She tilted her head and smiled up at the man she adored. 'I believe we agreed you would ask me a question today, Major.'

'That you can think of — '

'Kitty, my dear!' Mama's voice cut across their conversation. 'Are you better? I heard you had a contagious fever. Should you have come down?'

Kitty sent the major a droll look before responding to her mother. 'I am fully recovered, I thank you, Mama, and have Doctor Sanford's permission to come down for a few hours.'

'Indeed she does,' the doctor replied. 'I

wanted it to be a surprise.'

'It's certainly that,' Lizzy said, looking amused. 'You seem none the worse for your indisposition, Kitty.'

'And yet poor Lydia continues to suffer.' Mama shook her head. 'It seems most unfair.'

'That I should recover first, Mama?' Kitty raised a brow. 'Would it suit you better if I continued to languish in my bed, even when there is no need?'

'That is not at all what I meant, child.' Mama's eyes lingered on the major, still holding her hand, and her entire demeanour changed in a heartbeat. It was as though she had just recalled she had a match to promote and imagined it couldn't go ahead without her encouragement. 'In fact, now I come to think about it, Major Turner has been quite out of sorts without your society, is that not so, Major?'

'Indeed, ma'am,' Richard replied, sending Kitty the ghost of a wink.

Kitty closed her eyes for an expressive moment, wondering if Mama had any idea how much damage she caused her children in her misguided efforts to promote their causes. She inwardly sighed, hoping the major's love for her would prove to be as enduring as Mr. Bingley's was for Jane, or Mr. Darcy's for Lizzy. With his father adamantly opposed to the match, and the prospect of Mama interfering in their affairs at every turn, it would need to be.

'Kitty.' Her father approached and gave her a brief hug. By his standards, that was the ultimate display of affection, one she had seldom experienced before. 'I rejoice to see you amongst us again, my dear. Are you sure you are quite well? No ill effects?'

'I am unharmed, thank you, Papa,' she replied, glad that her bandaged wrist was hidden beneath her glove. It was the only physical reminder of her ordeal and one she would prefer not to have to observe for a while.

'Then at least sit down. There is to be music, I believe, and if Mary takes to the instrument, there is bound to be an unseemly scramble for seats as far away as possible.' Papa smiled broadly. 'Take my advice and get in early.'

Kitty privately agreed with her father's assessment of Mary's abilities but didn't think he ought to denigrate her quite so publicly. It had always been his habit to speak his mind and it had not occurred to Kitty before now to mind about it.

She sensed Mr. Turner, in conversation with Miss Bingley, watching Richard escort her to a chair. She elevated her chin, squared her shoulders and withstood his scrutiny. She even found the courage to send him a reckless little wave. Let him make of that what he would! After all she had endured today, she had no difficulty in countering his obvious disapproval.

While the musicians organised themselves, almost everyone else in the room whom she had not already seen, came up to Kitty and welcomed her back to the fold. Then, as predicted, Mary took her place at the instrument. Kitty listened politely but scarcely heard a note; correctly played or otherwise. She was in a plethora of nerves and anticipation, wondering if the major would take this opportunity to renew his address. He seemed perfectly composed and in no particular rush to do so. God forbid that he'd reconsidered, or blamed her in some way for her abduction.

'Meet me in the small sitting room,' he whispered when Mary's performance came to an end and a smattering of polite applause echoed around the room.

Everyone got up and moved around while Mrs. Hurst took her seat at the pianoforte and Kitty didn't think anyone noticed her leave the room shortly after the major. She didn't much care if they did. Hers and the major's was the worst kept secret in

Christendom. She doubted if there was anyone at Pemberley who didn't anticipate their announcement, if and when it came.

She felt nervous when she entered the room and he closed the door behind her, his tense expression drawing her gaze.

'What is it?' she asked. 'You look frightened half to death.'

'You frighten me, my love.'

'Me!' Kitty shook her head. 'But I have done nothing.'

'Unless you discount escaping from captivity, scaring the life out of those who love you, and then behaving as though nothing untoward had happened.'

Kitty didn't feel she should tell him that was partly because she thought his father might have been responsible for her capture and she wanted to show him she was no shrinking violet.

'Don't imagine I wasn't terrified. But the experience has taught me to grasp life and make the very most of it. After what happened to me today, there is nothing anyone can say or do to frighten me away from that which I most desire.'

'Dearest Kitty. Dare I hope you still desire me when I failed you in your hour of need?'

She offered him a radiant smile. 'How can you possibly doubt it? Thoughts of you, and how frantic you must have been when I was taken, made me doubly determined to escape. You see, I recalled there was a question you wished to put to me.' Ye gods, where had she found the courage to express herself so brazenly? 'And I most particularly wished to hear it.'

'And so you shall, my love. So you shall.'

Richard fell to one knee in front of her and grasped her hand. 'Kitty, I love you with a passion that defies understanding. My every waking moment is consumed by thoughts of you. Will you do me the very great honour of becoming my wife?'

Kitty laughed as she tugged him to his feet and threw herself into his arms. 'With all my heart and soul,' she replied, tilting her head back in anticipation of his kiss.

16

'When was their loss noticed?' Will asked Simpson, gazing at the breakfront case that housed his father's journals. Three were missing from the bottom shelf.

'Betsy was dusting this morning, sir. She noticed the cabinet had not been properly closed, which drew her attention to the gaps between the journals. She notified me and I immediately brought the matter to your attention.'

'Who would take them?' Lizzy asked, perplexed.

Will scowled at the space where the journals ought to be. 'Who do you think?'

'You imagine Wickham has been in the house?' Lizzy swallowed, gripped with fear. 'Why? And how could he have escaped detection?'

'As to the why, I have absolutely no idea how the man's mind works. How is more easily explained. We were in uproar yesterday, looking for Kitty. There were very few servants left in the house, and those that were here had additional duties. Is that not right, Simpson?'

'Indeed, sir. We were stretched, but that is no excuse. I take full responsibility.'

'Nonsense, man, no one is blaming you. We're merely trying to ascertain how this could have happened. We know Wickham is in the district and he knows the layout of this house well. It had not occurred to me that he would have the audacity to actually try and gain entry, otherwise I would have taken precautions to prevent it.'

Lizzy spread her hands. 'I still fail to understand what he could he possibly hope to achieve by taking such a risk for the sake of a few old journals?'

'I suspect we have stumbled upon his reason for coming to Derbyshire,' Will replied, storm clouds gathering behind his eyes.

'Which implies he had nothing to do with Kitty's abduction. That's something I suppose,' Lizzy said in what proved to be a futile attempt to cool Will's anger.

'It must be why he insisted Lydia meet Denny at a specific time,' Will said pensively. 'Although, of course, it was Wickham himself and not Denny who was actually waiting for her.'

'You imagine he wanted Lydia to help him gain access to Pemberley, or even to take those journals for him?'

Will nodded. 'Which would explain why he was so adamant she meet him alone. I dare say he knew she wouldn't agree to help him if he told her about his scheme before she left London. To Lydia's credit, she is a very different person to the rather silly girl whom he married and Wickham is no longer sure where her loyalties lay.'

'It grieves me that he must have seen Lydia thrown to the ground and did nothing to help her. I shall never forgive him for that. Never!'

And she would not. Lizzy realised now that she had been subconsciously trying to avoid the confrontation between her husband and his nemesis, to save Will's feelings and protect Lydia. But Will was right: matters had progressed beyond that stage and Wickham had to be prevented from interfering in their lives ever again, regardless of the awkwardness that would cause for Lydia.

'Wickham thinks of no one other than himself,' Will replied in a clipped tone. 'You, of all people, should be aware of that.'

'Of course I'm aware, but I had thought . . . Lydia is his wife, carrying his child.' She shook her head. 'I ought to have known better. But if Lydia loses her baby because he didn't go to her aid, then I shall not be held responsible for my actions. Not that his helping her would have made much difference, I suppose, but it's his ungentlemanly conduct, his total lack of empathy for his wife's situation . . . ' Lizzy paced the room, throwing her hands in the air as she gave vent to her emotions. 'I don't know how to put my feelings into words.'

'Calm yourself, my love,' Will said softly. 'Getting agitated will do no good.'

'I disagree. Agitation is sometimes the only answer.'

'Is Lydia likely to lose her child?' Will flexed a brow. 'I thought she was getting better.'

Fear for Lydia caused a shudder to vibrate through Lizzy's body. 'Doctor Sanford and Jane are with her now, and I'm about to go up. She's having a lot of pain, and well . . . ' She would spare Will the unpleasant particulars. 'We've been told to expect the worst.'

'Is Lydia herself in danger?'

Lizzy fought back tears. 'I pray she is not.'

'Go on up, my love. Leave me to worry about this business.'

Before she could move, a footman appeared in the open doorway. Lizzy knew he wouldn't presume to intrude upon a conversation between master and mistress and their butler without good reason and so, in spite of her need to be with Lydia, she waited to see what he wanted.

'What is it, Benson?' Simpson asked.

'Begging your pardon,' the footman replied, addressing his words to Will. 'One of the workmen from Doctor Sanford's house is here. They've noticed someone in the doctor's cottage and wondered what they ought to do about it. They weren't sure if the person had permission to be there, you see.'

Lizzy and Will locked gazes. 'Wickham!' they said together.

'I will deal with the matter personally,' Will said, grinding his jaw.

'No, Will, I beg of you!' Lizzy clasped his arm, anxiety affording her extra strength. 'Send others to bring him back here and explain himself. Don't go yourself. That is probably what he wants. It might be a trap.'

'You imagine I can't take care of myself and protect what's mine?' His eyes darkened with rage. 'What sort of man would that make me?'

'I don't doubt your capabilities in the least, but Wickham is desperate. Desperate men with nothing to lose are like cornered animals, unpredictable and dangerous. And we both know he's no stranger to underhand tactics.'

'The time has come to settle things

between us once and for all,' Will replied, his voice tight with a combination of controlled anger and steely determination. 'He will never leave us in peace until it is.'

'Then at least don't go alone.'

Will clasped her upper arms, gently loosened her grip on his own arm and smiled down at her; that slow, curling smile of his that lit up his features, caused the grip of winter to leave his eyes and regularly ignited Lizzy's passions. But her instinctive and rather inappropriate reaction at such a time was quickly extinguished by the fear that invaded every corner of her body. If she lost Will, her life would be over, too. She had always known that pride would be his downfall; stubborn, infuriating, adorable man that he was!

But the rational part of Lizzy's brain understood what drove him. Wickham was fixated upon Pemberley and looked upon Will's generous efforts to help him make his way in the world as a sign of weakness. Lizzy accepted now that he would never leave them in peace. It was almost as though he felt he had a claim upon the estate and it was time to disabuse him of that ridiculous notion once and for all. If she persuaded Will to let others deal with him, he would resent her for it and feel he was being cowardly.

How ridiculous!

Sighing, Lizzy accepted that she couldn't hold him back. This was something he needed to do and against her better judgement she wouldn't raise any more objections. Not because she didn't love him, but because she loved him too much.

'At least take someone with you,' she pleaded.

'Very well, to please you I shall take Fitzwilliam with me.' He kissed the top of her head, mindless of the fact that the servants were still in the room. 'Now go and be with your sisters. I shall be back before you know it and Wickham will never interfere at Pemberley ever again.'

★   ★   ★

Wickham had drunk more of Sanford's whisky than had been his intention, which led to prolonged bouts of love-making with Molly, which meant he fell asleep before he could finish the journals. He was awake now, far earlier than he wished to be, with a thumping head and a temper to match. He was halfway through the final journal and had found nothing, not a single mention of him or the future old Darcy had intended for him.

Damn it, he had been so sure! So very sure

there would be something he could use to his advantage. He would suspect Darcy of having destroyed the relevant passages, but the journals were intact. The only explanation was that his mentor had laid his plans earlier and the information he sought was contained in one or other of the journals that he had only skimmed while at Pemberley.

Journals he would never be able to get his hands on now without Lydia's help.

Wickham swore vociferously, conceding that old Darcy had probably not committed his wishes to his journals after all. That gentleman might or might not be his father, but he had made no provision for him, other than the promise of the living at Kympton when it fell vacant. Darcy had offered it to him, but he had decided by then against sermon-making and took financial compensation instead. Compensation that had long since been spent. His mentor was a forthright man who would have mentioned Wickham by name in his will, not trusting his son to carry out his wishes after his death unless he did so. He didn't need to acknowledge their relationship — a relationship which despite lack of evidence, Wickham still believed existed — in order to ensure the financial future of a man whom he had made no secret of favouring during his lifetime.

Wickham shook his aching head, conceding that his jealousy at being excluded from the party at Pemberley, combined with terror at the thought of being further trapped by fatherhood, had robbed him of his wits. If only Lizzy had not mentioned the journals in her letters to Lydia he wouldn't have thought about them and squandered his position with Gardiner. Now that he thought about it, that position had not been so very arduous, and at least it had kept him in London, at the hub of things, where he still had friends willing to lend him a helping hand, and where opportunities arose all the time for a man of education, wit and charm.

He had thrown away everything to look for proof that didn't exist.

Wickham was startled out of his self-pity when the door crashed open. He expected to see Sanford standing there but instead Darcy's loathsome form filled the aperture, a chilling cast to his expression. Wickham could see all the resentment and jealousy Darcy entertained for him etched in that expression and actually felt afraid for a moment.

But that was ridiculous!

Wickham reminded himself that although Darcy had considerably more money than he did, Wickham was his equal when it came to a physical contest and he would enjoy beating him to a pulp. In fact, he thought, slowly standing and flexing his muscles, he had waited a long time for this moment. Darcy had taken him by surprise last year and broken his nose. Wickham intended to revenge himself for that wrong, and so many others besides.

Molly, still lounging in bed in a state of semi-undress, screamed when she saw Darcy, with Fitzwilliam at his shoulder.

'Get dressed,' Darcy snapped at her without looking in her direction. 'Keep an eye on her, Fitzwilliam, while I deal with this.'

Darcy indicated Wickham with a look of such arrogant disdain as to rouse Wickham's anger.

'You've stolen my father's journals. I will have them back.' Darcy extended his hand. 'Then you will have the goodness to explain yourself.'

Wickham looked down his crooked nose at him. Damnation, his nose had been one of his finest features; now it sat at a slightly odd angle, marring his appearance. Darcy would definitely pay for that.

'I don't owe you an explanation,' he said dismissively.

'Then make one to the magistrate. You broke into Pemberley and stole my possessions. That is theft, whichever way you look at it. And you gave your companion,' he added scathingly, nodding towards Molly who had pulled a gown over her nakedness but still looked like what she was. Wickham was ashamed of her. Her presence was lowering the tone and putting him at even more of a disadvantage. 'You gave her your wife's jewellery. Even I, who know you for what you are, would not have thought you could stoop quite that low.'

'Of course you would not.' Wickham pulled himself up to his full height, wishing he was fully dressed. Instead he felt shabby and . . . well, unwashed, when facing Darcy who was, as always, impeccably attired. 'My wife will get her jewellery back,' he added untruthfully. The thought of returning it had not occurred to Wickham, but he wished Molly hadn't been so careless with it, providing Darcy with, Wickham supposed, justifiable cause for complaint. 'Whatever you think of me, our father instilled good principles into us both.'

'*Our* father?' Darcy elevated one brow, managing to convey a wealth of scepticism into the gesture.

'You know, of course, that my mother and our father were intimately acquainted. Very intimately.' Wickham tried to sound convincing. This was his only opportunity to make

Darcy see the truth and slim though his chances of success were, there was no other path open to him. If he could just light an ember, remind Darcy of how *their* father had favoured him. 'Suffice it to say, we are half-brothers.'

Darcy laughed in his face. 'Is that what this is about? You hoped to find some reference to our supposed relationship in my father's journals so you could force more money out of me.'

'You know as well as I do that it's true,' Wickham replied in a conciliatory tone. 'Why else would he have had us educated side by side and shown me so much favour?'

Dislike radiated from Darcy's dark eyes. 'Because you used your wits to ingratiate yourself and my father was taken in by your deferential attitude. I can assure you there is nothing to find in any of his journals to the contrary. I read every one of them, cover to cover, quite recently.'

Wickham shrugged, trying to hide his anger. He had supposed Lizzy would have mentioned the fact in her letters to Lydia if he had read them. It was a remarkable enough feat to be worthy of comment. But she had not said a word, and even if Darcy was lying, Wickham couldn't prove it. Nor could he now discover the particulars of his parentage he had come to find. All he could do was struggle to appear unconcerned in the face of Darcy's apparent sincerity.

'Then you must have hidden the evidence,' he said offhandedly.

'My father would not have left such a matter to chance. If what you say is true, he would have made proper provision for you in his will.'

Unfortunately, Wickham had reached the same conclusion. 'Perhaps he intended to but did not — '

'My father always acted upon his intentions. If you knew him as well as you claim, then you would be aware of that.' Darcy shook his head. 'But we are wasting time. Hand over my property and then you are coming with us.'

Hope flared inside Wickham. 'To discuss the matter at Pemberley?'

'Hardly that,' Darcy scoffed. 'There is nothing to discuss. You are coming to Sanford's house, from whence I shall send for the constable to take you in charge. You will answer to the magistrate for theft, and for breaking into this cottage.'

Wickham felt the colour drain from his face. Darcy clearly meant to do precisely that. 'You cannot. You're married to my wife's sister. The disgrace will tarnish your good name.'

'If it means I never have to see you again, it will be worth it.'

'And Lydia will be disgraced too.'

'Lydia will be better off without you. I notice you have not even asked after her health, even though you're well aware she was accosted and badly hurt.'

Dear God, he was in earnest! Wickham looked frantically about for something, anything, he could use as a weapon. He needed to get past the two men and escape. He had lived on his wits before, and could do it again. He would make his fortune by fair means or foul and then come back to deal with Darcy once and for all.

This was most emphatically not over.

Molly lugged her valise from the bedroom, causing just the distraction he required.

'Obviously our time together has come to an end,' she said to Wickham. 'Shame that. Now, which of you gentlemen would be kind enough to take me to the village?' she asked with the coquettish smile that always got her what she wanted. 'I suppose I shall just have to make my own way back to London.'

Fitzwilliam's gentlemanly instincts took over and he stepped forward to take Molly's valise. The doorway was now clear of obstruction, with just Darcy between Wickham and freedom. He shoulder-charged Darcy, knocking his feet from beneath him and, by the sounds of it, the wind from his lungs. He slammed the door shut behind himself, wishing he'd had time to do more damage to his foe, as he grabbed his coat and fled the cottage in the clothes he stood up in. A narrow pathway through the trees led to Sanford's house. But he wouldn't be safe there. People were working on it. Presumably one of them had noticed him in the cottage and warned Darcy.

He needed a horse, and he suddenly remembered, thanks to Lizzy's explicit correspondence with her sister, that Sanford had a supposedly fine stallion. Lydia had thought it a fine joke that Sanford had saved Lizzy and her son, then admitted the only other birth he had supervised had been that of the stallion in question. Wickham would use the beast to escape from the district. He knew the countryside like the back of his hand and by the time a search was organised, he would be long gone. He would then sell the stallion for enough to set himself up elsewhere.

Such thoughts buzzed through his head as he ran headlong, his heart thumping, blood pumping through his veins, his headache almost unbearable. He barely felt the branches that snapped at his face as he drew closer to Sanford's house, congratulating himself upon being able to think coherently enough to make plans under such dire circumstances. That Darcy would actually have him taken in charge caused renewed anger and determination to somehow get the better of the man to surge through him.

But first, he needed to escape and regroup. Darcy and Fitzwilliam were close on his heels but he had enough of a start to get to the horse. Sanford had always been a fine judge of horseflesh and if the beast was even half as fast as he dared to hope then no one would catch him once he was on its back. He yanked open the door to the stable, aware of voices shouting from the house for him to stop. He ignored them, just as he ignored the horse's snapping teeth. Its black coat gleamed with good health, while wild, rolling eyes and flaring nostrils hinted at its spirit. It was a beauty and would fetch Wickham a goodly sum.

With no time to look for saddle and bridle, he led the horse outside by its halter and vaulted onto its back. Darcy and Fitzwilliam arrived, panting, just as he turned the animal in the direction of freedom. He sent them a triumphant smile and a one-handed wave of farewell.

'Until we meet again,' he cried.

'Don't ride that horse!' someone from the

house shouted. 'He's cantankerous. No one can handle him except the master.'

Wickham ignored the warning. He was a first rate horseman, though he said so himself, and had yet to find an animal he couldn't ride. Besides, the alternative was unthinkable. He dug his heels into the stallion's flanks and encouraged him forward. He took off so fast that Wickham was almost unseated. He grabbed a handful of mane and regained his balance, concentrating all his efforts upon remaining upright as his mount headed for the narrow path leading to the road. Wickham ducked down to avoid overhanging branches, thinking the horse was not so very disobliging. Until it stopped dead quite without warning, let out a loud whinny and reared up so high that Wickham crashed his head against a branch and slithered to the ground.

His head hit something hard — a rock perhaps — and a starburst of pain exploded behind his eyes. He groaned, groggy and disorientated, but couldn't afford to linger. He must have taken worse tumbles in his time, although he couldn't recall precisely when. Be that as it may, he had to catch the damned horse and get away. Darcy and Fitzwilliam would reach him at any moment and the opportunity to escape would be lost to him.

He attempted to stand but just finding the strength to push himself up on one elbow was beyond him. His surroundings swam in and out of focus and something warm trickled into his eyes, blinding him. He touched his head and his fingers came away sticky with his own blood. He lay back and closed his eyes, just for a moment, waiting for the pain to abate.

Then next thing he knew, Darcy was crouching over him, no doubt revelling in Wickham's misfortune, at which point Wickham conceded defeat. He was tired; so damned tired. Yet again, fate had conspired against him and he couldn't seem to find . . . to find what?

'Wickham, can you hear me?' Tarnation, he could hear Darcy's voice coming from a long way off. 'Stay still. We're sending for help.'

Blood clogged Wickham's throat, making speech impossible, but he knew he was beyond help already.

'He's cracked his skull wide open,' he heard Darcy say. 'It doesn't look good.'

Wickham's last conscious thought before he died was that this was a better way out than going to a debtor's prison.

★   ★   ★

Lizzy and Doctor Sanford left Lydia's room together. Jane and Kitty remained with their sleeping sister with strict instructions to ring immediately if there was any change in her condition.

'I am so sorry, Mrs. Darcy,' the doctor said. 'There was nothing I could do to save the baby but at least I'm confident your sister will make a complete recovery.'

'No one could have done more for Lydia than you did.' Lizzy impulsively touched his hand. 'We are very lucky to have you here.'

'Thank you.' They settled into the small sitting room where they were less likely to be joined by other guests, most of whom were not yet down. 'I know you're worried about your husband, but you shouldn't be. He's perfectly capable of taking care of himself. Besides, Fitzwilliam is with him.'

'Will won't allow anyone else to deal with Wickham on his behalf.' She sighed. 'This has been a long time coming and I'm sure my husband will prevail. I would prefer to hear it from his own lips, that's all.' Lizzy anxiously pleated her fingers together in her lap. 'I just wish they hadn't been gone for so long. They ought to have been back long since. What could be keeping them?'

As though summoned by the power of Lizzy's thoughts, the door opened and Will and Fitzwilliam walked through it. Lizzy hurled herself into her husband's arms, mindless of the fact that they weren't alone.

'I was so worried,' she said. 'What took you so long?'

'I'm sorry, but Wickham's dead.'

Lizzy gasped, noticing the tension in her husband's features. 'You killed him?'

'Not me, but Sanford's horse.'

'What the devil . . . ' Dr. Sanford looked as confused and concerned as Lizzy felt.

Lizzy sank into a chair and listened, dumbfounded, to her husband's account.

'Poor Lydia. She's lost her baby and her husband on the same day.'

'I'm sorry about the baby,' Will said, sounding weary. 'But I can't pretend sadness at Wickham's demise. He never would have left us alone. He had decided he was my half-brother and stole the journals in the hope of finding an entry that would prove it.'

'Remarkable.' Lizzy shook her head. 'But at least we know why he was here and that he couldn't have taken Kitty. That's something, I suppose.'

'Yes, we know that much,' Will agreed.

'We sent for the constable who in turn called the magistrate out,' Fitzwilliam explained. 'That's why we have been so long. Fortunately, Wickham's actions were witnessed by several of the people working on Sanford's house as well as us, so there is no possibility of our account being disputed. Even so, there will have to be an inquest.'

'I am very glad Lydia is sedated and doesn't have to learn the news quite yet,' Lizzy said.

'That would be . . . ' Will looked up when Simpson entered the room, as though sensing more bad news. 'Yes, Simpson, what is it now?'

'The lad Jed has been attacked, sir.'

'Attacked?' Lizzy cried. 'Why? By whom?'

'He recognised the man who employed Miss Bennet's abductors, ma'am, and was attacked to prevent him from speaking up.'

'That man is here, in my house?' Will stood up, glowering. 'Turner, I suppose.'

'No, sir,' Simpson replied. 'Not Mr. Turner.'

'Then who?' Lizzy and Will asked together.

17

Richard faced his father across the width of the conservatory at Pemberley, resolute and determined.

'I am sorry you feel that way, sir,' he said. 'But my m-mind is made up. I h-have asked Miss Bennet to marry me, she has accepted, and there's an end to the m-matter.'

'And my feelings, the future of your family, mean absolutely nothing to you? I thought I had imbued you with a greater sense of duty than that.'

'My s-sense of duty has never b-een in question.' *Unlike that of my idle brothers.*

'If you go ahead with this inappropriate engagement I shall disown you.'

'That is r-regrettable,' Richard replied. 'But I shall not change my m-mind.'

'Then I shall have to take matters into my own hands.'

'There is n-nothing you can do to s-separate Miss Bennet and me.'

'Not that, you fool. If you want the girl, then take her, but you and she will never be welcome at Gaston House.'

'I h-had not supposed that w-we would be.'

'I shall just have to see to the succession myself.'

'You!'

'Miss Bingley.'

Richard was sure he must have misheard. 'Y-you are going to m-marry Miss Bingley?'

'I have not asked her, but when I noticed how taken you are with Miss Bennet I realised you might well forget your duty, and so — '

'B-but, excuse me, sir. Y-you are n-no longer a young man — '

'I am perfectly capable of siring more children, if that's what you're getting at, although I was hoping it would not come to that.'

'But, e-excuse me. Miss Bingley's f-family are l-less suitable than Miss Bennet's. T-they made their money t-through trade. My uncle w-would despair.'

'Miss Bingley conducts herself with appropriate decorum and wants to improve herself.'

'A-and she has a l-large dowry.'

'Mind your tongue, boy. This is all your fault.'

Richard was disgusted by his father's double standards and willingness to use Miss Bingley in such a manner. It would explain why he had paid her so much attention these past days and, in fairness, the lady had seemed to find those attentions welcome.

Perhaps they deserved one another.

'Y-you must d-do as you s-see fit.'

'Indeed I must. I shall make arrangements to leave here today and I doubt we shall meet again. If our paths should happen to cross, do not expect me to acknowledge you. We are now strangers to one another.' His father turned on his heel, disapproval evidenced in his ramrod straight posture. 'You have severely disappointed me, boy. I thought you understood what was expected of you, but it seems I . . . '

His words trailed off when Mr. and Mrs. Darcy joined them.

'The lad who rescued Miss Bennet has been attacked,' Darcy told them without preamble, his expression grim.

'Is he all right?' Richard asked.

'He has a nasty knock to his head,' Mrs. Darcy replied. 'Doctor Sanford is with him now. Thankfully he will recover.'

'He was attacked,' Darcy continued, 'because he recognised the man who employed Kitty's abductors.'

'Here in your house?' Richard shook his head, slow to absorb the implication, and then fixed his father with an accusatory look, damning him with his eyes.

'You cannot possibly think that I had anything to do with such an underhand scheme,' he said, looking genuinely shocked. 'I might disapprove of your intention to marry the chit but I would never behave in such an inappropriate fashion.'

'No, sir, we know it wasn't you.' Darcy's expression was as dark as pitch. 'It was your man Marsden whom Jed recognised.'

'Marsden?' The pater shook his head. 'Impossible. I gave no such orders, nor would I.'

'We have locked him in the cellar pending the constable's arrival,' Darcy said. 'That gentleman is having a busy time of it today. However, we spoke to Marsden and he confirmed you knew nothing about it.'

'So I should hope.' Richard's father fell back into his chair, looking older suddenly, and defeated. 'Marsden has been with me for years. I thought he was totally loyal.'

'He is,' Mrs. Darcy replied. 'That is the problem. He just told my husband he knew how opposed to the marriage you were but was equally sure the major would not back down. Apparently you were in your son's room and saw his sketchpad, full of drawings of my sister, and mentioned it to Marsden.'

'That's true. It was the point at which, excuse me, Mrs. Darcy, I knew I wouldn't be able to change my son's mind.'

'And so Marsden decided,' Darcy explained,

'out of a sense of misplaced loyalty, to take matters into his own hands. Apparently Mrs. Wickham asked Miss Bennet's maid to lay out her morning dress on the night of the ball when she didn't come down. She told Nora that she and Kitty would be going into Lambton early the next morning. Nora is something of a gossip and speculated in the servants' hall as to the reason for that excursion.'

'And Marsden overheard and t-thought it was too good an opportunity to dismiss, I would imagine,' Richard said slowly.

'Quite.' Darcy nodded. 'Marsden had already decided that he would apprehend Kitty if he possibly could, using the Spencer boys whose services were recommended to him when he paid a visit to Kympton inn. He had hired a curricle for that purpose and left it at the livery yard until it was needed. It was easy for him to sneak away early, before Kitty and Lydia left here, because you, sir,' he said, nodding towards Richard's father, 'would sleep later than usual after the ball. He was here to attend to your needs as usual when you woke, and you had no idea what plan he had put in place.'

'I most certainly did not.'

'He gave the men he hired specific instructions to take Miss Bennet's virtue,' Darcy added, grinding his jaw.

'The devil he did!' Richard balled his fists, ready to explode with rage.

'He thought that would be sufficient to deter your interest in her,' Mrs. Darcy said.

'Then he mistook the m-matter,' Richard replied savagely.

'Yes, I'm sure he did.'

'He attacked the boy who saved Miss Bennet,' the pater said slowly. 'Probably intended to kill him. I can scarce believe he would do such a thing.'

'He has admitted it all,' Darcy replied. 'There can be no doubt, I'm afraid. He wasn't even sure that Jed could identify him, but wasn't prepared to take any chances.'

Slowly Richard's father rose to his feet, walked across to Richard and extended his hand.

'Forgive me, my boy, if you possibly can. I should not have interfered and am ashamed of Marsden's actions. Marry Miss Bennet with my blessing. She will be a welcome addition to the family.'

Richard could see his father meant what he said, and it wasn't shock at his faithful manservant's underhand actions that had caused him to have a change of heart. He took his hand in a firm grasp and nodded, willing to accept his olive branch.

'Thank you, Father,' he said.

Epilogue

Lizzy rested her head on Will's shoulder, watching their baby son sleeping across his father's chest. Even though it was two weeks since all their guests had departed from Pemberley, it still seemed unnaturally quiet now things were back to normal.

'Will we ever give an uneventful party, do you suppose?' she asked.

Will smiled. 'It seems unlikely. But still, at least Sir Walter dealt with the inquest into Wickham's death as a formality and we were able to bury him quickly.'

'And he's been laid to rest here in Derbyshire, which he looked upon as his home.'

'And Lydia can make a fresh start.'

Lizzy sighed. 'I'm surprised that she declined our invitation to remain here at Pemberley.'

'She and your mother are close,' Will replied. 'She's the only member of your family, with the possible exception of Mary, who doesn't know Wickham for what he was. She will make a terrible fuss over Lydia, turn the whole thing into a Greek tragedy . . . '

Lizzy smiled. 'She will certainly do that. Still, I'm glad Lydia insisted Mama not be told about the baby. Only imagine how she would have behaved then.'

'Lydia will make a very elegant widow and I am sure, in time, she will want to take up your offer to live here with us.'

'I hope so. It will seem strange with Georgie and Kitty both gone.'

Will leaned up on one elbow and stole a kiss without disturbing the baby still sleeping across his chest. 'Kitty has her major, Georgiana will soon be married and Jane and Bingley are blissfully happy. Almost as happy as we are. Lydia has grown up no end and has been given a second chance. And best of all, the spectre of Wickham no longer looms over us. We are free of him at last.'

'I am so very glad, my dear, for your sake.'

'I would be a hypocrite if I pretended to be sorry he's dead.'

'Yes, I know.' Lizzy sighed. 'And the major and his father are reconciled. The major has not once stuttered since his father admitted he was wrong.'

'Turner spent his time trying to live up to his father's expectations, which made him nervous enough to stutter. Now the tables have been turned and the father respects the son.'

'So it would appear.'

'What is it?' Will asked, when Lizzy fell silent for some minutes. 'When you get that faraway look on your face, I know you're worried about something.'

'Oh, I expect I'm just being fanciful, inventing problems where none exist, but I still worry about Miss Bingley. It did cross my mind that she might somehow have arranged Kitty's abduction as an act of revenge. I would not put it past her. Still, I'm very glad Mr. Turner decided against marrying her. I still have trouble believing he was considering doing so for such vulgar reasons. I dislike her, but she deserves better than that, even if she does still look at you with as much hunger as she ever did.'

'Then she's wasting her time. I have you and Marcus. My life is absolutely complete.'

'Not quite.'

'What do you mean by that?'

'Well, I have a theory as to why your father favoured Wickham, if you are willing to hear it.'

'Go ahead,' Will replied warily.

'You describe your father as being aloof and proud — '

'All the things you described me as being when we first met because I followed his example.'

'Quite, but I think he was far more attached to you than he allowed himself to show. He regretted that you didn't have any siblings close to your own age, which is why he took such an interest in Wickham.'

Will nodded. 'Possibly.'

'Certainly. I have given the matter considerable thought and there is no other explanation. Wickham was personable and exploited your father's good nature. Why else would he go to the expense of giving him a gentleman's education, when he was obviously not born to be a gentleman? You said yourself that he encouraged your friendship and Wickham gave him every reason to suppose it existed, which it did for a while.'

'And my father's motives, if you're right about them,' Will said slowly, 'inadvertently gave Wickham false expectations.'

'Yes. I grew up in a large family, in a house a great deal smaller than this one, which is why I can imagine your father not wishing you to be alone here. I can't abide the thought of Marcus growing up alone either.' She offered Will a sultry smile. 'Don't you think we should concentrate our efforts upon giving him a sibling or two?'

We do hope that you have enjoyed reading this large print book.

Did you know that all of our titles are available for purchase?

We publish a wide range of high quality large print books including:
Romances, Mysteries, Classics
General Fiction
Non Fiction and Westerns

Special interest titles available in large print are:
The Little Oxford Dictionary
Music Book
Song Book
Hymn Book
Service Book

Also available from us courtesy of Oxford University Press:
Young Readers' Dictionary
(large print edition)
Young Readers' Thesaurus
(large print edition)

For further information or a free brochure, please contact us at:
Ulverscroft Large Print Books Ltd.,
The Green, Bradgate Road, Anstey,
Leicester, LE7 7FU, England.
Tel: (00 44) 0116 236 4325
Fax: (00 44) 0116 234 0205